Backup

Boyfriend

River Jaymes

The Backup Boyfriend
The Boyfriend Chronicles Book 1

Cover art by the Killion Group

ISBN-13: 978-0-9912807-1-1

Chapter One

Not far from Alec's intended destination, his motorcycle stalled at the stop sign and the elderly lady behind him gunned her vehicle, flipping Alec the bird as she roared by. Nothing like being insulted by a retiree before being left to eat her dust. Literally. Alec coughed as exhaust fumes and grit hit his face.

Clearly a cosmic bitch slap for ignoring the expert's advice and purchasing this bike.

An impulse buy triggered by a hellacious morning, sure. But being forced to push his classic— translation, *old*—Harley Davidson into said expert's garage? Not exactly a stellar start to a relationship with Alec's new-to-him motorcycle or his recently formulated plan to put the past behind him and get a life.

One that didn't include Tyler, his ex-boyfriend, at *every* turn.

A fresh wave of determination hit. Motivated, Alec raised himself up on his right leg and heaved his entire weight down on the kick start. The motor sputtered half-heartedly before dying, and two more tries produced the same results. Stumped, Alec frowned at the mound of metal between his legs.

"She's a fickle one, all right," a voice called out.

Alec's lips quirked at the suggestion he take the machine's uncooperative nature personally, and he sought the source with his gaze. In the front entryway of a metal building, beneath the words *Adams' Vintage Motors* printed in red, a man leaned against the doorjamb.

Dylan Booth.

Over the phone the mechanic's husky voice had slid over Alec like warm oil, but Alec's imagination hadn't done Dylan justice. Sporting grease-stained jeans and a black T-shirt, he had clean lines and classic good looks. Arms crossed, he appeared relaxed. Laid-back. But the keen eyes were alert, quietly assessing. On the inside he had to be laughing his ass off at Alec's self-induced predicament. Alec tried to care, but failed.

The current humiliation paled in comparison to today's news about Tyler.

The thought of his ex-boyfriend left Alec gripping the throttle with determination. After one more failed attempt at starting the motorcycle, he grunted in disgust and dismounted. Fortunately Dylan Booth kept any further comments to himself as Alec pushed the bike up the driveway, although the man had every right to be giving Alec hell.

"Nice to finally meet you in person." When he reached Dylan, Alec flipped the kickstand down and removed his helmet, grateful for the cool breeze. Striving to remain composed, he said, "I'm Alec Johnson."

The mechanic slowly wiped his hands on a rag as he stepped closer, the late afternoon sun reflecting off the greenest eyes Alec had ever seen.

With an air of reluctance about him, the mechanic stuck out his hand. "Dylan Booth."

Grease stained the whorls of Dylan's fingerprints. Fresh abrasions lined the top of his knuckles, as if he'd gotten into a fight with one of his vehicles. Alec reached out to shake Dylan's hand, and the rough calluses caught Alec by surprise.

Interesting. His experiences, such as they were, involved men like himself, those whose list of postnominal letters reflected the cost of an overpriced education. For a brief moment, his life to date felt way too tame, and he had to force himself to let go of Dylan's hand.

Alec shaded his eyes from the sun, feeling awkward, because now he had two reasons to feel self-conscious. "I decided against the starter bike you recommended."

"I can see that."

Alec waited for Dylan to add *what the hell were you thinking?* Or *serves you right, having to push your motorcycle into my garage.*

"I suppose Noah described my purchase as idiotic." Alec smiled grimly as he mentioned the mutual friend that had referred Alec to Dylan, because one of Noah's many missions in life included being the buddy that kept Alec humble.

"I think I heard the phrase 'dumb-ass decision,'" Dylan replied.

Alec knew Noah would never use those words. Dylan on the other hand...

His discomfort growing, Alec shifted on his feet and tried to lighten the mood. "He also claims the M.D. after my name stands for Massively Deluded."

Of course, when the personal life sucked, delusion held a certain appeal.

One beat later, Dylan's lips curled slightly in understanding. "Sounds like Noah."

Alec let out an amused huff. No friend of Noah's was safe from the man's opinions. Clearly Dylan had been on the receiving end as well. Unfortunately, Noah was friends with Alec's ex-boyfriend too. In fact, Tyler's presence touched every aspect of Alec's existence. His social circle. His professional life. They even worked at the same clinic.

Alec fought the familiar anxious tightening in his chest. The mechanic remained silent, and Alec realized the guy was waiting for the point of today's visit.

"Since you're the local expert on classic Harleys"—Alec gestured at his new purchase—"I hope you know a little about this particular machine."

"1964 Harley-Davidson FLH Duo-Glide. Last year they made this style."

Dylan's demeanor loosened instantly, and he stepped forward to run a reverent hand across the Harley's seat, caressing the leather. His palm traveled up the fuel tank before coming to a rest on the handlebar, affection in his gaze. And in his tone.

For a moment Alec considered suggesting Dylan get a room.

"They were used as police vehicles in the '60s," Dylan said.

Alec's eyebrows shifted higher. "Really?"

"I see the previous owner removed the windshield."

"I wouldn't know."

Christ, Alec.

He owned the vehicle. Had bought and purchased the motorcycle. He should be more familiar with its history. Then again, he should also be able to turn the damn thing on.

"Instead of removing the windshield," Alec said, "they should have fixed the kick start."

Dylan shot Alec a look he couldn't interpret. A reprimand for going against his advice to choose a newer model? A dressing-down for purchasing a vintage bike he couldn't start?

"This baby is a little complicated. Like most women, she has a few quirks to be aware of.

Especially when she's cold." Dylan crossed to where the large garage door gaped open. "Got a few things to finish before I close, so what can I do for you?"

Alec couldn't decide if the man was dismissing him or not. He probably wanted nothing to do with a newbie and his ill-advised purchase. Alec had no right to ask, but he did anyway.

Desperate times.

Desperate measures.

"I was hoping you could give my Harley a tune-up sometime before Friday," Alec said.

Dylan tugged on the chain, lowering the metal door with a squeak. "I'm booked every day this week."

Disappointment flared, and Alec forced himself to go on. "When is your soonest available appointment?"

"I can put you down for the first of next month."

Next month.

Better than an outright *no*, but Alec fought the pressing sense of urgency and eyed the recalcitrant bike. Not that Alec had pictured himself riding carefree through the streets of San Francisco in less than seven days. But, at some point in the next week, Tyler would return for the boxes he'd left behind. When his ex spied the Harley in the garage, Alec needed the motorcycle to run like a well-oiled machine. Or, hell, at least *start*.

"Any way you could squeeze me in sooner?" Alec said.

"Sorry, but I'm already behind as it is. Did you have her inspected before the purchase?"

Inspected? Alec sent Dylan a blank stare, which was probably answer enough.

Good God, this whole situation made Alec look like a moron.

Dylan paused in his efforts, the metal grating sound coming to a brief, blissful end just in time for Alec to hear Dylan let out a barely audible sigh. "Did you at least get the maintenance history on the bike?"

"Uh..." Alec scratched the back of his neck. "It was kind of an impulse buy."

"Candy, gum, and porno magazines are impulse buys," Dylan said drily. "Not motorcycles." Dylan's grip remained on the chain. And, although he sounded patient, the skeptical amusement remained firmly intact. "Especially a vintage one."

Just like I told you, the man didn't say.

Alec hoped he didn't sound defensive. "I did quite a bit of research a while back," he said. The day Tyler had walked out of their home for good, actually. "But this morning I found out..."

That my partner of two years has a new boyfriend.

Is dating a hottie.

That I've been replaced, after only fifty-six days...

Alec cleared his throat. "Today I found this for sale online and went and wrote the owner a check."

Dylan rubbed the faint stubble at his chin and stared down at the bike. "As impulse buys go, I suppose it could have been worse."

"How so?"

"Coulda bought the mechanically challenged Yugo." The reproof in Dylan's gaze went down easier with the hint of humor in his eyes. "On the plus side, Yugos had rear window defrosters." He hiked a brow meaningfully. "Mostly to keep your hands warm while you pushed the bastard to the nearest garage."

The indirect reference to his less-than-impressive motorcycling debut brought a grin to Alec's lips. "Now you're mocking me."

"'Course not."

"Are you sure?"

Clearly amused, Dylan went on. "If I wanted to mock you, I'd mention that a Yugo doesn't require skills with a kick start."

Alec let out a bark of laughter, surprising himself with the sound. He hadn't felt much like chuckling lately. Dylan resumed the noisy task of lowering the garage door, clearly locking up for the evening. But something in the man's demeanor felt approachable.

"Mind if I ask you a few questions?" Alec said.

"Fire away."

"Right." Ill-advised purchase or not, he needed to get back to the business of his goals. "So the bike tries to stall every time I stop. I have to keep my hand on the throttle to keep it running. Any suggestions on what I might be doing wrong?"

"Sounds like your carburetor needs adjusting. Just take a flat-head screwdriver to the fuel intake valve and—"

After scanning Alec's face, which most likely reflected his completely clueless state, Dylan dropped his hand from the chain, the massive garage door still halfway open. "Never mind. Won't take but a few minutes. How about I do that for you now?"

The tension in Alec's shoulders eased a bit. "That would be really helpful."

Dylan crossed back and righted the Harley, flipping the kickstand with a flick of his foot. As he pushed the bike inside the metal building, Alec followed behind, the position allowing him to freely study Dylan's form.

He guesstimated Dylan to be six two or so, two inches taller than Alec. His sandy hair was closely cropped on the sides, and the thick wayward strands on top looked more rebellious than messy. With each tiny adjustment in Dylan's position, the black T-shirt stretched tight across a broad back and his biceps, which were as well defined as the rest of him. With every shift of his thighs, his quadriceps lengthened and bulged slightly beneath his jeans.

No ogling the straight man, Alec. No ogling any man, period.

Alec pulled his gaze away and concentrated on his surroundings. The garage smelled of a mix of motor oil, exhaust, and dust. Several motorcycles lined the wall to the right.

"I really appreciate this," Alec said as he trailed behind Dylan.

"No worries."

"I'm just glad I didn't have to push the bike uphill for eight blocks. It weighs a ton."

"About six hundred and fifty pounds."

"You're kidding me." Alec came to a stop, the impulsive nature of his purchase hitting him all over again. "I had no idea it was that heavy."

Dylan shot Alec a questioning look, as if he couldn't fathom anyone being so uninformed about their vehicle. Normally Alec didn't make a move without a serious amount of research, a habit that used to drive Tyler crazy.

Dylan parked the Harley next to a shelf full of neatly arranged tools and turned, hands on his hips. "Spur-of-the-moment purchases are always risky."

The *especially when you don't know what the hell you're doing* went unsaid.

Alec let out a humorless bark of laughter. "Yes, but I needed a change. Today." Alec briefly glanced down the street, the knot in his chest expanding. After hearing the news this morning, he finally managed to speak the words out loud. "I just learned my ex has a new boyfriend. And I'm feeling…"

Humiliated that the man I thought I'd spend forever with has already moved on.

Demoralized that I've been replaced, fifty-six days after the breakup.

Fifty-six days.

The number felt tattooed on his forehead.

Dylan's facial expression froze in alarm. "Please don't say you're feeling suicidal."

This time Alec's bark of laughter was real. "No, not at all. Just wanted to shake up the routine." He shrugged, struggling to put his personal promise into words. "Reinvent myself, so to speak." In ways outside the reach of his memories of Tyler.

Dylan's comment consisted of a brief pause followed by a sharp nod before he crossed to the shelf of tools. "What kind of problems are you having?"

Christ, where to begin?

"Oh, you know. The usual," Alec said, surprised the man had asked. "Loss of appetite. Insomnia. I'm second-guessing every decision I made during our two-year relationship. We'd even talked about getting married—"

Alec caught sight of Dylan's almost horrified expression.

"Dude," Dylan said, "I meant what kind of problems are you having with the *bike*?"

Heat rushed up Alec's face, filling every available space.

Nice one, Alec.

He'd completed college in three years and aced his way through medical school. Had received several honors during residency. Had just been named the recipient of the prestigious Bay Area

Humanitarian Award for his work with the homeless.

Why couldn't he deal with a breakup?

Alec shoved his hands into his brand-new racing jacket. "So far just the stalling. But I've only driven it the few miles between the former owner's home and here."

"Most likely adjusting the carburetor will hold you over until a more thorough tune-up."

Dylan sorted through the well-organized tools that would make most men salivate. Alec concentrated on the display of Dylan's muscular back instead of the well-formed ass. Alec's sex life might be nonexistent of late, but checking the mechanic out wasn't a part of the make-a-new-life plan.

"I can put you down for a service check in my next available slot," Dylan said. "If you absolutely have to have the work done sooner, I can recommend a few people I trust."

"Will adjusting the carburetor help me get it started?"

"Maybe." Dylan lifted the lid to a massive toolbox. "But it also takes practice."

Practice.

Alec pursed his lips in thought and gazed at the far wall, where a muscle car sat on a lift, exposing the mysterious underbelly of the vehicle. Although well versed in the barriers of providing health care to the medically underserved, Alec wasn't mechanically inclined. Could barely operate a hammer and nail. Putting gas in his vehicle was as complicated as Alec could handle. Choosing to purchase the vintage Harley, aside from the cool-factor appeal, had been about pushing his boundaries and challenging himself to move beyond his comfort zone.

Despite this morning's epic fail, the decision felt right. Even after all the trouble with the bike, Alec still couldn't forget those first trouble-free minutes on the ride here. He'd felt almost...happy again. Nonetheless, for his new pastime to be successful, he needed someone's help in the beginning.

Decision made, Alec turned back to Dylan. "Do you ever give lessons?"

Dylan turned his head to look at Alec over his shoulder. "Lessons?"

"You know," Alec said, suddenly feeling awkward. The confused look on Dylan's face didn't help. "Pointers to people who don't know all the quirks to driving a 1964 Harley."

No need to mention his ignorance about motorcycles in general.

"'Fraid not." Dylan selected a screwdriver from the massive metal chest. "I'd make an exception in your case, seeing how you're a friend of Noah's and all, but my plate really is full at the moment." He shut the lid to the toolbox. "But I can give you the names of a couple of people who might be able to help you out."

A sense of satisfaction surged, and Alec grinned. "Perfect."

The green eyes held a hint of a smile in return. Given the horrendous start to Alec's morning, things were finally looking up. With any luck, facing Tyler again wouldn't be the disaster Alec had been envisioning for weeks.

~~~***~~~

The next day Alec tucked a towel around his waist, hair dripping as he padded out of the bathroom into his bedroom. He'd definitely taken steps toward making things better. The adjustment to the Harley yesterday had made a huge difference. Dylan had gotten the motorcycle started for Alec without any problem, proving that everything functioned properly. And the ride home had gone smoother, the trip proving Alec right.

He definitely didn't regret choosing the Harley.

This morning Alec felt better. Refreshed. More hopeful than he'd felt in a while. He'd put together a quiche and placed it in the oven, the first real cooking he'd done in ages. Even his daily jerk-off session in the shower had been satisfying.

Right up until he came, the moment ruined when an image of Tyler popped into Alec's head.

Alec's lips twisted. He'd started off as usual, visualizing David Beckham on his knees and getting nice and worked up imagining a strong body and hazel eyes so hot they could melt cold butter from twenty-five feet away. Alec liked a little stubble, the rough feel under his hand as he cupped a jaw while lips and tongue played him like an instrument. He and David had been so close to mutual satisfaction. *So close.* And then, like an annoying Internet ad that refused to close, up popped Tyler's face, staring at him like he had so many times before.

What a way to ruin a good orgasm.

But come Monday there'd be no more avoiding Tyler physically either. Between his ex's vacation and the medical conference Alec had attended, plus a whole lot of manipulation of the clinic schedule on Alec's part, he'd managed to avoid seeing Tyler at work since the split.

But they ran the Front Street Clinic together, for God's sake.

At this point, Alec figured he had two choices. He could man up, stop delaying the inevitable, and be the one to define the moment when they first met up. Or he could continue to avoid Tyler until the last possible minute, in which case the moment would define Alec.

And most likely not in a flattering way.

He towel dried his hair and shoved away the mental image of him blabbering like a fool in front of Tyler or standing there mute—either scenario an unfortunate possibility. Alec tossed the towel into the hamper with a determined *thump*. After almost two months of inertia, the time had come to seize the initiative. And that meant taking steps to ease them into their first day back in clinic together.

He'd call Tyler and tell him to stop by before Monday. No sense in ruining the entire weekend; tomorrow would be perfect. Lazy Sundays worked great for a mature exchange of words in which Alec's ex-boyfriend retrieved the last of his stuff from the garage.

The proactive decision cheered Alec up as he pulled on his clothes. Today he'd spend some quality one-on-one time with his recent purchase. No harm in practicing kick starting the Harley before Tyler dropped by.

Alec punched Tyler's name on speed dial with more force than necessary, hoping against hope that Tyler would answer.

Or not.

"Hello?" Tyler said.

Alec's chest filled with molten lead. "Good morning, Tyler."

"Alec."

There was an awkward pause as Alec relived the first time they'd met, during a medical conference in Hawaii. With Tyler's interest in treating HIV in indigent populations and Alec's additional training in street medicine, pairing up to create the Front Street Clinic to achieve their long-term goals had only made sense. Both personally and professionally. Now that the personal had ended the professional had just gotten ridiculously hard.

Christ, no more work relationships. Ever.

"Noah told me you bought a motorcycle," Tyler said.

Alec closed his eyes. Damn Noah and his big mouth.

"I did," Alec said. "I'm calling about the boxes you left in the garage. I thought you could swing by and pick them up tomorrow evening."

So far so good. He'd even managed a nonchalant tone.

"Can't," Tyler said. "I have plans."

Great. Now what? A bead of water ran down Alec's forehead, and he swiped at the drop. While Alec was trying to decide what to say next, Tyler went on.

"But I can come by today," his ex said.

Alec bit back the word *no*, but now that he'd set the strategy in motion, he didn't see a graceful way out. "Today's fine."

Today *sucked.*

Tyler said, "I understand if you're too busy."

"I can carve out a few minutes," Alec said. "What time this afternoon?"

At least Alec would have the morning to—

"I'll be there in an hour," Tyler said.

An hour? Perfect.

That left Alec just enough time to panic.

Chapter Two

"I can't get it—*her*—started."

The frustration in Alec Johnson's voice came across the phone loud and clear, and Dylan bit back a groan as, wearily, he raked a hand through his hair.

Hungry, tired, and up to his eyeballs in work, he didn't have time for Dr. Clueless today. What Dylan *did* have was a broken air compressor to fix, a tune-up to complete, and a meeting with Noah to discuss the details of the Fifth Annual Vintage Memorial Poker Run in memory of Rick. Dylan's chest gave a painful twitch.

Five years. His best friend had been dead for *five years*.

Dylan shook his head to chase away the thoughts. If Rick were alive today, he'd be laughing his ass off at the doctor's screwed-up situation of his own making. Of course, being the proverbial softie, Rick also would have been the first to help Alec out.

"Have you even owned a motorcycle before?" Dylan asked.

The pause was telling.

"I had a dirt bike when I was a teen," Alec said.

Dylan rolled his eyes. Figured. Most likely the Harley would wind up parked in Alec's garage, unused. Left to fall into disrepair. What a waste. At least Alec hadn't purchased a crotch rocket and gone out and gotten himself killed on his first day.

Alec went on. "I know you don't have time for lessons, Mr. Booth—"

"Dylan."

"Dylan," Alec repeated. "But I wondered if you could stop by my place and help me get her started."

Was this guy for real? Wasn't adjusting the carburetor enough?

"I'm not a doctor," Dylan said. "I don't make house calls."

"I know," Alec said. "But my ex is dropping by today. And I'd really appreciate you making an exception, despite my...dumb-ass decision."

Dylan gripped his phone, refusing to let the sincere words and hint of self-deprecating humor change his mind.

But Noah had sent the doctor to Dylan for help, and Dylan owed Noah big time. And despite his friend's flippant attitude, Dylan knew the man had nothing but total respect for Alec's work with the homeless.

The *homeless*, for fuck's sake.

Dylan closed his eyes. From the ages of fifteen to eighteen, he'd lived on the streets, every day a fight to survive, his only "family" being Rick. They'd stuck close together. Looked out for one another. With Rick's tendency to get sick and Dylan's propensity to get into injury-producing fights... *Jesus*, they could have used the services of someone like Dr. Alec Johnson.

Dylan reached for his keys. "Give me your address."

Ten minutes later he was motoring down the road on his favorite motorcycle, an Indian Blackhawk. As he turned off of Sloat Boulevard and onto Highway 1, he considered turning around. When he entered Alec's family-friendly neighborhood, the urge grew stronger. Why had he agreed to this?

Just get the motorcycle started and then get back to your massively growing to-do list.

Alec's well maintained home had been meticulously restored, like the rest of the 1920s-era houses that lined the street. The Mediterranean style residence had large bay windows, a brick driveway, and a beautiful yard, a nice combination. Kinda homey, if one was into that kind of thing.

Which he wasn't.

The garage door yawned open, and Alec stood inside, staring down at his Harley. Dylan pulled up and parked his motorcycle in the driveway.

"I've been trying for twenty minutes to get her started," Alec said as Dylan entered the spotless garage, not a tool in sight.

Man, how did the dude function without tools?

"I really appreciate you coming," Alec said.

"No worries."

Alec tucked his hair behind his ears. The automatic gesture looked like a well-established habit. The thick, brown waves hung to his chin, just long enough to fit neatly behind his ears. He looked like a young, hippy college professor, his blue gaze open and honest, filled with an obvious intelligence.

Gone were Alec's jeans and brand-spanking-new riding jacket from yesterday. Instead, Alec wore khaki pants and a polo shirt more fitting the academic lurking beneath.

Alec planted his hand on his hips, eyeing the Harley. "I can't decide if it's the bike or if it's me."

"I have a 1942 WLA that's a bitch to start too."

Alec's gaze ticked up to Dylan's. "Should I be taking her reluctance personally?"

"Absolutely."

Alec chuckled and sent Dylan a smile. Despite the fatigue and this morning's inconvenient timing,

Dylan felt the urge to return the grin and was left wondering why. A buzzer sounded in the background, interrupting the moment.

Alec tipped his head toward the house. "Do you mind? I just need to turn the oven off."

"Go ahead."

Alec opened the door into what looked like the kitchen as a delicious smell drifted into the garage. Feeling on edge, Dylan shifted on his feet as he scanned his surroundings, trying to remember why he'd agreed to make the trek to Alec's house.

A sense of obligation, mostly. Curiosity too, about the man Noah had been mentioning for several years now. Dylan had expected serious and boring and uptight, not the self-deprecating sense of humor from yesterday. Pushing the motorcycle into the garage had to have been humiliating. Hard not to admire how Alec handled himself with dignity in the face of one embarrassing moment after another. And every interaction left Dylan a little more curious...

He rubbed his jaw. But he still had work coming out his ears and a bike rally to organize in honor of Rick.

Frowning, Dylan glanced at the far wall that contained a framed, poster-sized picture of a crowd of people holding signs. He stepped closer, intrigued.

The protest looked well attended. Dylan had no trouble figuring out the subject, a rally to support gay marriage. Posters dotted the scene with slogans such as *Down with DOMA* and *Don't Hate, Overturn Prop 8*. And then he spied Alec in the picture holding a sign that read *Jesus had two Dads and he turned out okay.*

Dylan bit back the grin and turned to look at Alec as he reentered the garage.

"Nice slogan." Dylan pointed at Alec's sign.

Alec followed Dylan's gaze and another easy smile appeared. "I didn't come up with the phrase, but I felt it was worth repeating."

"Definitely a winner."

"It appeals to my love of irony."

Dylan let out an amused grunt. "I know what you mean."

He was about to turn away from the poster when he spied a middle-aged woman in the picture, standing to Alec's left. Same brown hair as Alec's. Same blue eyes. Dylan leaned in to read the woman's sign. On top, the huge placard read *Waiting for my son and his partner to attain equal rights*. Beneath was a blown-up picture of a wedding invitation.

Alec Walter Johnson and Tyler Michael Hall request the pleasure of your company...

Surprise widened Dylan's eyes.

"My mother," Alec said.

Dylan cleared his throat, trying to think of a response. "Supportive."

He certainly had to admire her creativity. *And* the irony.

"You have no idea," Alec said drily. "She's still celebrating the death of DOMA." Alec blew out a breath. "Unfortunately, she's also holding out hope she gets to use that invitation one day."

The pause lengthened and turned uncomfortable, and Dylan felt pressured to fill the silence. What was he supposed to say? Hats off to you for your part in lifting the ban on gay marriage? Sorry your boyfriend left and now you can't enjoy the fruits of your labor?

Or maybe: congratulations, you won the war...but lost the battle.

Dylan stuck a hand in his back pocket. "The Harley."

"Right," Alec said. "She's being stubborn."

Grateful to get back to business, Dylan said, "So the bike is cold. Which means you'll need to turn the fuel tap." He crossed back to Alec's motorcycle to point out the various parts as he continued. "The choke needs to be all the way down. After giving her a few primer kicks, then you return your choke to one click below. Key on, one quarter throttle"—he touched the handle of the Harley—"and she should fire right up."

At the lost look on Alec's face, Dylan hesitated. Did the guy even know the purpose of the choke? Seriously, the man had no business owning a vintage bike. He should have started with a friggin' moped.

"Remember, this machine has a lot of compression," Dylan went on. "You gotta respect her. The kickback can throw you over the handlebars."

Alec's expression shifted from slightly lost to vaguely concerned, and Dylan suppressed the sigh. The "quick" visit was going to take longer than he'd thought. And certainly more time than he could afford.

First things first, Booth.

"Why don't you let me show you how to start her?" Dylan said.

Dylan mounted the motorcycle and ran through the process, explaining each step as he went and firing her up on his second try. Satisfaction rolled through him, and he revved the engine for a moment, enjoying the lumpy rumble unique to a Harley.

"I'll take her for a spin to warm her up," he said over the noise. "It'll be easier for you to practice when she's not so cold."

Alec nodded, and Dylan backed her out and headed down the driveway.

Instantly, he relaxed, cruising up the street. Despite his totally clueless state, Alec had managed to choose well. Dylan settled back on the leather seat, getting more comfortable. What a sweet ride. With all the crap piled high on his current schedule, when was the last time he'd taken a trip with no destination in mind, just for fun?

Felt like forever.

Dylan tooled up the road and around the block, enjoying the agility and smooth suspension before returning her to the driveway. While the bike continued to idle, vibrating beneath Dylan, he glanced at Alec, who appeared to be having second thoughts about his purchase. Not being able to start her would definitely put a damper on things.

"Listen," Dylan said over the rumbling engine, "if you want, this week after work I can teach you all her quirks."

In what spare time?

Dylan pushed the annoying thought aside. If nothing else, the Harley deserved an educated driver. He could afford an hour at the end of his day. Besides, Alec wasn't the total stick-in-the-mud Dylan had envisioned. Despite going against Dylan's advice, the man's dedication to his purchase was beginning to grow on Dylan.

Alec looked relieved. "That would be great."

"Since tomorrow's Sunday, we'll start in the morning." Dylan nodded at the Harley. "You ready to give her a whirl?"

"Yeah," Alec said, reaching for the handle. "I just—"

Alec's gaze caught and held on something in the distance, his lips tightening, and he briefly closed his eyes before facing the road. Dylan glanced over his shoulder and discovered the reason for the interruption.

An athletic looking guy in running shorts and shoes closed the driver's door of a sleek Range Rover now parked across from Alec's house. A second man exited the car. Dylan killed the switch on the Harley, and the motor died, the last rumble vibrating in the air.

"Christ," Alec murmured. "Tyler brought his boyfriend."

Tyler, as in the *Tyler Michael Hall* listed on the wedding invitation. Well, that explained the wigged-out look on Alec's face. They watched the two men open the trunk of the Range Rover.

"I can't believe he brought his new boyfriend," Alec said again. "*Damn it.*"

Stunned by the force behind Alec's whispered words, Dylan turned back to Alec. The dude who'd gracefully faced total public humiliation on the streets of San Francisco seemed to be losing his shit. Anxiety shimmered in his eyes. Apparently, his composure and sense of humor evaporated when facing his ex.

"How am I supposed to act?" Alec whispered forcefully. "Friendly? Coolly cordial? Or do I just ignore the new boyfriend? I know one thing for sure. I definitely don't want to act like the desperate ex." Alec shoved his hair back from his face, the rising panic rolling off him in waves thick enough to choke a horse. "And, good God, what was I thinking asking Tyler to come get his stuff?"

Unfortunately, Alec rambled on, and Dylan shot a glance at the two men now approaching. Just what he didn't have time for, getting sucked into the middle of a goddamn soap opera. Alec's disjointed mumblings finally died out as Tyler made his way up the driveway.

Alec's voice sounded strained, but at least all signs of his babbling had vanished. "Hey, Tyler."

The ex, in contrast, looked completely unruffled.

"This is the motorcycle you bought?" Tyler had black hair, cool gray eyes, and a tiny crease of concern between his eyebrows. "Are you trying to get yourself killed, Alec?"

Color tinged Alec's cheeks, his expression open, exposed, reminding Dylan of Rick. And the age-old need to protect bristled through Dylan. He forced himself to grip the handles of the Harley.

He'd spent his adolescent years using his fists to defend his friend against homophobic bullies, but Tyler wasn't one of those. And this wasn't Dylan's fight. Besides, the ex was right. Clearly Alec was as green as they came. But for some reason the trace of alarm in Tyler's tone ticked Dylan off, mostly because Tyler looked completely in control while Alec seemed too agitated to reply. Though preferable to babbling, Dylan hoped Alec's tongue-tied state wouldn't continue. Because somebody needed to say something...

The awkward moment stretched to the point where Dylan couldn't take the pressured silence anymore. "Alec is handling her just fine," Dylan lied.

"Fine" being a relative term, of course. But he chose to ignore the *are-you-kidding-me?* look Alec lobbed in Dylan's direction. No false bravado from

the man. What followed was a hint of skepticism in
Tyler's eyes that raised Dylan's hackles further.

"How well do you know Alec?" Tyler asked.

For the life of him, Dylan couldn't stop the
words that scraped from his mouth next. Maybe
because, with the simple lift of a brow, Tyler had
more or less called Dylan a liar—which wouldn't
have pissed Dylan off so much except for the fact it
was true. Maybe he was irked by the smooth tone of
Tyler's voice while Alec looked so friggin' miserable,
the seeming imbalance of power always triggering
the reflexive action.

Protecting Rick had been Dylan's most
important job. But using his fists was no longer an
option. Words, however, were.

Which often popped out of Dylan with zero
advanced planning.

"I know him well enough," Dylan said, hoping to
bring Tyler down a peg or two, level the playing field
for Alec, so to speak. "Alec brought me home and
fucked my brains out last night."

Whoa, that felt all kinds of weird coming from
his mouth.

The silence that followed lasted just long
enough for Dylan to register Alec's jaw go slack and
the blank expression on Tyler's face. The new
boyfriend pressed his lips together and looked away.
Dylan couldn't be sure, but the man might have been
laughing.

Finally, Tyler studied Dylan, his gaze drifting
over his holey jeans, faded T-shirt, and work boots.
"Alec slept with you last night," Tyler said, a question
mark buried at the end.

Was he daring Dylan to confirm the statement?
Dylan crossed his arms, fast losing patience with the
man for calling him out on his lies.

"Yes." As if his previous statement hadn't been crazy enough, Dylan found himself upping the ante. "We've been pretty hot 'n heavy for a while now."

"Interesting," Tyler said, his expression unreadable. Two beats passed before Tyler glanced at Alec. "So I assume he'll be attending Noah's cocktail party as your date?"

A *date*?

Alec's mouth opened, but no sound came. As the man's mute state continued, Dylan shifted on the motorcycle, the awkward tension making his muscles tight. The look on Tyler's face was clear. He didn't believe a word Dylan had said, and the answer to the party question was simply a test. If Dylan said no, Tyler would be proven right.

But if Dylan said yes...

Jesus, what was he thinking? He couldn't say yes. Dylan knew plenty of people who swung that way, and Rick had been as gay as they came, but Dylan wasn't sure he could even fake an attraction to a guy. 'Course, he was an expert at bullshitting his way through just about anything.

You don't have time for this.

Dylan opened his mouth to refute the ridiculous "date" idea and then glanced at the expression on Alec's face. The man was bleeding vulnerability. And after three years on the streets with a friend who'd been a constant target, Dylan couldn't change now, the protector-mode as ingrained as breathing. The words shot out before he could stop them.

"Yep, I'll be there. I wouldn't miss Noah's party for the world," Dylan said.

Fuck. He could just imagine the hysterical laughter coming from Noah now.

Alec's voice was strained. "Yes, Dylan will be attending with me."

Well, double fuck. Alec made a lousy liar. The light in Tyler's eyes transmitted his complete skepticism. He didn't believe either one of them. And Dylan decided the man must be a total douchebag.

An extremely *astute* douchebag, but a douchebag nonetheless.

"I'll just collect the last of my things," Tyler said.

Alec waved at six neatly stacked boxes in the coroner of the garage. "Help yourself."

As soon as Tyler and his boyfriend left, each carrying two cartons as they headed for the Range Rover, Alec leaned in Dylan's direction.

"What the hell did you say all that for?" Alec whispered, blue eyes blazing.

Dylan ignored the churn in his stomach as he wondered exactly the same thing. "He was pissing me off," he said, hating that he felt so defensive. "How the heck did you spend two years with that asshole?"

He frowned as he watched Tyler arrange the boxes in the back of his SUV.

"He's not normally an asshole." Alec rubbed his forehead. "I think seeing you in our—*my*—driveway really threw him for a loop."

Dylan pointed at the blond-haired boyfriend helping Tyler load the Range Rover. "Like flaunting his new piece of ass is any easier on you?"

Seriously, what was *wrong* with him today?

Dylan dropped his arm and reined in his anger. The ex returned to the garage, alone, and Alec attempted to appear unaffected by his presence—a spectacular fail. Dylan hoped the good Dr. Johnson excelled at his work, cuz he sucked at starting motorcycles and picking up the pieces after a failed relationship. And he really sucked at pretending he was okay around his ex.

Dylan shot Tyler a huge smile, determined to make the man uncomfortable, if such a thing were possible. Maybe then Tyler wouldn't notice how miserable Alec looked.

"Need any help with those last two?" Dylan asked.

"No, I've got them," Tyler said.

"I don't mind."

"No need to trouble yourself."

"No trouble at all. I'm feeling pretty motivated," Dylan said. "Cuz the sooner you leave, the sooner Alec and I can get back to that sex swing."

Tyler paused in the midst of picking up the remaining boxes. "Alec doesn't have a sex swing."

The grin that hijacked Dylan's face was huge. "He does now."

Man, he'd really rolled out of the evil side of bed this morning.

Alec sounded defeated. "You just don't know when to shut up, do you?"

"It's a gift," Dylan said.

Or a curse, depending on the day.

For a brief moment, the unflappable Tyler looked uncertain, less sure of himself. Good, let the bastard have doubts. Finally, Tyler shook his head, the unruffled expression returning as he held the last two boxes in his arms.

"Guess we'll see you both at Noah's party," Tyler said as he passed by.

Dylan's grin returned. "Looking forward to it."

Chapter Three

Thirty minutes later Alec blew out a sigh of relief when he heard the *beep, beep, beep* of the combination to the front keyless entry of his home, and Noah swept inside with a flamboyant flourish. A tightly wound bundle of energy in a compact five-foot-ten-inch body, he looked casually dressed, but Alec knew the outfit by Hermes had cost a fortune. Noah's lean frame sported a long-sleeved, cashmere T-shirt and fitted black jeans.

Alec just hoped the man had brought his powers of persuasion along.

Noah closed the door and paused, assessing Alec and Dylan where they sat in the living room. "I need a Bloody Mary."

"It's only eleven o'clock in the morning," Alec said.

Though, God knows, after Tyler's visit and Dylan's maverick mouth, Alec felt the need for a drink too.

"Yes, a bit of the hair of the dog and all that," Noah said as he smoothed a black strand of hair from his forehead. "Couldn't this have waited until a better time? Like next year?"

Alec said firmly, "No."

The first thing Alec had done after Tyler left was call Noah and insist he come over. Normally Alec would have taken pity on his friend, but this time Noah's hangover-fueled protests went unheeded. Alec needed him to talk some sense into Dylan. Besides, it was only fair. Noah was the one who had sent Alec to Dylan in the first place, and Noah had neglected to mention the man was insane.

Alec would have remembered such a description.

Noah crossed the living room toward Dylan, where he stood at the minibar, mixing the Bloody Mary.

"Remember, Noah," Dylan said, "this afternoon's meeting about the poker run can't run any longer than forty-five minutes, tops."

"I'll do my best." Noah accepted the drink with a murmured thanks. "But I can't make any guarantees."

Dylan pointed a finger in Noah's direction. "Don't make me pull out a timer."

"Deal," Noah said. "As long as you don't make me drink alone."

Dylan obligingly pulled a beer from the tiny refrigerator, and Alec got the distinct impression the mutually tolerant pattern of interaction had been forged ages ago.

"I saw last week's blog," Noah said to Dylan. "I have to say, your post was inspiring."

Surprised, Alec glanced at the mechanic. "You have a blog?"

"Yep." Dylan twisted the top off his bottle with a hissing *pop*. "About vintage bikes." He flipped the cap between his fingers, and it hit the stainless steel garbage can with a *ping*, plopping inside.

Noah grinned as he watched the procedure. "That never fails to amuse me," he said, turning to Alec. "Isn't he just the butchiest thing you've ever seen?"

Instead of answering, Alec addressed Dylan instead. "What do you write about?"

"Last week I explained what produces the unique sound of a Harley, starting with an explanation about the four cycles of power generation." A faint grin slipped up Dylan's face. "The suck, the squeeze, the bang, and the blow."

"Sounds like my night last night." Noah sent Dylan an innocent expression. "The suck and the squeeze were good. But the bang and the blow were phenomenal."

"We don't want to hear about it," Alec said.

"Sweetie, that's because you're not getting laid regularly anymore." Noah gestured at the bay window. "You live in San Francisco, for chrissakes. There's a great big gay world out there with plenty of men to go around." His gaze settled on Alec, his voice dropping an octave. "It's time, Alec."

It's time, Alec.

The words reverberated through Alec's head, and he shifted his attention to the window and the Harley parked in the driveway. Up until this point, he'd been avoiding Noah's hints about moving on— the loss of a sex life the least of Alec's problems. But, deep down, he knew Noah was referring to something more important.

Clinging to memories of better times with Tyler was fruitless, but Alec had invested two years of his life into their relationship. *Two years.* And letting go of his hopes for forever had proved harder than he'd ever imagined.

Noah interrupted his thoughts. "You need to start dating."

"True," Alec said. But after being so wrong, how could he ever trust his choice of a potential partner again? Alec pushed the thought aside. "Except now Tyler thinks I'm sleeping with Dylan."

Noah choked on his drink, his face turning red as he struggled for breath. For a moment Alec thought he'd need to help clear his friend's airway.

"Dylan's as straight as they come. You can't even get him drunk and take advantage of him." Noah pretended to look dejected. He hadn't earned the nickname the *Diva of Drama* for nothing. "Trust me, I tried and failed."

Dylan rolled his eyes. "That was a long time ago. And we all know how much you love confusing intoxicated heterosexuals."

"Everyone has to have a hobby. Besides, a little flirting never hurt anyone," Noah said with a dismissive hand before he turned to Alec. "Why would Tyler think you're sleeping with Dylan?"

"Because I told him we were," Dylan said.

Noah gripped his glass, frozen, the only movement a slow blink of his eyelids. When he finally recovered, he dropped into a chair. "Now I'm confused."

"Join the club," Alec muttered.

Not that sleeping with Dylan was a repulsive idea. Who wouldn't admire the classic good looks, killer body, and confident attitude? Dylan was daring, unapologetic, and so rough around the edges he made tree bark look like polished glass. The earthy rawness made for an impressive animal magnetism.

"What's there to be confused about?" Dylan said. He took a pull from his bottle, his Adam's apple doing a mesmerizing slow rise and fall. "I come to the party and pretend to be Alec's main squeeze."

Alec's head pounded, the beginnings of a killer headache coming on. "You're not really coming."

"Hell, yeah, I am," Dylan said in protest. "I'm not letting that asshole call me a liar and get away with it."

"But you *were* lying," Alec said.

"Hah." Dylan pointed his bottle at Alec. "But he can't prove that, now can he?"

Alec squeezed his forehead between his thumb and his index finger, hoping to thwart the budding migraine. My God, the man really wanted to go through with the ridiculous plan.

Alec turned to Noah. "He's *your* friend. Can't you convince him not to go?"

"Me?" Noah pressed his hand to his chest. "I wouldn't miss this fake-homo show for all the Gucci shoes on Rodeo Drive. Besides, once Dylan Booth gets an idea in his head, the threat of hell and high water pants won't change his mind. Hetero or not, he'll make a fabulous backup boyfriend."

Dylan tipped his head. "Backup boyfriend?"

"You know," Noah said. "The boyfriend substitute, at least that's how I use the term. He's not a real boyfriend, just a convenience. For display purposes only. Sometimes used to make the ex jealous."

"I don't want to make the ex jealous," Alec said. "That's a junior high school move."

"Yeah?" Dylan said drily. "Well, my inner twelve-year-old would love to see Tyler jealous."

Noah turned his gaze to Alec. "You know how much I admire Tyler's dedication to the Front Street Clinic."

Alec mentally winced, but not because of the whiplash change of subject. Alec had acclimated to Noah's hectic, non sequitur ramblings long ago. But the new topic left Alec worried what would pop from his friend's mouth next. With Noah, danger lurked around every benign-looking corner.

"Tyler's a great guy and a fantastic physician. Almost too dedicated to his patients if you ask me," Noah continued. "But he's always so...coolly detached. I swear if his pulse got any lower, we'd have to have him declared dead." He lobbed a look at Alec. "I never thought he was right for you."

Christ, how had his friend known the truth while Alec had remained so oblivious? When Dylan had opened his mouth and lied about their relationship, Alec's first instinct had been to deny, deny, deny. Mostly because he knew how much further the lie took him from reconciliation.

Yes, he understood they were over, and he had too much self-respect to cling to someone who'd so obviously moved on. But a small part of him kept thinking if Tyler came back, then Alec hadn't really spent two years being so *wrong*...

A smile crept up Noah's face. "I'd like to see Tyler jealous too. In fact, nothing would entertain me more than watching Dylan ruffle the Ice Man's implacable feathers."

"Then I'll simply skip the party," Alec said.

"You can't," Noah said calmly. "I planned it specifically for you and Tyler."

Dylan shot Alec a confused look, but Alec was too mentally exhausted by the idea of an evening with Dylan, Tyler, and the new boyfriend in the same room to explain its origins. Noah, on other hand, was a perpetual energy machine.

Noah's enthusiasm showed in his voice. "The Front Street Clinic is receiving the humanitarian award from the Bay Area Council on HIV."

"And...?" Dylan asked.

"And I'm throwing a party to celebrate," Noah said as if the answer should be obvious. "Tyler and Alec and I worked our asses off getting that clinic up and running. A one hundred thousand dollar check earmarked for our housing project and a tacky plaque inscribed with Alec's and Tyler's names should be celebrated in style."

Alec glanced at Noah. "You could cancel the party."

"But I bought enough caviar for a hundred people," Noah said. "What would I do with such a large order of fish eggs?"

"Donate it to a local food bank?" Alec suggested hopefully.

"Goodness, no," Noah said, as if Alec had announced they should all eat gazpacho with their fingers. "The order is coming from Caviar House and Prunier in London. This demands a palate that can appreciate quality."

"Quit pretending to be a snob, Noah," Dylan said.

"Hon, I'm not pretending."

For once, Dylan was right. Noah was mostly show. Alec had long suspected Noah's claim of chasing straight men bordered on being a huge exaggeration.

Questionable sexual conquests aside, Noah used to serve on the Bay Area Council on HIV, which is how Alec had met him. When Alec and Tyler had first envisioned a clinic for the homeless, Noah had worked tirelessly behind the scenes to ensure they had adequate financial support. The man's energy was amazing, if not exhausting.

"Well, if you're not canceling the party, I'm going," Dylan said.

Noah narrowed his gaze at Dylan. "This isn't your beer-and-a-bucket-of-chicken-wings kind of affair. You up to the task?"

"Definitely," Dylan said.

"Seven o'clock, two weeks from today," Noah said. "My place."

"I'll be the one in the leather dog collar," Dylan said.

Noah laughed, Dylan grinned, and Alec let out a groan.

Christ, this was going to be a disaster.

Chapter Four

The next morning, after days of typical non-stop fog, the wet blanket had lifted, and the rising sun celebrated by stretching streamers of pink and orange across the sky. Dylan had been itching to hit the road since he'd parked his and Alec's motorcycles on the trailer behind his truck and driven them east toward Livermore Valley. Two such beautiful bikes deserved a kick-ass route, and Dylan had chosen accordingly. The wine country's rolling, vineyard-covered hills offered the perfect place to practice Alec's skills. Dylan had unloaded the bikes with anticipation, but so far, the ride hadn't lived up to his expectations.

In fact, the trip kinda sucked.

As Dylan followed behind, they headed over a patch of rough road, and Alec's Harley shook like a washing machine on spin. Dylan bit back the words crowding his throat. He hated sounding like a broken record. But he'd dragged his butt out of bed before the ass-crack of dawn on a Sunday to give Alec the promised lesson, and, bloody hell, he had every intention of following through.

No matter how moody the student.

"Dude, I told you," Dylan said into the microphone in his helmet. "You need to relax your grip and let the front wheel adjust to the terrain. That's what it's supposed to do."

Instead, Alec's hands seemed to tighten around the handles. Dylan could practically see Alec's knuckles bleeding color from the effort. Frustration pierced Dylan in the gut, mostly because he knew the man wasn't nervous or uncomfortable or acting out of defiance.

No, Alec simply looked pissed off.

They'd been on the spectacularly scenic road for an hour now, enjoying cooler morning temperatures and the scent of earth and all things green, yet Alec appeared no closer to relaxing than he had when Dylan arrived at his house. At first he figured Alec wasn't a morning person, passing off the man's one-word responses in the truck as a sign of not enough caffeine. Dylan had hoped getting out on the motorcycles would ease Alec's tendency toward one-syllable replies. Once they'd gotten started, Dylan had coached Alec via the wireless headset. Alec, however, then chose complete silence.

Single word responses were apparently too much for him now.

Alec's shoulders looked rigid as he steered through the turn, and Dylan sighed into his microphone. "You're too tense."

No response.

"You know," Dylan said, lips twisting wryly, "in case you hadn't realized, the wireless setup in our helmets works both ways."

Dylan thought he heard something that sounded like an amused huff.

"Stop overthinking things and just relax," Dylan went on. "The bike will turn more effectively if you're not so stiff."

"I'm trying."

The clipped words were almost worse than the silence, and Dylan didn't bother keeping his sigh silent as he followed Alec down the deserted, backcountry road. They came to a crossway and slowed to a stop, intent on turning onto a strip of road Dylan loved to go wide open on. In front of

Dylan, Alec rested one foot on the ground and leaned slightly to adjust his mirror, and Dylan saw the potential fuckup in the making.

He opened his mouth to call out a warning, but Alec's bike began to tip, and the words died, too late to do any good. Gravity and the weight of the Harley overcame Alec's attempts to remain upright. The machine fell to the ground, taking Alec along and pinning his left leg under the bike.

Dylan pulled up beside him and stopped, flipping up his visor. "The bike feels especially heavy when she starts to tip."

Alec didn't respond. He simply killed the switch to the Harley, the engine dying, and removed his helmet. Dylan had dropped a bike a time or two himself in his early days, and he remembered wanting to crawl under a rock and hide from the humiliation.

Dylan pulled off his helmet. "You need some help picking her up?"

"No." Alec slid his leg from beneath the Harley. "I'll be fine." He stood, refusing to look Dylan in the eye.

But something about the set of his shoulders and the firm line of his mouth told Dylan that Alec wasn't embarrassed. Just like the day he'd pushed his bike into the garage, Alec accepted his limitations with a graceful dignity Dylan couldn't help but admire. The same kind of lack of shame Alec exuded now. Nope, he definitely didn't look humiliated.

But he sure as hell still looked pissed.

No doubt about it. Alec was mad at Dylan. They weren't friends, so Dylan shouldn't care, really. But for some reason he couldn't explain, he did.

Dylan tucked his helmet under his arm. "You gonna spend all week making me pay for telling Tyler we're fucking?"

Jesus. Twenty-four hours later and Dylan still couldn't believe those words had shot from his mouth. Alec's response consisted of a flicker of a frown as he brushed the gravel from his jeans and removed his jacket before tossing it aside.

Dylan sighed, a cool breeze ruffling his hair as the silence of the vineyards surrounded them. Might as well get comfy cuz he'd be here a while for sure. He flipped the kickstand down and settled back against the seat, watching Alec grip the Harley and pull, attempting to lift his motorcycle.

His technique sucked. No way would this end in success. But Dylan knew Alec wasn't too keen on taking instructions at the moment. Dylan had spent the last hour and a half picking up on that big friggin' clue.

Dylan waited patiently for the man to ask for help. The furrow between Alec's brows and the firm set to Alec's lips didn't speak of him changing his mind anytime soon.

"Because if you're intent on making me pay, just let me know." Dylan hooked his helmet on his handlebar. "So I can plan ahead."

Alec flicked a curious look in Dylan's direction.

"Next time I'll bring some music, so I won't have to listen to you giving me the silent treatment," Dylan said.

A ghost of a grin came and left Alec's lips, and his gaze dropped back to his bike. Face set, Alec adjusted his hold on the motorcycle as if all he needed was a better grip and the bike would lift easily. And then he heaved with all his might. The tendons in his neck stood out, his biceps bunching as he strained. He didn't have much bulk, but his lean frame held enough muscle to get the job done, if using the proper technique.

Alec ceased the futile attempt and propped his hands on his hips, finally meeting Dylan's gaze. "It was an asinine thing to say to Tyler."

Dylan felt his brow crinkle. So the man *could* put more than three words together.

Unfortunately, those words pushed an uncomfortable prickle up Dylan's neck. "Yeah, well your ex was acting like an ass." Well, that didn't sound defensive at *all*.

"Maybe so. But I'd expect, as a grown man, you'd have better control over your own tongue."

Dylan hiked a brow, amused. "You could have told Tyler the truth. Oh, wait, that's right," he said drily. "You couldn't say anything at all."

Alec huffed again—and Dylan definitely detected the self-deprecating humor in the sound—and went back to his futile attempt at lifting the bike.

And so what if the ex had pissed Dylan off? Their relationship was none of Dylan's business. He shouldn't have let himself get backed into a corner about the damn party.

Alec adjusted his grip on the handle bar and the seat and heaved. The bike barely budged. Dylan bit his tongue, determined to wait for Alec to ask for help. Dylan had already offered. Damned if he was gonna offer again and get turned down. But the guilt about his actions yesterday still needled him...

"You could tell Tyler the truth now," Dylan said.

"Except I'd look like an idiot for going along in the first place."

Jesus, what did the man want from him?

"Then we go and pretend were doing the horizontal mambo," Dylan said.

"I know absolutely nothing about you. How am I supposed to pretend we're in a relationship?"

Seriously? Was that what had the man's boxers tied in a knot?

Dylan suppressed the smile. "I didn't tell your ex we were in a *relationship*." The word felt foreign on Dylan's tongue. "I told him we were having sex. There's a difference."

"Not for all of us," Alec muttered and returned his attentions to his reclining bike.

The statement burrowed its way deeper into Dylan's head, and the picture hanging on Alec's garage wall flashed through Dylan's mind. Did Alec think Dylan's claim had killed the last chance to kiss and make up with his ex? Was regret making Alec so moody now? And why did the idea make Dylan feel like shit?

Guilt rolled through his gut again, this time creeping up his chest, and Dylan swiped his hand through his hair. Man, he really needed to stop working so hard. His fatigue was probably a good explanation for how yesterday had played out. Tired and cranky from a lack of downtime, he'd slipped into protector mode—defending a man who would have survived without his help—and then taken Tyler's behavior personally.

With a silent groan, Dylan dismounted. Clearly he needed to burn off a little steam and kill the grumpiness with some satisfying speed. And no way was that happening anytime soon while Mr. Happy Homemaker here tried to lift the bike the *wrong* way.

Dylan crossed to stand beside Alec, who simply paused in the midst of another attempt, his biceps straining as he frowned up at Dylan.

"Quit sulking," Dylan said, his tone easy.

"I'm not."

"You are. And it's not an attractive look on you."
Dylan gently pushed Alec over to make room for
himself. "I'm helping. Unless you want to throw a
disc and wind up in bed unable to move. You're a
doctor. You should know to use your legs, not your
back. Like this." Dylan faced away from the bike and
crouched down, hooking his hands on the seat.
Using his thighs, he walked backward, lifting the
motorcycle as he went.

Alec stared at the now upright Harley. "Your
muscles are bigger than mine."

"I think we've established the same about my
mouth."

Alec's gaze lifted to Dylan's. "Is that your way of
apologizing?"

Yes.

"No," Dylan said.

Alec's eyes crinkled in amusement as if he'd
heard the contradiction, and a flush of
embarrassment heated Dylan's stomach. While Alec
looked as if he were contemplating a smile, Dylan
carefully laid the bike back down on the road.

"Give her a whirl," Dylan said.

Alec turned and mimicked Dylan's previous
actions, achieving success on the first try.

"Excellent." Dylan clapped Alec on the back.
"You have muscle enough."

The rigid set to Alec's shoulders finally eased a
bit, and Alec actually grinned. A small one, but the
first since this morning. For some bizarro reason,
Dylan felt as though he'd accomplished something
huge and found himself grinning back. Jesus, he was
definitely working too hard. Why else would a small
exchange of smiles make him feel this good?

"Now," Dylan said, eyeing Alec, "let's get back
on the bikes and try to enjoy ourselves, okay?"

"Sounds like a plan."

The backup boyfriend situation had gone unresolved, but Dylan decided to simply appreciate the ease in the tension. Once out on the road and following Alec again, Dylan twisted the throttle. With a roar, his motorcycle shot forward. He spared a brief glance at Alec as he pulled up beside him on the highway lane. Although the man's moodiness was gone, unfortunately Alec still traveled ten miles an hour under the speed limit. Dylan had been chafing all day, longing to hit the throttle on the straightaways.

"How about a race?" Dylan said into the mike.

"Are you kidding me?"

"No."

After a split-second pause, Alec said, "If you don't want to continue the lessons, just say so. No need to try and have me killed."

Even over the wireless headset, Dylan could hear the wry amusement in Alec's voice. Ah, the good Dr. Johnson was well and truly back from his sulk. A grin spread up Dylan's face.

"Now that you've finally relaxed, your technique is solid," Dylan said. "And, dude, getting you killed would be a bad plan. Noah would never let me hear the end of it. That alone is incentive enough for me to keep you alive."

Alec's laugh echoed in Dylan's helmet, bringing them another step closer to their initial easy-going interactions.

Feeling encouraged, Dylan said, "Sure I can't convince you to a race on the straightaway? There's no traffic. Little chance of getting hurt. And I'm not talking about high rates of speed. I was thinking more along the lines of actually reaching the speed limit."

A pause, and then, "How far?"

"Just to where the bridge crosses the road up there. Think you could handle that?"

After a few seconds of silence, Alec leaned forward and twisted the throttle, pulling ahead of Dylan before responding. "If I die, I hope Noah hounds you for life."

Dylan chuckled and increased his speed. As the trees whizzed by at increasing rates, the wind whistled past Dylan's helmet. His motorcycle revved beneath him, sending a familiar vibration he found comforting.

He loved this stretch of open road. This was where Dylan came when life got tough. Nothing soothed like the achievement of speed and eating up the ribbon of highway in front, the blur of scenery disappearing behind. Out here there were no disappointments.

Nothing to be taken away.

In a way, it was nice to associate the stretch of road with a good memory, replacing so many bad. Dylan maintained his position just behind Alec and to his right.

"Looking good," Dylan said.

"Feeling good."

They passed beneath the bridge, and Dylan eased up on the throttle, following Alec as he pulled onto the side of the road and parked. Alec removed his helmet. Cheeks flushed, eyes shining, the man sent Dylan the kind of smile that seemed to bubble up from the toes and escape with a burst.

"That was fantastic," Alec said.

Alec's enthusiasm pulled another grin from Dylan. "I knew you'd enjoy a little speed. So..." Dylan hooked his arm across his handlebar. "We good now?"

For the life of him, he couldn't figure out why the answer felt so important.

Alec leaned back on the seat of his Harley, looking fit, easy, and relaxed. "I don't think 'good' is a word that should be used in reference to you," Alec said drily, the words eased by the light in his eyes. "But we've definitely reached a truce."

The acute flush of pleasure left Dylan feeling strangely on edge, but he chased away the doubts and clapped on his helmet with a grin. "Then prepare to be schooled on the finer points of steering on the way back."

~~~***~~~

A week and a half later, Alec steered the Harley into Adams' Classic Motors, the lumpy rumble bouncing off the concrete floor and metal walls of the building as he parked inside. Crouched beside a motorcycle, grease smudging his arms and coating his hands, Dylan had his fingers buried in the decrepit looking vehicle's insides. Alec killed the Harley's motor and waited for the sound to die, muscles tense.

You just came to ask him about his plans for tomorrow, to invite him along for a beer and to catch the game on TV. Friends do that sort of thing all the time.

Even though Dylan had clearly enjoyed the daily lessons, so much so he'd continued well past Alec's need for instruction, uncertainty over their connection left Alec hesitant. The relationship felt like friendship, but Dylan was a hard man to read.

But the thought of watching tomorrow's football game alone bordered on depressing.

Alec pushed the feeling aside. "That's a Triumph TR5 Trophy you're working on. The kind of bike driven by James Dean," Alec said. "Doesn't get any cooler than that."

Hands still buried, Dylan raised his brows. "I'm surprised you recognize the make."

"Manufactured from 1949 to 1958. The 'Trophy' part of the name came from the three bikes built for the International Six Day Trial in '48, which won the manufacturers' team trophy."

Dylan stared at him as if he'd sprouted three heads, and Alec shrugged. "Research is a family passion." In fact, his parents were more obsessive than their son.

Though Dylan didn't grin, his green eyes flickered with humor. "A family passion, huh?" He nodded at Alec's motorcycle as he went on. "How she running today?"

"A little rough, but not so bad."

"Tell you what," Dylan said, pulling his hands out of the Triumph. "Why don't we give her a tune-up? Won't take but a couple of hours."

Caught off guard by the offer, Alec spent the next three seconds studying Dylan.

Since the first motorcycle lesson, they'd seen each other every day, Alec stopping by the shop after work or Dylan making the trek to Alec's house. Once he'd even stayed for dinner. When Alec had pulled the eggplant Parmesan out of his oven after the lesson, the growl from Dylan's stomach had made both of them laugh. Food definitely tasted better with company, and Alec hated eating alone.

"I appreciate the offer, but what about the Triumph?" Alec asked.

"It'll keep until tomorrow. I'll tell the owner of the bike I'm running a day behind schedule."

"Won't your boss get mad?"

"Dude, *I'm* the owner," Dylan said. "I can do whatever I want."

The news sent Alec's hairline reaching higher. When Noah had sent him to see Dylan, Alec hadn't given the ownership of the business any thought. "I assumed you were an employee."

"Hell, no," Dylan said. "You think I'd work this hard for someone else? I own this bucket of grease, lock, stock, and barrel of used motor oil."

"Then why isn't it called Booth's Classic Motors?"

Dylan's face went blank, and he turned back to the motorcycle, plunging his fingers back inside. Dylan might be a hard man to read, but right now the tension in his shoulders spoke volumes. Several seconds passed by until Alec began to wonder if Dylan would answer the question.

"My best friend's last name was Adams. We used to talk about opening our own business restoring vintage motorcycles." Gaze fixed on the Triumph, Dylan gave a tiny shrug. "So I guess it's a way of making sure Rick got what he'd always wanted."

Alec rested his palm on the handle of the Harley, unsettled by the news.

"Rick," Alec said slowly, the pieces of the puzzle slowly slotting together. "As in Noah's old boyfriend?"

"Yep."

Alec didn't know much except that Noah had dated a man who had died of HIV, hence Noah's commitment to the community. But the news that Dylan's friendship with Noah had been forged through that relationship came as a complete surprise.

In retrospect the information explained a lot about the connection between Dylan and Noah, complete opposites in many respects. From the first moment Alec had watched the two interact, he'd been curious. Alec could tell the bond went deep. He just hadn't known why.

Crouched by the bike, Dylan continued with his task, and Alec searched for something appropriate to say.

"That's a nice way to keep his memory alive," Alec said.

"Mmm hmm," Dylan said, keeping his eyes on his task. "Every year on Rick's birthday we used to take a road trip. The poker run is a way of remembering him and raising money for HIV research at the same time."

So not only had Dylan named his business after his dead friend, Dylan had started a fundraiser in honor of him as well. Still waters did indeed run deep. Dangerously deep.

"Bring the Harley over here and we'll start with an oil change," Dylan said.

The subtext came across loud and clear: conversation over, time to move on.

Alec dismounted, pushed the motorcycle closer, and parked next to the Triumph.

The next two hours came as a complete surprise and were much more entertaining than Alec would have predicted. Every time Dylan sent Alec to fetch something, Alec tried to help, but his ignorance about basic tools was impossible to hide. When Dylan had to describe what a Phillips screwdriver was, the mechanic could barely contain his laughter.

After that, Dylan's good-natured teasing became a part of the process. So Alec shamelessly used his photographic memory to spout random motorcycle facts he'd picked up during his research—the first time since college that Alec's ability to recall useless information had come in handy.

As Dylan set the bucket of used motor oil aside, Alec finally worked up the courage to ask the question that prompted today's visit. "Tomorrow I'm planning on having a beer at Danny's Suds and Sports and catching the football game on TV. You want to come along?"

Alec hated that he held his breath while waiting for an answer. One of the few things he and Tyler had shared outside of work had been college football. Alec considered himself a serious fan. Tyler maintained an interest as well, enough to humor Alec, anyway. And with the start of the season tomorrow night, the first since their breakup, he couldn't stomach the thought of watching the game alone.

Christ, he hated rattling around an empty home.

"When is the game?" Dylan asked.

Dylan stood and placed the bucket of old oil on a table before returning to kneel by the motorcycle, this time right at Alec's feet. The scent of spicy soap and musky man and motorcycle hit, reminding Alec of Dylan's intent to pose as his new boyfriend. Alec's nervous system sparked, his thoughts stumbling.

"Seven o'clock," Alec said.

"College or pro?"

"College."

"Which team?"

Alec absently studied the sweat staining the collar of Dylan's T-shirt and the smudge of motor oil on the back of his neck, a result of the messy process and the state of Dylan's hands.

"College Bay University," Alec said.

"The Tigers?" Dylan winced. "Somehow, I never pictured you as a glutton for punishment."

"I know," Alec said, a smile overtaking his face. "But they're local. Besides, I like cheering for the underdog."

"If you support the Tigers, you must get off on cheering for the losing team as well." Dylan leaned back on his heels, bringing him closer to Alec's legs, and sent him pointed look.

Unfortunately, now those green eyes gazed up at him from a position that brought to mind all sorts of scenarios involving Dylan on his knees, and Alec's body went still. His traitorous mind pictured sweat-slicked arms and messy fingers reaching out to cup Alec's crotch. Unzipping his zipper...

And before Alec could stop them, more graphic visions barreled past. Dylan's callused hands stroking Alec's cock. That pink tongue circling his head. Dylan's mouth stretched wide around him, hot and slick and taking him deep. Alec gripping that grease-stained neck as he thrust hard, coming in the back of Dylan's throat.

Holy shit.

Heart thudding painfully, Alec gave a single shake of his head and forced the images from his mind.

Alec didn't trust himself to date just yet. And he'd be crazy to get involved with someone looking for nothing more than a quick fuck. Alec had never been the one-night-stand type, a sure route to frustration and heartbreak. But fantasizing about an unattainable straight man?

The epitome of ludicrous.

Dylan gave a sharp nod. "Okay. I'll come."

Alec ignored the thrill jetting through his veins at Dylan's unintentional double entendre.

"Good." Alec cleared his throat awkwardly. "I'll go dump the bucket."

He picked up the pail and headed for the used-oil barrel, feeling slightly unsteady.

So far he'd had no trouble admiring Dylan's drool-worthy attributes with an almost detached, clinical air, like one did of someone completely out of reach. But time had changed things. Clearly there was more to Dylan's rough-and-tumble attitude and sharp tongue than Alec first appreciated, namely learning his bark lacked serious bite. Not to mention his dedication to his friend's memory.

Alec bit back a sigh. Enjoying his time with Dylan was fine. Admiring his loyalty was good too. And Alec felt no shame recognizing that the man brought a new level of standards to the phrase "sex on two legs."

But there was something slightly alarming the way Dylan, without even trying, pressed a hidden nerve inside Alec. A nerve he hadn't known existed. Dylan had unlocked a sweaty, tough-guy fantasy Alec had been better off *not* knowing he harbored.

And now, when he looked into Dylan's gaze, Alec suddenly longed to see heat in those green eyes as they peered down at him from a very inappropriate position.

Christ. And he'd thought his life couldn't get any more screwed up.

~~~***~~~

Packed, the sports bar hummed with fans hoping against hope their team could pull off the impossible and actually win a game. And if someone had told Dylan he'd wind up hanging out with a guy who knew every statistical fact about the Tigers, he'd have sworn he needed to get a life.

Alec, however, had no shame whatsoever as he leaned closer to Dylan to be heard. "Their quarterback had a 135 passing efficiency rating last season, up from 129 the year before."

"Your knowledge would be more impressive if it included the stats of a *winning* team."

Alec clearly didn't care. "So who's your favorite?"

"Whoever's the best bet on the TV set."

"You're a love-the-one-you're-with kind of guy."

"Absolutely."

"That's sad, Dylan," Alec said with mock sympathy. "Very sad."

"No." Dylan sent his friend a huge grin. "I prefer a sure thing."

When the quarterback got sacked on the big screen hanging over the bar, Alec let out an exuberant groan. The dismayed Tiger fan to Dylan's left slapped the counter, jostling his beer in the process. Dylan slid his mug and his stool an inch closer to Alec's. Although Dylan preferred pro ball to college, he had zero regrets about coming tonight.

Watching Alec's reactions was almost as entertaining as the game itself.

At halftime, Dylan turned to Alec. "How did starting the Harley go this morning?"

"Got it on the first try."

Alec's satisfied little-boy grin brought an odd flush of pleasure through Dylan's chest. Alec had grown much more adept at turning over his motorcycle, with an eighty percent success rate of getting her going even when cold. Just like their backcountry race, every kick start of the Harley brought a flare of excitement and satisfaction to Alec's eyes.

And why was the sight so fucking amusing?

Probably because most of Dylan's serious biker buddies lived fairly far away. Outside the occasional trip to a rally or an organized run, Dylan's contact consisted of the rare phone call and a meet-up once, maybe twice, a year.

Dylan paused and then tossed out the idea that had been churning in his head for the past several days. "You should come on the poker run with me," Dylan said. "Plenty of awesome bikes to see."

Alec let out a skeptical snort. "I've owned my motorcycle a little over two weeks. I'm not exactly a pro."

"Don't need to be. The weekend is all about fun."

The doubtful look on Alec's face grew bigger. "I'd hate feeling pressured to keep up."

"No pressure, man," Dylan said.

Alec tapped his fingers on the counter. "I think I better pass."

The pretty brunette waitress set down two more beers and took the empty chicken-wing basket away, and Dylan sent her a nod of thanks before turning back to Alec. "Let me know if you change your mind. As I said, lots of awesome bikes to drool over." Dylan cocked his head as he went on. "You never did tell me why you chose your Harley."

Alec crossed his arms. "It was an impulse buy. I'd spent some time doing research, thinking I'd choose a duo-sport because I wanted something light enough to pick up. You know"—Alec's lips quirked as he took a bite of his French fry—"in case I fell over or anything."

Dylan played dumb. "Now who'd do a lame-ass thing like that?"

Alec laughed, his eyes crinkling at the corners. Since the first lesson, Dylan had learned that a smiling Alec was good. A laughing Alec? Even better. Alec's refusal to participate in the poker run left Dylan feeling vaguely unsatisfied. Clearly he'd have to work on the guy and get him to change his mind.

But before Dylan could decide how to make that happen, or why he cared so much, his cellular buzzed, and he pulled the phone from his back pocket. He eyed Noah's incoming number and groaned, letting the call go to voice mail.

He pointed his iPhone at Alec. "This is why I need you to say yes."

Alec tipped his head in confusion.

"To keep me from killing Noah at the poker run," Dylan went on.

"And you thought that would provide me with incentive?" Alec said drily.

A chuckle escaped before he could stop it. "This year Noah volunteered to be in charge cuz I want to actually enjoy myself instead of running around taking care of last-minute details. Unfortunately, he's been driving me friggin' crazy."

He never should have let his friend volunteer to head up the annual run this year. For some reason Dylan had yet to explain, the fifth anniversary of Rick's death seemed... significant, for lack of a better description. Although he appreciated Noah stepping up to the plate, Dylan was beginning to have regrets.

Serious regrets.

"At least Noah's organized," Alec said.

"Yeah, but his attention to detail is driving me batshit crazy." Dylan's lips twisted in a mix of irritation, amusement, and affection—the standard reaction triggered by his friend.

From Alec's earlier response, no doubt he felt the same way.

"And Noah didn't know how much work the event involved, so he's been a queen bitch about the whole thing," Dylan said.

"I'm not surprised you two have vastly different ideas about how the weekend should play out. Noah's as gay as they come, and you're"—Alec waved in Dylan's general direction, clearly struggling for the right words—"very much not."

Amused by Alec's description, Dylan licked the hot wing sauce from his fingers and wiped his fingers down his jeans. "I sure as hell don't spend as much on clothes."

"He does give the Kardashians a run for their money."

"How the hell would you know that?"

"Don't tell anyone." Alec leaned in close and lowered his voice. "I hide my *People* magazine in the middle of my stack of medical journals."

Dylan tipped back his head and laughed. Apparently the good doctor's research fetish extended to pop culture gossip as well. "Your secret is safe."

Alec steadily held Dylan's gaze and set his drink down, blue eyes lit with humor. "Go ahead and say it."

"Say what?"

"That reading *People* magazine makes me a girl."

Dylan pressed his lips together, smothering the smile, and gave Alec a lingering once-over as if the ridiculous statement deserved serious consideration. Alec didn't have an overly muscular build, but the slim, well-toned physique filled out his button-down shirt just fine. Clearly, the man was in good shape. His angular face lacked any hint of femininity, but something about those blue eyes softened the features, and it wasn't just the thick lashes. No, the effect came from an underlying openness and humility.

A vulnerability that Dylan found strangely compelling.

"Nope, you're definitely not a girl." Dylan nodded at a table with two females who'd been casting looks their way since they arrived. "*Those* are girls."

"Women."

"Whatever."

The blond sent a sexy smile and turned in her chair to face him—or maybe Alec, Dylan wasn't which—offering up a view of an impressive pair of breasts. Any other night Dylan would have been all over the offer, making his choice and enjoying himself until the sun came up. Right now he preferred hanging with Alec. Dylan hadn't had this much fun since...well, since he couldn't remember when.

Huh. He really needed to stop working so hard and get out more.

"They're looking this way too." Alec nodded at two men facing them on the other side of the bar, both studying them as well.

A military man, complete with buzz cut, sported an I'm-a-badass posture. The second guy had more muscles and tats than the cover of a bike rally magazine.

"Sorry." Dylan shook his head and picked up his mug. "Does absolutely nothing for me. But don't let me stop you. Take your pick and have at it."

"They're eyeing both of us. I think they want a foursome."

Dylan choked on his sip of beer. "You gotta be fucking kidding me." He blinked, staring at the two men. "Four?" Dylan didn't consider himself a prude by any stretch of the imagination. He liked a good kink as much as the next guy. But still... "Man, how does anyone keep up with what goes where?"

"I wouldn't know. I'm into monogamy."

"Yeah." Dylan eyed Alec over his mug. "The poster in your garage provided a pretty big clue."

Alec tipped his head. "Have you *ever* been in a relationship?"

"Hell, no. I'm all for monogamy. But I subscribe to the only-one-woman-a-night version. And I sure as hell don't want to be tied down to one person. Ever."

The halftime show got underway, a band marching across the field on the big screen, and Dylan decided to take advantage.

"You sure I can't talk you into the poker run?" This time Alec's hesitation lasted longer, so Dylan went on. "I guarantee you'll have fun."

"What if I fell over in front of a crowd of die-hard bikers?"

"Dude, people fall over all the time."

Which wasn't entirely true, but anyone with Alec's enthusiasm would always be welcome among Dylan's riding friends. Besides, Dylan would be around to keep any assholes in line.

"Okay." Alec blew out a breath. "I'll go."

Pleasure flared, and he bumped his shoulder against Alec's. "Good."

The grin on Dylan's face must have made him look like an idiot because suddenly Alec was staring at him with an odd expression. An awkward pause swelled during which Dylan tried to figure out what the hell he'd done wrong.

Awareness washed over him slowly. A welcoming warmth. A pleasing pressure. The contact, in some weird way, reassuring. Slowly he realized their shoulders were still pressed together. And, as Dylan got caught up in the blue eyes, Alec's gaze briefly ticked to Dylan's mouth, the dark lashes dipping.

The glance hit Dylan like a blast from his acetylene torch, sending sizzles of heat skittering confusingly up his limbs, only to finally concentrate, fuck his life, in his groin.

Background noises faded, but Alec shifted his attention to the TV so quickly that the loss of the return gaze left Dylan feeling...unbalanced. As if he'd lost an anchor and been set adrift. And it also left him wondering if he'd imagined the whole thing. Alec's profile filled Dylan's vision, and he couldn't seem to pull his gaze away from Alec's mouth. Would his lips feel as soft as they looked? Would they taste good?

Jesus, what the hell was wrong with him?

Dylan turned to face forward, pretending to watch the commercial on the big screen as his heart spent several minutes knocking beneath his ribs, trying to beat some sense into him from the inside out.

Dylan was no homophobe. A number of his acquaintances were gay, a byproduct of his friendships with Noah and Rick. And those who were straight knew better than to use the words faggot or queer around Dylan.

Being touched by another man didn't threaten Dylan's masculinity. He knew who he was and what he liked and hadn't really considered much outside the female persuasion. So why the confusing response to such a simple glance at his mouth?

Man, he really needed to get laid.

"You still coming to the party tomorrow night?" Alec asked.

Party?

Dylan seized the churning cauldron of his thoughts.

"Look, you really don't have to go," Alec said. "This whole backup boyfriend thing isn't necessary."

Going will be a mistake.

The words echoing in his head held an edge of concern, and Dylan gripped the handle of his mug.

Since their first motorcycle lesson, Alec had tried multiple times to talk him out of attending Noah's party. And every time Dylan had refused. He'd originally gone along with the scenario because he'd felt compelled to come to Alec's defense. Being bested by Tyler didn't sit so well with Dylan either.

But the more time he spent in Alec's company, the more important going became. He hated the thought of a miserable, speechless Alec facing his bastard of an ex and the new boyfriend alone. Someone had to be around to metaphorically kick Tyler's ass should the need arise.

And which Alec would show up tomorrow night? The tongue-tied man from the garage? Or the easygoing, confident guy with a research fetish and shameless obsession for *People* magazine?

If you go, you could kiss him for real. Find out if those lips are as soft as they look.

Desperate to ease his suddenly scorched throat, Dylan picked up his mug and tossed back the rest of his beer. "I told you before, and I'll tell you again." He set his mug down with a determined thud, refusing to let the dumbass thoughts in his head scare him from his decision. "I'm going." He glanced back at the burly dude with tats.

Nope. Nothing. Not a goddamn flicker.

All kissing Alec would prove was that men did nothing for him.

Dylan relaxed in his seat, finally spotting the furrow of concern on Alec's brow.

"Listen," Dylan said, "I'll follow your lead. If you're relaxed and happy, I'm relaxed and happy. No big deal." In fact, he'd make sure it wasn't a big deal.

Alec sent him a skeptical look. "You can keep your mouth shut if necessary?"

"Absolutely," he lied.

Alec pursed his lips and slowly nodded. "Okay," he said. "A little company would certainly be welcome. Tyler and I have conveniently avoided each other as much as possible. But passing him in the hallway at work and the brief meetings we've had so far have gone okay. Incredibly strained, but okay."

"Sounds like we're ready for tomorrow night then."

Alec shot Dylan a confident smile. "I'm definitely ready."

Chapter Five

Oh God, he was so not ready.

Like millions of downed electrical wires, Alec's nerves crackled as he trailed Dylan down the posh hallway to Noah's condominium. Located in Pacific Heights, Noah's place overlooked San Francisco Bay and the Golden Gate Bridge, as exclusive as Noah's taste in clothing. Dylan, in a surprising show of conformity, had dressed for the occasion. The sight was distracting, not to mention a complication Alec hadn't considered when he'd assumed he was mentally prepared for tonight.

As they drew closer to the condo, the sound of laughter and muted music drifted from under Noah's door. Dylan turned to face him and suddenly Alec needed air, so he tugged at his tie, hoping for relief.

"Quit fidgeting," Dylan said.

"I can't help it."

"Dude, you have got to lighten up," Dylan said. "You look as tense as a trip wire that's two seconds from triggering an explosion. And remember..."

Dylan stepped forward to adjust Alec's tie, bringing his green gaze close and those callused hands even closer. Alec wished he knew which spicy soap Dylan used, and how was relaxation even possible with Dylan around?

"Just pretend you can't keep your eyes off of me." Dylan gave the tie an awkward pat, his gaze shifting away as he stepped back.

Pretend. At this point Alec would hardly be pretending.

Dylan had shown up at Alec's place wearing nice slacks, a dressy leather jacket, and a blue button-down shirt that did crazy things to the color of his eyes. Eyes that brought to mind The Look.

The moment in the bar when Alec's brain had suffered a complete meltdown.

It was wrong, so wrong to be crushing on his new friend. Especially when said crush had Alec seeing things that *weren't there*.

Like Dylan engaging in The Look, as if he returned the attraction.

Tyler and his boyfriend had taken a backseat to Alec's more pressing concerns. Despite his previous promise, Dylan was a wild card. Who knew what the man would pull? Even worse, how was Alec supposed to engage in small talk when all he could think about was that imagined heat in Dylan's eyes?

Dylan pressed the doorbell, and the door opened.

"Finally," Noah said, gripping them both by an elbow and pulling them into the marble foyer. "I'm glad you're here." In the large living room beyond, people milled about in cocktail dresses and suits.

Noah leaned in, whispering conspiratorially. "FYI. Tyler brought that sweet piece of ass of his. And, sweetie"—Noah shot Alec a sympathetic look—"Logan is gorgeous. Everyone adores him. Did you know he produces documentaries and won a Sundance Film Festival award?"

"So what?" Dylan replied, tossing a casual arm around Alec's shoulders, and every cell in Alec's body hummed happily. "Alec has me and a sex swing."

Alec's body went from humming to buzzing in alarm, and Noah let out bark of laughter.

"Christ, I need a drink," Alec mumbled.

"You'll need several." Noah winced. "Some of the talk revolves around how Tyler replaced you so quickly..."

At this point, who cares?

"No worries. I've got this." Dylan steered Alec into the living room.

The next hour passed in a tense montage of guests coming by to congratulate Alec on the award, and he smiled and thanked them, introducing Dylan. Dylan, for his part, behaved. And while he didn't do the small talk Noah's usual crowd enjoyed, conversations revolving around art and theatre and overseas vacations, Dylan had won over just about every guest that stopped by. Including Jack Davis.

As a member of the board at Charity Regional Hospital, he was one of the richest men in the Bay Area and had come to the party accompanied by his wife. Dylan had told a joke that just skirted the edges of raunchy, and Sylvia Davis had laughed so hard Alec feared she'd undo all the Botox work she'd clearly had done.

Dylan's easy, earthy charm—not to mention the good looks begging to be plastered across advertising billboards—won him the hearts of most of the women and quite a few of the men. Even Jack Davis, a codgery old bastard most people avoided, had liked Dylan.

Just when Alec was beginning to think he had the night in the bag, reality returned with a bitchy vengeance when he caught sight of his ex's jet-black hair.

"Alec," Tyler called smoothly from across the room. He placed his hand behind the blond-haired man at his side as they made their way in Alec's direction. "Good to see you."

The buzz of conversation around them dropped several decibels. Every guest studied the two during his ex's approach, as if expecting—hoping?—for an embarrassing scene.

Dylan must have noticed. "Goddamn vultures," he murmured as he threw his arm across Alec's shoulders again.

Unfortunately, the rubbernecking taking place made the comparison just a little too accurate.

Dylan pulled Alec closer, leaning in to whisper at his ear. "Remember, don't let him get to you." Dylan's warm breath sent goose bumps fanning down Alec's neck. "You only have eyes for me."

God, it was enough to make sweet baby Jesus cry.

"I'm fine," Alec whispered firmly.

Except for the part that involved Dylan touching him.

Alec tried to put some much-needed space between them, but Dylan's arm held fast as Tyler drew closer. Alec attempted a smile, painfully aware of the hard bicep pressed against his shoulder, the scent of man and spicy musk and something he couldn't quite identify.

When the two men stopped in front of him, Alec said, "You remember Dylan?"

Tyler's cool gaze landed on Dylan. "Of course."

The two shook hands and seemed to be sizing each other up. Jockeying for position. Preparing for confrontation. Tyler's iron control matched up against Dylan's little boy, poke-it-with-a-stick-to-get-a-reaction style. A pounding throb set up house behind Alec's right eye.

"This is Logan," Tyler said.

Alec reached out and shook Logan's hand. "Nice to see you again."

Dylan's hand on Alec's shoulder shifted possessively to the back of Alec's neck, like a high school football player might grip his girlfriend, claiming his territory. Alec used to hate the jocks with their cocky bluster and swagger and territorial nature. With Dylan, the posture was strangely thrilling. Alec suppressed a sigh.

Christ. When had he morphed into a teenage girl? And how could he focus with Dylan's thumb stroking his skin?

"I heard about the Sundance Film Festival award, Logan," Alec went on. "Congratulations."

"I've been lucky."

Logan wore a genuine smile, and Alec should probably resent his ex's new boyfriend for being so nice.

"I'm sure luck only played a small part," Alec said. "How did you get started?"

"I attended Duke University's Center for Documentary Studies at the same time Tyler went to medical school there. In fact, I just learned he grew up one county over from me. Our high schools were rivals."

"Small world, huh?" Alec said.

The conversation hit a lull, and the low-grade tension climbed another degree. At this point, Alec would have gladly given away a kidney just to have the conversation over.

Looking as unruffled as ever, Tyler said, "What high school did you attend, Dylan?"

"I didn't," Dylan said easily. "By age fifteen, I was living on the streets."

The words bowled over Alec's discomfort, and he whipped his gaze to Dylan, almost wrenching his neck in the process.

Dylan used to be a street kid?

Mute, Alec stared at the hint of a grin on Dylan's lips.

Logan managed to clarify the question on Alec's mind. "You were homeless?"

"Yep."

Alec struggled to process the news. In fact, the nonchalantly delivered admission had clearly caught the entire group off guard. Tyler's face looked blanker than usual as he remained silent, as if the information didn't compute. Or maybe he simply couldn't understand Dylan's cheerful delivery. Tyler hardly ever lost his cool. Alec had spent two years admiring his composure in the face of adversity. And Dylan appeared to be enjoying Tyler's expression. Obviously Dylan still considered Alec's ex-boyfriend a challenge.

Logan interrupted Alec's thoughts. "That must have been tough, Dylan."

Dylan hiked a shoulder. "Got my GED, some technical training, and then on-the-job experience before opening my own shop restoring vintage motorcycles."

"My brother and I are hardcore Ducati fans," Logan said. "Tyler and I met when Steve wrecked his bike and Tyler stopped to help."

"I'm curious..." Tyler flicked his gaze to Dylan. "How did you meet Alec?"

Alec's chest froze. Tyler knew.

His ex definitely knew Alec and Dylan were faking.

Alec could tell by the look on Tyler's face. Those coolly assessing eyes landed on Dylan's palm cupping the base of Alec's neck, and an uncomfortable heat flooded his stomach. A gentle squeeze of Dylan's fingers followed, mostly likely meant to be reassuring, but the pressure created all sorts of images of those hands closing around other areas of Alec's body.

Concentrate on Tyler, not the hand at your neck.

"Dylan's been helping me get the Harley into shape," Alec said.

Tyler held Alec's gaze. "About time you developed an interest outside of work."

And defeating Proposition 8, Tyler didn't add, probably because they'd had that debate a number of times before.

"I've been trying to convince you of that for over a year," Tyler went on.

Alec refused to let Tyler claim any ownership over the decision to buy the Harley. "You also spent two years trying to get me to accompany you on your daily run, partake of your morning spinach smoothie routine, and commit to an organic, vegetarian diet," Alec said drily.

"You didn't take me up on any of those ideas either."

"Maybe I just needed the right incentive," Alec said.

"Namely, me." The cocky smile that slipped up Dylan's face should have been a warning. "Although..."

The look Dylan sent Alec set him on edge.

Dylan continued, gaze lit with amusement. "I had a devil of a time getting this relationship kick started."

Alec repressed the urge to roll his eyes, his lips twisting wryly instead. "It was the sex swing that finally sold me."

Dylan tipped back his head and laughed while Alec admired the smooth skin of his neck, the faint stubble on his jaw. Christ, he really was gorgeous.

"And yet," Tyler murmured, "you two seem like such an unlikely pair."

Obviously annoyed by the continued challenge in Tyler's tone, Dylan narrowed his eyes, and Alec's stomach grew tight. Oh God. This wouldn't end well.

"That's funny." Dylan crossed his arms, his voice so low only the four men could hear. "Cuz ever since Alec and I met we've been fucking like Energizer bunnies on Viagra."

Alec almost choked on his tongue. "Excuse us."

He gripped Dylan's elbow, dragging him to the far end of the room, weaving through the crowd as he went. Once they reached the other side of the living room, and safety, Alec leaned against the wall.

"You really don't know when to shut up, do you?" Alec said wearily.

"I told you," Dylan said. "It's a gift."

Alec let out a humorless bark of laughter. He supposed he should be grateful Dylan had behaved for so long. And Alec couldn't decide which was worse, Dylan's mouth, the fact that Tyler saw through their facade, or the effect Dylan's presence had on Alec's body. Alec absently watched his ex lean over to whisper in Logan's ear.

"Dude," Dylan muttered, stepping too close for comfort.

The man's hand settled in the small of Alec's back, and Alec's nervous system went berserk, snapping and sparking to life. He could practically smell the electrical fire. Christ, clearly Dylan's presence constituted the bigger problem here.

Dylan's forehead crinkled with concern. "Are you still hung up on Tyler?"

Alec rubbed his brow, trying to ignore Dylan's palm along the base of his spine. "No."

Dylan shifted another hair-raising step forward. "Then what's wrong?"

You're standing way. Too.

Close.

With monumental effort, Alec wrestled his biggest concern into a mental lockbox and met Dylan's gaze, which brought to mind The Look. Unfortunately that meant problems number two through ten fell from Alec's lips unchecked.

"Everyone here knows Tyler and I still run the clinic together," Alec said, trying to ignore Dylan's scent. What was that delicious smell anyway? "Most of these people are friends or donors. Some are both." And while Tyler's presence had at one time turned Alec into a mute fool, apparently Dylan's proximity left him with a severe case of verbal diarrhea. "And they help keep the Front Street Clinic's doors open, but they're a little too interested in our breakup. I mean, *way* too interested. Did you see the people staring at us?"

"Alec—"

"It's like being placed under a microscope."

Dylan's fingers began a soothing rub, sending seductive signals Alec knew were false, but his brain short-circuited anyway, his voice climbing an octave.

"Everyone is waiting for my reaction," Alec went on, the words stumbling out. "Probably hoping for me to break down. And I *know* he knows we're lying, Dylan. I can —"

"Stop," Dylan said, stepping close enough to kiss.

~~~***~~~

Alec seemed incapable of stopping. All Dylan could do was watch his friend continue, that mouth moving faster and faster, desperation in his voice. Guilt settled beneath Dylan's breastbone. The blame lay squarely on his shoulders. The whole backup boyfriend had been his idea. Alec had been awesome about facing Tyler tonight, easily holding his own with that wry sense of humor. Until Dylan opened his big, fat mouth.

If Dylan hadn't insisted on this whole charade, Alec would be handling the party better. The feeling in Dylan's chest responded, as if on cue, with a little protective twitch of anxiety.

Dylan tuned back in to Alec's ramblings.

"...I see it in Tyler's eyes. I can hear it in his tone." Alec was really worked up now, as if the first few minutes had only been the warmup. "I can feel it in the way he looks at me. I can feel it in the way he looks at *us*."

Dylan placed his hand on the wall by Alec's head and leaned in to catch his gaze, trying to block the view of his ex. "Alec, man, you gotta relax—"

Blue eyes wide, Alec looked really agitated now. "And, Christ," he squeaked out, literally *squeaked,* "what does that make me?"

Jesus, the man was going supernova.

"I'll tell you what that makes me," Alec said, that mesmerizing mouth moving faster. "It makes me the ditched, desperate ex-boyfr—"

Dylan did the only thing he could think of. He leaned in and kissed him.

You wanted to know how this felt.

While Dylan told the voice in his head to friggin' shut the hell up, he realized Alec had gone completely still.

For a few heart-thudding moments, Dylan thought Alec was going to freak out, so Dylan placed his free hand on the man's chest, confining him against the wall. Hoping to give Alec time to pull himself together. Willing his friend to calm the fuck down.

Keeping his mouth trapped against his.

Besides, Dylan had come to the party as the boyfriend. No shame in an innocent display of PDA. And when he finally allowed his brain to process the sensations darting around his nervous system, he noted how supple Alec's lips were. How soft.

Just like he'd imagined.

Oh, *man...*

Their lips locked, and his pulse spiked higher, the incident lasting longer than he'd intended. Dylan had started out with the intent of a simple peck on the lips, just to put an end to Alec's babbling and hopefully show Tyler a thing or two. And Dylan had been so caught up in congratulating himself on the brilliant idea—two birds, one fucking brilliant stone—he hadn't considered the repercussions. He'd been too busy to listen to the thoughts whispering in his head, like his need to *know* how Alec tasted.

Jesus, something that he couldn't *un*know now.

The disturbing thought fled when Alec gripped the edges of Dylan's jacket and lifted his chin to meet the kiss head-on, shoving the moment from way-better-than-expected to *smokin' hot*. The change was entirely too much to process, so Dylan closed his eyes and turned his brain off.

He increased the pressure, and Alec's lips opened willingly beneath his. The surge of satisfaction had Dylan shifting closer, instinctively tipping his head to seek a better position. First left. And then exploring from the right, gathering more of that mouth with his. A stream of sensations whizzed by like the blur of scenery at high rates of speed. The sensations included heat and moisture and softness, as well as hot, damp breath and the faint taste of a fruity wine.

Enjoying the hard chest beneath his hand, Dylan slid his palm lower, past the flat abdomen and landing on the lean jut of Alec's hip. Alec let out a tiny whimper, and Dylan just managed not to haul the man closer.

Not a trace of disgust pricked Dylan's conscious. In fact, his body grew frustrated by the limited contact, so he opened his mouth wider, pressed deep. Alec moaned beneath him, as if asking for more.

Oh God, no. No tongue. No *way* was Dylan up for tongue.

The entire event couldn't have lasted longer than five seconds, maybe six—okay, more like ten—but then Alec touched his tongue to Dylan's lower lip, right before giving it a gentle nip. The pleasure nearly crippled Dylan, and he groaned.

Jesusfuckingchrist.

Dylan drew back, stunned. Body smoking. Blood boiling. Limbs singed.

What the *hell*?

Blue eyes blinked up at him. "Sorry." Alec cleared his throat. "Got a little carried away."

Dylan wiped his mouth, surprised to find his fingers shook a little. "S'okay, man." He swiped a hand through his hair and hoped he appeared calmer than he felt. "I'm the one who started the whole lip-lock idea."

Several seconds passed by as Dylan tried to get his act together while Alec looked as if he was in pain.

Alec finally spoke again. "I need another drink."

And all Dylan could think was *I need about twenty*.

~~~***~~~

Two shots of tequila later, with the stability of his knees still in question, retreat seemed to be Alec's only option.

Three uniformed servers bustled across the hardwood floor of Noah's kitchen. The impressive room contained restaurant quality appliances, eleven-foot ceilings, and huge windows overlooking the bay. Silver platters of appetizers lined the granite countertop. Although the space also included a full wine refrigerator and the bottle of Patrón Alec had pulled from the cupboard, he appreciated the solitude the most. He needed to focus on recovering from the feel of Dylan's mouth pressed against his.

For the first few seconds of the kiss, all Alec could think was *this isn't real*. Of course Dylan wanted to show Tyler up. But the longer the moment had gone on, the more genuine the scenario felt, until Alec had begun to envision how the night could end, with Alec on his knees in front of Dylan. Or vice versa. And, oh God...

He pressed his lids closed, rubbing his eyes.

"Alec."

He looked up and met Tyler's gray gaze, his ex leaning against the doorway to the kitchen. Alec's heart picked up its thudding pace, and he braced for the encounter.

Wasn't a make-out session with Dylan in front of fifty of Noah's friends—not to mention the fallout from the event—enough to contend with for one night? And exactly when had Alec's life turned into a headline worthy of *People* magazine?

Alec took a deep breath, trying to ease the tension in his chest. "Tyler—"

At the same time, Tyler said, "I want to—"

They both paused, and the heavy atmosphere grew more oppressive. A muscle in Tyler's jaw twitched, a habit that Alec remembered from the early days of their relationship. Every time they'd met with an organization to request financial support for their newly founded clinic, Tyler had been well prepared. Cool. Confident. Sharply dressed and in total control. Except for the small tic that had been the only clue to Tyler's discomfort.

The same tic that had appeared the afternoon Tyler told Alec goodbye.

Alec's pulse increased to an uncomfortable rate. He'd fought hard for the right for them to marry. All he'd ever wanted was to share his life, his home, with someone special. *Commitment*. Tyler knew that the day he'd moved in. And was that too much to ask?

Apparently Tyler thought so.

"Actually, I just wanted to say I'm sorry for the way things went down," Tyler said as he entered the kitchen. "I realize me leaving seemed to come out of the blue. And I know how hard that can be."

For the first time since the breakup, Alec let his anger take the lead. "Do you?" The whiplash turn of events had left Alec stunned. He'd never even had a chance to save the relationship. "Everything seemed fine, and the next thing I knew, you were gone."

Tyler glanced out the window. "In college, the same thing happened to me." He crossed his arms. "I never did figure out what went wrong."

Alec leaned back against the counter. "This is news to me."

Tyler had mentioned he'd dated a guy in college. From Tyler's expression now, Alec knew the relationship must have been serious. But why was he just learning this now?

"Memphis Haines and I were together for a year and a half before he broke it off without warning," Tyler said.

Alec almost laughed at the bitter irony until he recognized the name. "Memphis Haines the stunt guy?"

"He wasn't famous back then. But that's not the point I'm trying to make."

Alec held his ex's gaze, struggling to control the resentment that had been festering for over two months. "What *is* your reason for being here?"

"To say that I should have given you a little warning. But we'd grown too comfortable, I think. I knew you'd talk me out of leaving." The hint of a smile lacked any real humor. "The path of least resistance and all," he said. "But tonight I—"

Something flashed in Tyler's eyes just before he shifted his gaze to one of the large bay windows. Alec remained silent and studied Tyler's profile as the source of that brief emotion finally connected, an emotion Alec had never seen on Tyler's face before.

Jealousy.

Tyler was *jealous*.

Alec swept a hand down his face, hoping to hide his surprise. Christ, Dylan should be here to witness the sight. And Alec wasn't above admitting a small part of him—the side permanently stuck in adolescence, no doubt—took some satisfaction from the knowledge. Since the split, Alec had experienced a whole host of emotions, from shock to disbelief to anger.

But the self-satisfied, junior high schooler thoughts were definitely new.

The sound of someone clearing his throat interrupted the moment. Alec looked over to where

Dylan stood in the doorway, studying them both with a guarded expression.

Finally, Dylan's gaze settled on Alec. "You okay?"

Shit. He couldn't answer that question until *after* this conversation with Tyler.

"Yeah." Alec's gaze flicked back to Tyler. "We were just setting a few things straight."

Dylan hesitated before giving a sharp nod. "I'll let you two get back to it then." With one more questioning look in Alec's direction, he turned and headed back toward the party.

Tyler watched Dylan go. "He's a little..."

Smart-mouthed? Insane? Too beautiful for words? No sense in adding the excellent-kisser label. Alec pushed the memory of the moment from his mind.

"Rough around the edges," Tyler finished.

Alec stared at the doorway, remembering the feel of Dylan's calluses against his skin. Just the thought sent goose bumps popping up along his spine. Why the sudden fixation with rough hands?

"I have to admit the man is definitely good looking." Tyler's gaze steadily met Alec's. "But he doesn't fit your usual MO."

You mean my attraction to men who are actually gay?

This time the bitter laugh escaped. No need to share the tidbit about Dylan's orientation with Tyler just yet.

"Is this the new you?" Tyler leaned against the far counter. "A man into sex swings and no-strings-attached fucking?"

Anger flared higher.

You made your choice. And it wasn't me.

"That's none of your business anymore," Alec said.

"You're right. But I still don't think he's what you want."

After all those months of Alec attending every gay marriage demonstration he could, Tyler had *known* what Alec wanted. He'd thought the fight worthy of his dedication, every moment of his day taken up by either the clinic or the next demonstration.

When Noah called to discuss the clinic—which he did, frequently—Alec made a point of being available. When his mother informed him of another demonstration, Alec had stepped up and participated.

He'd believed the time a wise investment in the future. *Their* future.

"What should I want?" Alec said.

"What you've always wanted," Tyler replied. "A committed relationship."

"Commitment didn't work out so well for me."

"So you've decided to change your priorities now?"

"Maybe," Alec said, struggling to maintain a cool tone. "Maybe not."

Tyler held his gaze, and Alec read a whole host of emotions contained in the single crease in Tyler's forehead. Anger. Genuine puzzlement. Even a hint of concern.

"I think you're making a big mistake," Tyler said.

This seemed particularly damning coming from a man who didn't know Dylan's true orientation.

"If so," Alec said evenly, "it's my mistake to make."

Alec pushed up from the counter and left to go in search of more alcohol...and Dylan.

Chapter Six

Crap, this wasn't going at all like he'd planned.

Dylan gripped the same whiskey he'd been nursing since the kiss that had kicked him in the ass. He longed to slug the rest back, along with about twenty more. But someone had to remain in control because Alec looked totally buzzed. Correction, Alec seemed a stone's throw away from *sloppy*.

Served Dylan right for being so spiteful. If he hadn't felt the need to put Tyler in his place, Dylan wouldn't have deepened the kiss and—

Jesus, who was he trying to convince here?

Dylan knew his time on the streets had honed his abilities as a master bullshitter, but bullshitting himself was another thing.

Since Alec had bitten Dylan's lip, Dylan had been fighting to recover from the nip that had taken the moment from surprisingly hot to *not nearly enough*. And just when Dylan had decided he was okay with how the whole thing went down—cuz, really, what choice did he have?—and was ready to act as if everything was normal, Alec had headed straight for the kitchen.

And then Tyler had followed Alec.

For a second Dylan hadn't known what to feel, the thoughts bumping around as if the gears in his brain had been stripped. A part of him had been happy for Alec, glad his friend might be winning back the man he'd lost. But another part of him had been friggin' annoyed.

He pushed the feelings away. Time for a reality check.

There were friends, like Noah, and now Alec. And then there was sex, provided by *women*, a mutually satisfying exchange of the baser needs in life. Dylan liked sex. Lots of it. And he carefully selected companions who wanted the same and nothing more.

Dylan didn't know a thing about dealing with exes because he'd happily managed to avoid anything remotely resembling a relationship. A status he had every intention of maintaining, thankyouverymuch. Five years later and Noah still hadn't recovered from losing Rick. Alec looked miserable and uncomfortable around Tyler.

Who needed that kind of grief?

And while Dylan had been thrown off kilter by the scene in the kitchen, never mind the lingering effects of the kiss, it appeared his newfound friend was no better off. After reentering the living room, Alec had headed straight for the bar and tossed back a shot of tequila.

Followed by three more.

With every drink Alec had gotten a little looser, until his demeanor was way too relaxed. So Dylan had corralled him in a corner, successfully keeping the guy away from most of the guests. Alec was leaning against Dylan pretty heavily now, and Noah was currently shooting Dylan heated questions with his eyes—as if he blamed the current fucked-up state of affairs on Dylan.

"See?" Beaming, the doctor threw his arm around Dylan's neck, pulling him closer. "I can't keep my eyes off of you. How am I doing?"

Try as he might, Dylan couldn't pry his gaze from Alec's lips. Dylan wasn't going to waste time lying to himself anymore. The man had a fucking beautiful mouth, especially when it looked like it had at the end of their kiss, roughed up, red, and spit slicked...

Dylan briefly pressed his lids closed. "You're doing great," he murmured.

Although Alec felt a little too close for comfort.

And while he'd hoped the kiss would feel dry and papery—and less than inspiring—he hadn't seriously contemplated his world reversing course on its axis.

Arm around Dylan's neck, Alec snuggled his head into the crook of Dylan's neck and let out a sigh. Dylan was considering what to do about the current predicament when Alec's free hand cupped Dylan's ass, sending sparks dancing across his skin.

Man, he'd created a monster.

"Ya know," Alec said, his words slightly slurred as Dylan discreetly pulled Alec's hand from his butt, "this party turned out a whole lot better than I'd expected."

"I should get you home," Dylan said.

"Excellent idea."

Alec's smoldering look made Dylan nervous.

Before Dylan could decide what to do next, Alec clutched the front of Dylan's shirt, pulling him in the direction of the foyer.

Leaving. Yep, leaving would definitely be good.

Hoping to make an exit with as little attention as possible, Dylan simply trailed behind. The crowd in the living room had grown, yet Alec managed to thread his way through without stepping on toes or tripping over shoes. When they exited the living room, Dylan spied Tyler and his boyfriend in the foyer.

Crap.

With Alec in his current condition, passing those two would mean trouble for sure. A few drinks and the normally mild-mannered Dr. Alec Johnson became very outspoken. And kinda handsy. Dylan pulled Alec's palm from his chest and linked their fingers together, hoping to keep them from wandering to more inappropriate areas.

While Dylan eyed the space between the front door and Tyler, sizing up the distance and trying to decide how best to escape, Noah arrived from the kitchen, stopping at Tyler's side.

Fuck.

Noah shot Dylan another what-the-hell? look, and Dylan veered sharply left, changing course to lead Alec down the deserted hallway and into Noah's office. At least here Dylan could keep Alec from groping him in public. They could wait out Tyler's departure, and Dylan could slip Alec out the exit without having to pass by Noah.

"Let's wait for the crowd at the doorway to clear before we leave," Dylan said.

"Perfect."

Alec closed the door. Before Dylan could register the intent in his eyes, Alec gripped Dylan's jacket and stepped backward until his shoulder blades hit the wall, pulling Dylan close.

"I'm good with that," Alec said.

"Come on, man." Dylan gripped Alec's wrist and pried it from his chest, totally ignoring how smooth the man's hands were. "You've had too much to drink, and you don't know what you're doing."

"Bullshit," Alec muttered, leaning in to kiss Dylan.

Dylan briefly froze. But, hell, if they started that up again, no telling where they'd wind up. Possibly on that futon along the far wall. Dylan turned his head to avoid the kiss, but Alec kept going, his mouth landing on Dylan's neck instead.

Hot breath fanned across Dylan's skin. Lips nibbled at his now skyrocketing pulse. And Dylan's dick gave an interested twitch.

Fuck a duck.

He needed to remind himself that this was his *friend*, a friend who was acting out of frustration after watching his ex all evening. Or maybe Alec was still reeling from the scene in the kitchen with Tyler. Had they made out? Had Alec put his hands on Tyler's ass too?

Dylan chose not to dwell on the possibility, and right now Alec didn't seem to be thinking too much about Tyler. Lips whispering across Dylan's throat, Alec groaned out Dylan's name and placed a hand on his abdomen, just above the waistband.

Beads of sweat broke out along the back of Dylan's neck. Blood rushed through Dylan's veins, confused as to whether to supply his conflicted brain, his limbs for escape, or more urgently *needy* areas. Dylan's dick now demanded more than its fair share.

No sense in denying the truth. While he'd been hitting first base with Alec, not only had Dylan not been grossed out or disgusted, not only had the act turned him on, the moment had planted ideas in Dylan's mind. Ideas about Alec and...uh...more than just kisses.

Dylan slammed his lids closed.

Before his muddled brain could process Alec's next move, Alec's hand landed on Dylan's zipper and flicked it open. A searing jolt shot through Dylan's veins, and his eyelids popped open.

Jesus, had he said something about those ideas *out loud*?

"No touching the junk," he scraped out as he reluctantly pulled the hand away. "Come on, Alec. Get your shit together, man."

Get your shit together, Booth.

Fingers gripping Alec's wrist, Dylan tried to prevent further crotch groping. He pressed his other palm against Alec's chest to keep the man from plastering their torsos together, trying not to enjoy the hard plane of lean muscle.

Distance. That's all he needed, just a little distance.

He was so busy congratulating himself on his success he forgot about the rigid hard-on confined beneath his briefs, bulging along the open zipper of his pants. Alec abandoned his attempts at a kiss and dropped to his knees to press his open mouth to Dylan's cock.

Dylan sucked in a strangled breath.

Paralyzed by the surge of pleasure, he stared down at the arousing sight, the damp heat of Alec's breath seeping through the briefs. Pushing Alec away would be a hell of a lot easier if Dylan wasn't so turned on. Alec nibbled his way from the base of Dylan's erection to the tip and gently scraped his teeth across the sensitive head.

Dylan gripped Alec's shoulder, shaking with the need to force him back and thrust closer, all at the same time. "Alec," he said hoarsely.

Ignoring the admittedly questionable protest, in one swift motion, Alec pulled out Dylan's dick and swallowed him whole.

And that was the end of life as Dylan knew it.

Dylan's eyes rolled back, and somewhere close by a meteor must have crash-landed cuz the floor beneath them wobbled. Alec bobbed his head up and down, spit slicking the way, and what was supposed to be an attempt at another objection came out of Dylan sounding faded and weak.

"Fuck."

One hand wrapped around the base of Dylan's cock, Alec pulled off to lick from base to tip again. "We'll get to the fucking, I promise."

The words briefly brought Dylan back to his senses, but not enough that he had the strength to end the pleasurable sensations. Hopefully he was capable of speech. And he had to try and get Alec to see reason. Dylan couldn't stand the thought of his friend hating him tomorrow.

"Alec, listen man," he said, "this isn't what you want."

But, Jesus, Dylan was a powder keg full of *want*.

"It'll be s'good," Alec said. Lids heavy, he looked up at Dylan. "Topping is like the Sky Rocket of roller-coasters, but bottoming is like a wild ride on the Screamin' Demon Express. I promise, you'll love it."

Fire shot through Dylan's veins, leaving behind the scorched remains of his good intentions. His legs felt like overcooked pasta. Dylan swayed, placing a hand on the wall above Alec, propping himself up. Mesmerized, he stared down at the top of Alec's head, the waves of brown hair. That beautiful mouth...

Full. Spit-slicked. Slowly stretching wider as he slid back down Dylan's cock.

Dylan wasn't sure, but he might have let out a whimper. Alec was currently sucking him off as though he'd waited all his life to get his hands and mouth on Dylan.

He'd never felt so worshipped.

"You taste perfect." Alec licked Dylan's slit, making Dylan's vision blur from the shock of pleasure. "Like leather and whisky and salt."

Several seconds passed with the aching promise of more, and Dylan fought to uncross his eyes. The rasp of a zipper broke through Dylan's dazed state. And when Alec pulled out his own cock and gave several tugs, Dylan definitely whimpered.

No. Please, just...no.

A part of him demanded he close his eyes again. That he should be picturing a woman kneeling before him. But, God help him, he wanted to watch Alec and the blissful expression on his face. That expressive blue gaze and wide mouth. The quiet *slap slap slap* of his hand as he stroked himself. Dylan let out a groan, mentally tossing in the last towel.

At this point he might have to hurt anyone who tried to end to this.

Alec's head was bobbing in earnest now, as if he couldn't get enough. The wet warmth of his mouth, the reverent stroke of his tongue, and that incredible, incredible suction dragged Dylan closer to the inevitable end. Alec seemed determined to suck the orgasm from Dylan, willing or not.

Panting, throat raw, Dylan fit his palm to Alec's face and scraped his thumb across the smooth cheek, stroking closer to the mesmerizing lips stretched tight around him. Alec moved up and down along the slick skin, taking him deep. When Dylan's finger touched where their bodies met, Dylan almost came.

"Alec," he groaned.

He should let himself blow his load so this would be over.

But if he let himself come *this would be over*.

And then Alec released Dylan with a wet *pop*.

"No," Dylan rasped out.

Mouth parted, Alec moaned out his orgasm, thick ropes of white shooting from Alec's slit. Dazed and uncoordinated, he absently mouthed Dylan's cock as he slowly recovered. Dylan wished he could say the same, because no blow job, ever, had been this good, and he hadn't even come yet. Alec getting off on *Dylan* getting off took the experience to a whole new level. And the moment was hot as hell.

Whatever Alec wanted, he could have.

That fucking glorious mouth swallowed Dylan back down. Alec's sticky fingers returned to stroke the base of Dylan's dick, and something inside him broke.

Jesus, Mary, and Joseph, he needed—

He buried his fingers in Alec's hair, shoving the brown curtain back for a better view, and clutched the side of Alec's head for leverage. Cautious at first, Dylan began to rock his hips. When Alec hummed in encouragement, Dylan gripped Alec's head tight and thrust deep, once, twice.

Intense heat flashed from his groin, a goddamned solar flare shooting from his dick, and Dylan let out a harsh cry. He pressed his forehead against the wall in relief as he emptied himself inside Alec's throat for what felt like forever. Until Dylan felt heavy. Wrung out.

Bled dry.

Several seconds passed by before Dylan's endorphin-saturated brain switched back on, and he became aware of the sound of rustling clothes.

When he regained the use of his muscles, Dylan glanced down. Alec sat on the floor at his feet, back against the wall. Eyes closed, he had a content look on his face. Somewhere along the way, Alec had made himself more presentable, his pants now zipped. Unfortunately, they still needed to get the hell out of here. And they would.

Just as soon as Dylan could breathe without making so much noise.

Someone laughed down the hallway, and Dylan tensed, fumbling to fix the front of his pants. If Noah found them here, there'd be hell to pay.

Dylan reached down and pulled Alec to his feet. The man swayed a moment, and guilt sliced Dylan deep. Alec was in no condition to be making important decisions, like whether he wanted his ex-boyfriend or the fake one. Or who to be giving blow jobs to.

Damn.

"We need to get you home before you pass out," Dylan said.

"Not gonna pass out," Alec said, eyes still closed. "Just enjoying the post-orgasmic buzz, you know?"

Heck, yeah. Dylan knew.

"I think you're buzzed enough," Dylan said drily.

Hand on Alec's elbow, Dylan opened the door and steered him down the hallway, hoping against hope they wouldn't run into anyone along the way. But when the two of them rounded the corner, Tyler, Logan, and Noah were still standing in the foyer by the front door, talking. All three turned to look at Alec and Dylan.

Busted.

Tyler's face looked totally blank, Logan looked amused, and Noah...

Noah looked ready to kill them both. Cuz, yeah. The tangle of Alec's hair, his rough, reddened lips, and the dazed expression on his face gave them away.

"That was the best party *ever*," Alec said in a lilting voice.

Inside, Dylan winced, but he kept his expression bland. "He's had a little too much to drink."

Logan laughed. "And we can guess what he's been drinking."

Dylan pretended like crazy his face wasn't heating up into one hell of a blush, maintaining an even tone. "Thanks for the hospitality, Noah." Dylan refused to meet his friend's gaze. "Nice to meet you, Logan."

"Good night, everybody." Alec waved, a smile on his face as Dylan practically dragged him toward the front door. "Dylan, promise me we'll do that again when we get home."

Behind them, Logan laughed. Dylan barely suppressed the groan as he hustled Alec out of the condo, closing the door on the accusing look on Noah's face.

~~~***~~~

The next morning awareness rose in layers. The faint throb in Alec's head had him cautiously cracking an eyelid open, light not the most welcome of sensory inputs right now. His hand flexed against a rock-hard thigh, and his morning wood pressed low on Tyler's back. He opened the single eye wider, taking in the striped comforter on his king-sized bed and the cobalt blue walls and mahogany dresser beyond. But something felt off.

Alec frowned at the shoulder blade with a line of puckered skin, a purple scar that had healed ages ago. But...Tyler didn't have a scar on his back. And that wasn't the only thing that didn't compute. The hair seemed too light and the shoulders too broad and the skin too tanned and—

And Sweet Jesus, Tyler didn't live here anymore. Neither was he as large as the man in his bed.

Dylan.

Alec's chest contracted, squeezing the air from his lungs as the previous night came back to him in a rush. Dylan looking good enough to eat in his dress clothes. His arm around Alec, the hard muscles, and his fabulous smell. Being trapped between Dylan and the wall.

The kiss.

Sucking him off.

Heat pricked Alec's neck. And then there'd been the ride home. He had vague memories of his hands being all over Dylan. Honestly, how had the man managed to drive his truck? And when they'd entered Alec's house, he...

Shit.

Alec had practically dragged Dylan into his bedroom and pushed him down on the bed, pouncing on the guy like the zombie apocalypse loomed close and Alec was determined to wring as many orgasms from Dylan as possible beforehand.

Granted, Dylan Booth was bigger and stronger than Alec. He had at least two inches and a good thirty pounds on him, all muscle. At any point during Alec's mortifying actions, if Dylan had wanted to overpower Alec and push him away, he could have. But, still, Alec remembered enough to realize that he'd been attacking Dylan's clothes as if they were an affront to nature. All the while listing out the ways he was going to make Dylan come. How good being fucked felt. How much Dylan would love being a bottom.

Explaining in great detail exactly *how* he'd top Dylan.

But after getting sidetracked by a moment of frottage—and coming, *again*—Alec had slumped to the bed, exhausted. He had fuzzy memories of Dylan cleaning him up and wondering how such a rough-and-tough guy could be so gentle, just before he had proceeded to pass out.

Why Dylan hadn't up and left him was a mystery. At three a.m., Alec's pounding headache had interrupted his sleep, so he'd gone for a bottle of water and three ibuprofen. Fortunately, his middle of the night prowling now meant his headache was reduced to a dull thud, but the remaining dregs of his hangover were the least of his problems.

Now he had to figure out what to do about Dylan.

Alec's cellphone buzzed on the nightstand, and he peered over Dylan's shoulder. Noah's number flashed on the screen before going to voice mail, and Alec realized he now had twenty-five unread messages. No need to wonder who had sent them.

Alec's gaze dropped to Dylan, the thick lashes out of place on the rugged face. One hand under his pillow, the other resting beside his head, Dylan looked relaxed in sleep. Alec's palm on the man's thigh was a problem, and Alec wasn't even going to touch on how his cock was deliriously happy pressed along the top of Dylan's ass.

Alec ignored the scent of sweat and semen and man, because he needed to get out of this bed. But when he went to withdraw his hand, he paused. Before he could stop himself, his finger lightly traced the scar lining Dylan's shoulder blade.

"Morning," Dylan said.

Alec swallowed hard and mimicked Dylan's easy, we-didn't-just-sleep-together tone. "How did you get the scar?" The question felt infinitely easier than asking what would happen when they left this bedroom behind.

"Stab wound from a broken bottle," Dylan said.

"How old were you?"

"Fifteen."

Fifteen. Alec stared down at the linear scar. The answer opened up a whole new line of questioning he'd been dying to pursue. At that age Dylan had been homeless.

"What happened?" Alec said.

The pause that followed was long, and Alec wondered if Dylan would answer.

"I'd been on the streets for six months when one night I came across a kid about my age," Dylan said. "The guy he was with was getting really rough, so I stopped to help."

The final piece of the puzzle slid into place. "Rick."

So that was how the two men had become friends.

"Yeah. I got the scar in the scuffle, but I managed to give the abusive prick a run for his money," Dylan said.

Alec knew the answer before he even asked. "Was Rick turning tricks?"

As Alec waited for an answer, somewhere down the street a neighbor honked a car horn. A dog began to bark in answer. Another lazy Sunday morning in Alec's neighborhood. But nothing about today felt ordinary.

"He was doing what he had to do to survive," Dylan answered, a defensive thread in his tone. "He showed me a better place to sleep, and I showed him the best places to find food."

After a brief moment of internal debate, Alec decided he had to ask.

"Did you love him?" Alec said.

The tone of Dylan's voice changed every time he talked about his dead friend. And a part of Alec hoped there *had* been some romantic feeling on Dylan's part, because if he'd loved a man before, that meant there was hope that he and Alec could have more.

And he should not be entertaining such stupid, *stupid* thoughts.

"No, not like you're thinking," Dylan said.

Alec tried not to let his disappointment show. "But you still miss him."

"Every goddamn day."

Seconds passed into minutes, until the reality got too much for Alec. He was in bed with a man, had had sex with a man who could never really be more than a fake boyfriend. Escaping suddenly seemed like a necessity.

He went to pull his hand from Dylan's thigh, but Dylan reached back and trapped Alec's palm beneath his, accelerating the pulse in his wrist.

"You promised you'd show me how it felt," Dylan said.

For the first time since they'd started talking, Dylan rolled his head to look up at Alec. The man had a seriously sexy case of bed-head hair, his eyelids still heavy with sleep. But his gaze smoldered with awareness.

"But you passed out before you could follow through," Dylan went on.

Alec blinked, forcing his mouth to work. "How what felt?"

Dylan arched his back, the base of Alec's hard cock now pressed tight against the top of Dylan's naked ass, sending a thrilling jolt up Alec's spine.

"Christ, Dylan." The rough words rushed out, unchecked. "Last night was crazy. The tension at the party was epic. You were totally trying to prove Tyler wrong." Alec rubbed his face. "Not to mention that really awkward moment in the kitchen, and then I had too much to drink. I practically forced you—"

"Screw that," Dylan said with a scowl, ending Alec's string of words. "You didn't force me. And if I wanted to be gone, I would have left."

"You shouldn't be sleeping with me." Alec amended the statement. "I shouldn't be sleeping with *you*."

A lazy eyebrow rose. "Little late to be deciding that now."

Shouldn't the man be more disturbed by the events? And did that mean something more? The hope had Alec dropping his forehead to Dylan's shoulder.

"Shit," Alec whispered.

Too late summed the situation up perfectly. Too late to take back all he'd done with Dylan—well, perhaps *to* Dylan was a more appropriate description. Too late to return to a time when Alec thought of Dylan as just a smart-mouthed mechanic instead of a man who'd not only survived the streets but gone on to start a successful business. A man who'd risked his life to defend a complete stranger.

"No sense in pretending you don't want me," Dylan said, and Alec could hear the amusement in his voice. "Last night was kind of a giveaway."

Despite everything, Alec smiled against Dylan's shoulder. "Which part?" He lifted his head to peer down at Dylan again. "When I attacked you in Noah's office or when I pinned you to my bed?"

"Yes to both. And then you went on and on about what bottoming felt like. You were rambling." Crinkles framed his green eyes when he smiled. "You do that sometimes when you're nervous."

"Sorry."

"Don't be." He grinned. "I figured out one way to get you to stop, although the kiss kinda caught me by surprise. But, seriously? The blow job blew my mind." Dylan raised an eyebrow. "You're really good at that."

Alec's throat felt as dry as yesterday's toast. "As Noah said, a guy's got to have a hobby."

Christ, what an inane thing to say.

Dylan faced forward, no longer meeting Alec's gaze. "I'm not much for porno talk during sex, but during our, uh..."—he cleared his throat—"mutual grinding session, you went into explicit detail about exactly how you were going to fuck me."

Alec closed his eyes. Thank God Dylan had used the word mutual. Alec hated to think he might have used Dylan as a humping post.

"I'm not too proud to admit the words were a total turn-on," Dylan went on.

Alec's lips twisted wryly. "I guess that means you don't subscribe to the theory that taking it up the ass makes you less of a man?"

"Heck, no. It's just sex. It doesn't mean anything."

It's just sex. It doesn't mean anything.

Well, damn. The words weren't comforting. Alec knew his crush had taken a nosedive into deeper levels the moment they'd kissed. He wasn't ready to admit the truth, that he might have fallen a little for Dylan during his refreshing candor about his limited education and his refusal to feel less than because of it. Completely unselfconscious and at ease with his past, Dylan was proud of his life. That kind of self-confidence was endearing and incredibly sexy.

And apparently prevented any lingering hang-ups about sex.

Dylan leaned forward and opened the drawer on Alec's nightstand, pulling out the lube and several condoms.

When Dylan looked over his shoulder and caught Alec's surprised look, he said, "Last night you showed me where you kept your supplies."

Of *course* he had.

Heat climbed Alec's face. There was no time to dwell on the embarrassment because Dylan scooted backwards until Alec's cock pressed along the crack in Dylan's ass again, and the hit of pleasure paralyzed Alec.

Dylan seemed to notice Alec hadn't moved.

"Do you want me to go away?" Dylan said.

"We shouldn't be doing this."

"Not what I asked. Do you *want* me to leave?"

Alec wanted lots of things, like Dylan's lips opening beneath his in a *real* kiss. To trace that scar on Dylan's shoulder with his tongue. To feel Dylan come in his mouth without the dulling effects of alcohol. Dylan on all fours, with Alec behind him. Yeah, he wanted a lot of things.

Dylan leaving wasn't one of them.

"I want you to stay," Alec said.

Dylan released a breath and rolled onto his stomach, spreading his legs. He folded his arms and planted his forehead on his wrists.

The beautiful sight of Dylan splayed before him in such a vulnerable position made Alec's fingers clumsy. After two tries, Alec finally flipped the lid to the lube open. Mindful of Dylan's relative inexperience, Alec applied a generous-to-the-point-of-messy amount of liquid on his fingers. Alec brushed his hole, and Dylan tensed.

Alec leaned forward and pressed his mouth to the scar, tracing the ridge of purple flesh with his lips. "Easy," he murmured against Dylan's skin.

And as Alec ran his mouth along the corded muscles of Dylan's back and stroked the puckered hole with his thumb, Dylan slowly melted, his body going lax. A few minutes passed, and Alec felt confident enough in Dylan's state to take the next step. He breached the ring of muscle with his finger, and a light shudder ran through Dylan's body, as malleable in Alec's arms as he was hard-nosed out of them. Humbling Alec with his trust. Empowering him with such complete submission.

For two years Alec had been happy letting Tyler take control in bed. But this...

Alec knew sex with Dylan didn't line up with his long-term plans. Yet he couldn't bring himself to care. For once Alec wanted everything, wanted to be greedy and careless and rash, despite the fact the need was equal parts scary and exhilarating.

Letting Dylan grow accustomed to the feel, Alec spent more minutes than necessary with just one finger, fucking him slowly. He watched as Dylan's breathing grew more labored, his arousal obvious. The view left Alec feeling invincible, which only made him more determined to make this good for Dylan.

Alec advanced to two fingers, encouraged when Dylan remained silent, no protest in sight. In fact, Dylan began to thrust his hips against the bed, and the occasional whimper escaped, the sounds barely audible. All that changed when Alec brushed his prostate.

Dylan hissed, and his hands shot forward to grab the headboard. "Jesus," Dylan groaned, arching his back.

"Feeling okay?"

Dylan's answer came in the form of a moan, and he tipped his ass up in a silent beg, pushing against Alec's fingers. Alec smiled. The man might not be much for talking during sex, but the noises that rumbled from his throat were sexier than all the explicit words in the world.

God, too bad last night's memories were veiled by the buzz of alcohol.

"You're description didn't do it justice," Dylan murmured.

"Description?"

"Prostate."

Alec had no idea what he'd said last night. But he knew exactly what Dylan was talking about.

"You mean this?" he said, and brushed the sensitive bundle again.

Dylan stiffened and dropped his forehead to the mattress. "God, yes," he said. "Just...*yes*."

With the addition of a third digit, Dylan grew impatient. So Alec increased the pace, and Dylan seemed satisfied. But not for long. Soon the rock of his hips was as much about taking more of Alec's fingers as seeking friction against the bed.

"Alec," Dylan whispered hoarsely, his fingers gripping the headboard. "What the hell are you waiting for?"

Need and anticipation pounded through him, and Alec briefly pressed his lids closed. Struggling to rein in his emotions, he applied the condom and some more lube. With one hand he lined up his cock at Dylan's asshole and, as gently as he could, eased inside.

The taut muscles gripped his cock, remained tight, and then Alec breached the ring, sinking deeper. His eyes nearly crossed from the pleasurable pressure and the heat and *damn, damn, damn* he needed to get his act together before he completely lost control.

He settled for low, shallow thrusts to get Dylan used to the sensation of being filled beyond capacity, gradually taking more as he increased the pace. Sweat glistened along Dylan's back. Drawn by the sight, Alec tasted the salt-sweat of his shoulder. He couldn't see Dylan's face to gauge whether or not he was hurting. But the silence from Dylan was a change from before.

"Are you in pain?" Alec asked.

"No," Dylan said, his voice tight. "It's just not...."

Alec lifted Dylan's hips, pulling the man to all fours. "On your elbows, Dylan," Alec said, hand gently pressing on Dylan's back.

Dylan complied, placing his elbows on the bed, ass high in the air. And, Christ, the sight nearly did Alec in. Once Alec controlled his breathing again, he pulled back, palm pressed between Dylan shoulder blades, and thrust deep.

"There," Dylan yelped. "Right goddamn there."

The new angle allowed Alec to hit Dylan's prostate with almost every stroke. At least Alec thought so because the mewling sounds now escaping Dylan's mouth with every thrust had the high-pitched, keening sound of one about to blow his load.

"Oh God," Dylan said with a shaky breath, lowering his face to the bed. "I can't..."

Everything about Dylan's position—forehead pressed against the sheets, legs spread—screamed for more. The sight almost pushed Alec over the brink. But the words coming in pants from Dylan's mouth now left Alec concerned.

"Can't what?" Alec continued to pump his hips.

Over his shoulder, Dylan looked up at Alec. Eyes wild, cheeks flushed, mouth parted and gasping, Dylan looked like a man on edge. And the vision, the very fact that Alec was the one who could bring Dylan to such a state, thrilled Alec to the core. But the word *can't* slipped from Dylan again, bringing Alec back to reality.

Alec pulled back until his erection almost popped free but couldn't bring himself to withdraw completely. He hated the thought of disappointing Dylan as much as he hated the thought of bringing this to an end.

"Do you want me to stop?" Alec asked.

Sweet Jesus let him say no.

Chapter Seven

Too far gone to mutter a *hell no*, Dylan reached back and pulled on Alec's hip until his cock was buried to the hilt. The small bundle of hungry nerves went haywire again, as if they'd been waiting forever for this particular meal, and Dylan's lids fluttered closed.

God, this was worth the initial discomfort. So *friggin'* worth it.

Chest heaving, he kept his hand clamped on Alec, their bodies pressed tight as Dylan fought off the orgasm that threatened to come too soon.

Last night during their grinding session, Alec's teasing fingers on Dylan's hole had been a revelation. Between the sensation and Alec's words, a picture of them in this very position had popped into Dylan's brain, and he'd instantly shot his load. The fantasy had surprised the hell out of him.

Through the years, he'd enjoyed more than his fair share of blowjobs and rubbing one out with a woman. His past experiences made it easy to write off last night's pleasurable activities as understandable, even familiar.

But this? Dylan dug his fingertips into Alec's hip, holding him close. This he'd never considered before.

Dylan finally felt in control enough to groan out the words. "Don't. Fucking. Stop."

A breath *whooshed* from Alec, his hand steadying Dylan at his back.

"Thank God," Alec rasped out.

And then he began to fuck Dylan in earnest, Alec's lean hips digging deep, deep, deep.

Dylan's eyes rolled back. Ditching any pretense of holding it together, he let out a long, low moan of appreciation. Or thanks. Or a plea for more. He didn't know which. And he sure as heck didn't care. Knuckles tight, Dylan fisted the sheets, now feeling so wide, so open he began to literally beg, blubbering out an embarrassing string of half-formed words.

He liked having Alec surrounding him. On top of him. Pinning him to the bed.

Holding him *down*.

"I..." Dylan let out a gasp.

Sweat slid down his temple. The intensity threatened to topple him, bigger than anything he'd ever experienced before. His knees grew shaky, his back straining to maintain a position that provided just the right angle for the maximum of pleasure. His muscles screamed for relief. His body screamed for release.

Alec gripped Dylan's back tight, his hips driving forward with a forceful snap.

And the orgasm hit with a blindsiding blast, stripping Dylan of the last of his strength, and he collapsed. Alec followed him down, pushing up on his arms and ramming Dylan's ass as he came too. Dylan pulsed and pulsed until he thought his brains had been liquefied and ejected from his body. Gone. Absorbed into the sheets.

Never to be found again.

He couldn't have blanked out for more than a second or so, but it might as well have been a lifetime. When Dylan came back to his senses, he felt as if he he'd moved away years ago and then tried to return home... a home he'd left behind for so long that everything looked different when he got back.

Alec's chest pressed against Dylan's back, their sweat-slicked skin sliding against each other as they both struggled to suck in enough oxygen.

"Jesus, Alec," Dylan croaked, "you forget to mention the part where I'd feel like I got hit by a speeding semi. A very *big* speeding semi." He bit his cheek, hoping he wasn't about to sound like a total slut. "When can we do that again?"

He felt Alec smile against his neck. "When do you think you'll recover?"

Dylan gave a tired scoff. "Next week, if—"

The *clink* of glass on glass came from the living room, and they both froze. Before Dylan could process what the sound meant, Alec had vaulted from the bed, his cock making an impressive exit from Dylan's ass and causing his muscles to spasm painfully.

Dylan hissed in protest.

"Christ, I'm sorry," Alec said before crossing to look out the window toward the street. "Noah's car is here."

With a groan, Dylan buried his head in his arms. All he wanted was to enjoy the feeling of having the shit kicked out of him sexually before he had to deal with what this meant to his and Alec's friendship. And now he had to deal with *Noah*?

The man who'd become Dylan's foxhole buddy during the battle to keep Rick alive and then during Rick's slow slip toward death. During those dark days, Dylan would have lost his friggin' mind without Noah. But Dylan knew their shared history wouldn't save him from his friend's opinions.

Dylan reluctantly rolled over and pushed up from the bed, glancing at Alec. For some reason, he didn't want Alec hearing what Noah was bound to say.

"You go take a shower," Dylan said, looking around for his clothes. When that failed, he crossed the floor, grabbed a towel from the bathroom, and ran it under the tap to clean himself up. "I'll handle Noah until you get done."

Dylan knotted a second towel around his waist and waited for Alec to disappear into the shower. Tense, but determined, Dylan padded down the hallway, planning his defense in anticipation of facing his opinionated friend.

After Alec had passed out on the bed last night, Dylan had spent all of thirty minutes on the computer Googling bisexuality before giving up. He'd started out curious. Twenty-five minutes later, he'd been struggling not to freak the fuck out. He'd gone from a small sliver of self-doubt to a super-sized serving of batshit-crazy confusion.

What was with all the labels? Homosexual and heterosexual, great. Bi-curious and bisexual, fine. But then came pansexual, omnisexual, polysexual, and...fluid. *Fluid*. What the heck did that even mean?

Seriously, how had a fairly simple concept become so complex? Only one thing Dylan knew for sure. He wasn't transgender or transsexual. He liked boobs and appreciated their aesthetic qualities, but he sure as hell didn't want to wear any.

Unfortunately the single discovery hardly helped. So he'd shut down Alec's computer and resorted to his life-long motto: fate liked to kick the shit out of people, which meant when you found something that felt good, *go for it*.

Up until that point, everything with Alec had definitely felt great. So Dylan had wisely crawled back into Alec's bed, anticipating this morning, and in return had experienced the oh-holy-shit-gasm of a lifetime. Yes, returning to Alec's bed had been a very wise decision.

Except for the part where he'd forgotten to bolt the front door...

With a resigned sigh, Dylan reached the living room and leaned against the doorway. Beyond the leather furniture centered around a glass coffee table, Noah was at the minibar pouring tomato juice into a glass. Noah wore jeans and a form-fitting sweater that hugged his lean frame, and his shoulders looked tense.

"How long have you been here?" Dylan asked.

Noah whirled to face him, blinked, and slowly set his glass on the counter. "Long enough to catch the sound of the final act."

Dylan remembered how he'd gone nuclear there at the end, picturing his brains leaking out onto the bed. And Noah was staring at Dylan as if he'd lost his mind.

Uh, yeah. About that...

"What the hell were you thinking, Dylan?"

Dylan's face burned, and he secured the towel tight around his waist as several sarcastic replies came to mind.

I was tired of playing for the same team.

I suddenly had the urge to experience life as the little spoon.

I wanted to be able to wear the You Suck, And I Like That In A Man *T-shirt you gave me.*

But Dylan knew a flippant answer would only make matters worse. Instead, he simply stared at Noah and waited for him to go on.

"Wait, scratch that." Noah picked up his tomato juice. "Obviously you *weren't* thinking."

"No need to get your silk panties in a wad, man," Dylan said. "Ease up a little."

"I do not wear silk panties," he said. "And, *no*, I will not ease up. You're taking the substitute-boyfriend gig way beyond what any rational human being would consider reasonable. I might have heard the two of you, but Tyler was too far away to appreciate how loud Alec groaned when you. Fucked. Him!"

That last sentence started out as a statement and ended up an accusation.

Hating that he felt defensive, Dylan crossed his arms. "I didn't fuck Alec. He fucked me."

Noah's face went positively goldfish, bulging eyes, gaping mouth, and all. Apparently not only had he heard the finale, he'd assumed a lot about their position as well.

Noah finally blinked, coming back to life and crossing the thick rug on the way to the couch. "Have you been drinking?"

"No."

"Taking poppers?"

"*No.*"

"Abducted by queer aliens?"

The bark of laughter almost hurt. "No. I asked him to fuck me."

Noah's legs appeared to give way, and he dropped onto the leather couch with enough force to trigger a *swish* of air from the cushion. For the first time since Rick had introduced them oh so many years ago, Noah remained speechless for a full five seconds. Dylan hadn't thought the man capable. The sight was almost worthy of the mess Dylan now found himself in.

Almost.

"I don't understand," Dylan said. "Technically I should be the one freaking out here. But, honestly, I don't think there's any reason to make a big deal of the whole thing." Besides, wigging out now was sorta pointless. Dylan entered the room and sat down, proud of his awesome reasoning skills and his nonchalant tone. "Sleeping with men is normal enough for the two of you."

"Yes, but we sleep with men who are *gay*," Noah said.

"That's not what you've told me in the past."

"Nice try," Noah said. "But we're not talking about me right now."

"Yeah." Dylan's lips twisted wryly. "Funny how we never talk about you. Why is that, Noah?"

Noah offered nothing more than a blank stare, which changed when Alec appeared in the doorway. Good, Dylan could use a little help here. Dark hair damp, and in jeans and a T-shirt, Alec took one look at Noah's now frowning face and grimaced.

"I need coffee," Alec said and pivoted to head for the kitchen.

"Get back here, girlfriend," Noah said and Alec slowly turned around, clearly preparing for battle. Noah went on. "We need to set a few things straight."

After a two second pause, Alec entered the living room. And suddenly Dylan wasn't up for dealing with Noah anymore, especially with Alec so clean and smelling so good and looking as though he needed Dylan to get him all sweaty again. Dylan let out a sigh.

Jesus, he really was a slut.

~~~***~~~

Alec had learned long ago that humoring Noah made things easier in the long run, so he settled against the wall. Although he wanted to get this confrontation over with, he desperately needed some caffeine. Retreat sounded rather appealing too.

Retreat from Dylan's hot, knowing gaze. From the confusion twisting Alec's gut in knots. And nothing good ever came from a Noah that called him *girlfriend*.

"I suggested you start dating again," Noah said, frowning at Alec. "*Not* jump into bed with a straight man."

"You sleep with straight men all the time," Alec said.

A bark of laughter shot from Dylan, and Noah tossed the man a look. Dylan pressed his lips together, clearly struggling to smother the rest of his amusement.

"We're not talking about me," Noah said. "We're talking about you, Alec."

"This conversation is sounding very familiar," Dylan murmured.

Noah ignored him. "I'm very aware of Dylan's tendency to fuck anything that moves."

"Hey!" Dylan shot up in his seat.

Was his protest due to the accusation being false or because Noah had shared the truth? Alec tried hard to pretend the answer didn't matter.

"Okay, so you're not quite the manwhore," Noah said to Dylan, and Alec's shoulders eased. "During the week, I practically have to drag you out of that garage of yours. But on the weekend, all bets are off. You're with a different woman every Friday and Saturday night, Dylan. You can't even commit to one make of motorcycle, for chrissakes."

Alec let out a huff, amused by the words, until Noah's focus shifted again.

"And you..." he said to Alec, and Alec's muscles tensed for battle. Noah stood and began to pace as he went on. "You are just getting out of a two-year relationship—a relationship you were mourning just weeks ago. And now you've gone and hooked up with Dylan?" Noah came to a stop in front of Alec. "Could you get any more idiotic?"

Probably not.

"Give me a minute," Alec said drily. "I'm sure I'll think of something."

Dylan chuckled again, and Noah frowned at him. "This isn't a laughing matter."

Clearly struggling to restrain a smile, Dylan rubbed his chin and glanced at Alec, probably hoping for a bit of solidarity while dealing with a seriously worked-up Noah. But Alec was too busy getting lost in the green gaze and remembering the wild look on Dylan's face as Alec pounded into him from behind.

He *still* couldn't wrap his mind around the sight.

Several seconds ticked by, and Dylan's eyes grew dark, dropping to Alec's body. The drag of his gaze was like a physical touch, stealing Alec's breath. And, for one insane moment, he thought Dylan was going to cross the room and haul Alec back to the bedroom.

Christ, he was still worn out and buzzed from this morning. Noah was right. Dylan's libido clearly operated at full throttle.

Alec was trying to decide if that was a good thing—or bad—when Noah stepped into his line of vision, blocking Alec's gaze.

"Stop the eye fucking, you two." Noah turned to face Dylan. "Dylan, are you bisexual?"

The words knocked the breath from Alec, and Dylan looked thrown by the question.

His answer was slow in coming. "No."

Noah planted a hand on his hip. "Are you interested in a relationship?"

This time there was no pause on Dylan's part.

"Hell, no," Dylan barked.

Alec's chest grew tight, and Noah shot him a see-what-I-mean? look before turning back to Dylan. "Why don't you go make coffee while I chat with Alec?"

"Gladly," Dylan said.

Alec relaxed a fraction, feeling relieved. Knowing Noah, Alec didn't want Dylan to hear what came next. Once Dylan was gone and the sound of puttering drifted in from the kitchen, Noah addressed Alec.

"I know you, Alec." Noah took a step closer. "You think because you managed to wring all those noises from Dylan's mouth that, somehow, he's in to you." Noah's expression had morphed from ticked off to concerned.

Alec bit back the groan, preferring a wrathful Noah over the sympathetic one. And Alec certainly didn't want to touch on the fact that his friend was right. After this morning's round in bed, Alec had begun to imagine a future that included dating Dylan.

You knew this would happen.

Using both hands, Alec raked his hair from his face. "I really don't want to talk about this right now."

"Too bad." He steadily met Alec's gaze. "You know as well as anyone that a good proportion of men's orgasms—whether they're gay, straight, or chock-full of angles—are brought about by their right hand."

When had this discussion turned to masturbation?

Noah stuck up his palm as if displaying Exhibit A in his case against Alec. "I don't know about you, but I regularly get off to something that I have absolutely *no* attraction to."

Alec almost winced at the words. Christ, no mystery where this topic was headed.

Noah went on. "Essentially we're all just a bunch of walking hard-ons in search of the big O. And Dylan is no different. Dating is one thing, but you do not need to be jumping into bed with anyone just yet, much less Dylan. Not when you're already carrying around enough baggage to rack up a five-hundred-dollar charge on Delta Airlines."

Baggage? Alec opened his mouth to protest.

"No, seriously, Alec." Noah's face was grim. "You're a mess. Not to mention a hopeless romantic. Before you shacked up with Tyler—a move I was against from the start, if you remember—you fell in love with every one-night-stand who managed to convince you to sleep with him."

Having his past thrown at him so aggressively had Alec raising his hands in surrender. Having said past illustrate the very point Alec had tried to make to himself before sleeping with Dylan was painful. "Okay, okay. I get what you're saying, all right?"

Alec knew he'd screwed up big time. He didn't need his friend to beat him about the head with the idea.

Noah apparently didn't care. "And I know Dylan even better than I know you. He'll seek out the pleasurable activity without a second thought. And you, my friend, are incapable of fucking a guy for fun and keeping your heart out of the way."

Alec struggled with the need to close his eyes, refusing to share that his heart might already be involved.

Prolonging the end will only make this worse.

Alec dropped his hands to his sides. "Fine," he said before turning and heading off.

"Where are you going?" Noah asked.

"To the kitchen."

"What for?"

Alec kept walking, his feet feeling a hundred pounds each. "To tell Dylan goodbye."

~~~***~~~

As the stainless steel coffee machine sputtered out the last drops into the carafe, Dylan scanned the room containing white tile, mahogany wood, and enough gadgets to supply a kitchen store. Dylan knew the dude liked to cook, but *seriously*. Somewhere in this well-stocked kitchen there had to be coffee cups. After several tries, Dylan managed to find the right cabinet and filled a mug. He propped his hip against the counter and sipped the black brew, enjoying the scent and the much-needed shot of caffeine.

He was just wondering if Noah was done raking Alec over the coals—and whether it was safe to return to the living room—when Alec entered the kitchen, his bare feet silent against the floor.

Noah's presence had allowed for zero time to discuss the happenings in Alec's bedroom, and the low-grade tension now made Dylan uneasy. Without a word, he reached into the cabinet with the mugs and filled a second cup, passing the coffee to Alec.

"Thanks," Alec said, adding cream from the refrigerator.

The man seemed to be having trouble meeting his eyes.

Damn, this wasn't what Dylan wanted.

"I didn't mean to—" Dylan began, just as Alec said, "I shouldn't have—"

They both fell silent, and Dylan raised his coffee in Alec's direction. "You first."

"Noah's right. Last night was a mistake."

Annoyance started its engines low in Dylan's gut. He wasn't sure why Alec's statement ticked him off so much. Yes, he'd had the same thought. Yes, he was now feeling more awkward and antsy than a prostitute at Sunday mass. And, okay, so they were just now starting to sort through the consequences of their actions. But, damn it...

Dylan refused to regret his choices.

"I think we should take a breather," Alec said.

Dylan frowned in confusion. A *breather*?

"I mean..." Alec rubbed his eyes. "I think we shouldn't see each other for a while."

Dylan set his mug on the counter with a *clunk*. "Why not?"

Holy Christ on a stick, now he sounded like a clingy woman.

"Come on, Dylan. Things are weird enough. I don't think continuing with the one-on-one motorcycle lessons is a wise move."

Dylan massaged his forehead, ignoring the headache blooming in the background. "Why don't we just chalk the whole thing up to some Guys Gone Wild thing and pretend the night never happened?"

"You can do that?"

Heck, no.

"Absolutely," he said instead.

The flash of emotion in Alec's eyes was brief but still managed to twist Dylan's gut into knots. Great, now the vulnerable look on Alec's face was courtesy of *Dylan*, not Alec's ex. And the knowledge didn't sit well.

"Maybe in a couple of months we can see where we are," Alec said, but Dylan got the distinct impression Alec had no intention of following through. "But, for now, I think it's best if we don't see each other."

Alec was giving Dylan the brush-off. Politely, of course. But still a brush-off.

An unfamiliar sensation crept up Dylan's spine. Hunh, so this was how it felt for a woman when he reminded them that one night was all he'd agreed to. In the future, he'd have to remember how much it sucked to be on the receiving end.

But, for some reason, Dylan wasn't ready to give up. "What about the poker run?"

Dylan wasn't sure why, but he really wanted Alec around for the fundraiser.

"Maybe next year I'll sign up to participate," Alec said.

Fuck. Bad enough this was the fifth anniversary of the run. Now the event Dylan had been looking forward to for weeks felt less and less like the much-needed distraction he'd require to survive Rick's birthday without going bonkers.

Still, even though sleeping with a guy didn't threaten Dylan's masculinity, acting like a clingy, psychotic girlfriend sure as heck would.

"Okay, man. If that's what you want," Dylan said. He studied Alec's blue eyes before moving his mug to the sink. "See ya around."

Without looking back, Dylan headed out of Alec's house.

Chapter Eight

Two weeks later, Dylan parked his motorcycle in front of the Front Street Clinic.

Jesus, he was turning into the clingy, psychotic girlfriend.

But, damn it, he wasn't stalking Alec. After days of no contact, Dylan was simply dropping by to ask if Alec had changed his mind about the poker run. Man to man. Friend to friend.

Nothing girly about that at *all*.

He dismounted, pausing before he flipped the kickstand down. The neighborhood skirted the edges of questionable, so he pushed his bike up the walk, grateful he'd driven his beater Yamaha instead of something he valued more. A large RV was parked on the side street, the words Mobile Medical Unit in red lettering on the side.

After a few seconds of deliberation, Dylan left his motorcycle along the right side of the building's walkway and pulled open the front door. Done in basic, boring gray, the office just met the standards for functional. Scuffed linoleum. Basic furniture. The walls were blank other than a few posters proclaiming the importance of using condoms.

Dylan passed through the empty waiting room and headed for the utilitarian front desk. A middle-aged lady sat in front of a computer, her salt-and-pepper hair pulled back. The baggy sleeves of her scrubs flapped at her shoulders as her fingers flew across the keyboard.

Without even looking up, she said, "Can I help you?"

"I need to speak with Dr. Johnson."

"Do you have an appointment?"

"Uh, no," Dylan said. "Can you tell him Dylan Booth is here to see him?"

Her fingers finally stopped clacking away on the computer, and she shot Dylan a lethal look she'd probably spent years perfecting. Dylan adopted his most charming smile. Unfortunately, she was less than impressed.

She peered around his shoulder before returning that fierce gaze to his. "The walkway isn't a parking lot."

"Huh?"

"It's a walkway." When Dylan simply blinked in confusion, she continued as if participating in a spelling bee. "W-A-L-K—"

"I know how to spell walkway," Dylan said drily.

Man, the dragon lady was one tough customer.

He smiled again. "If you'll just speak with Dr. Johnson—"

"I'm sorry, but you'll have to make an appointment."

She returned her focus to her computer with more concentration than a Friday afternoon at five o'clock deserved. Either she was an overly dedicated employee or she was intentionally giving Dylan the brush-off. Heck, much more of this and his ego would start taking all these rejections personally.

Dylan leaned his elbows on the counter. "Just tell Dr. Johnson his boyfriend is here," Dylan said and had the distinct satisfaction of watching Dragon Lady's expression freeze.

The sight was definitely worth the risk Alec would consider Dylan the backup boyfriend that wouldn't go away.

"What did you say your name was again?" she asked.

His grin grew bigger. "Dylan Booth. D-Y-L—"

"All right. All right." Dragon lady pushed her rolling chair back from the desk. "No need to be a smartass." She waved her hand at the empty waiting room consisting of a dozen plastic chairs and end tables with piles of magazines. "Have a seat."

Dylan shot her his most charming smile. Again. "Thanks."

She lifted her eyes heavenward in a what-a-piece-of-work expression.

Fifteen minutes later, Dylan fidgeted against the hard seat. He'd done a lot of thinking lately and come to the conclusion that, for the first time in his life, he had regrets.

Or more accurately, one very big regret.

Which was a strange feeling after a long-standing commitment to living in the present—because screw the past. She was a done deal. And screw the future cuz she was a fickle bitch. No getting around the truth though. He'd messed up royally, because as much as he'd enjoyed the life-altering sex, he'd found he missed Alec's company more. Enough that he'd trade in the un-fucking-believable memories just to have Alec back in his life.

As someone who appreciated good sex and happily spent most of his downtime alone, the thought was friggin' disturbing.

"Dylan?"

Dylan looked up and did his best to keep the groan from escaping. How many conversations was he gonna have to suffer through before he spoke with Alec?

Tyler stood in front of him. His smooth, black hair just reached the tops of his ears, and the man looked watchful, all emotion carefully barricaded behind those iced-gray eyes.

"I'm here to see Alec," Dylan said.

Well, duh, no shit, Sherlock.

A small smile briefly flickered across Tyler's face. "I guessed as much," he said. "I know the relationship started out fake. But you two looked pretty serious by the end of Noah's party."

Dylan had already decided not to dwell on that particular memory.

Tyler's dress pants, necktie, and button-down shirt looked crisply professional. And, for the first time, Dylan studied Tyler's athletic build. The dude clearly took his training seriously. Dylan could appreciate why Alec had hooked up with his colleague. But, try as he might, Dylan couldn't fathom why Tyler had moved out. And while Dylan preferred living alone, sharing a house with Alec must have been awesome.

"I assumed you and Alec had called things off," Tyler went on.

Dylan shifted in his seat, hating the perceptive nature of Alec's ex. "What made you think that?"

"His usual good mood has taken a leave of absence."

And while Dylan felt bad about Alec being unhappy, on the other hand...

Thank God Dylan wasn't the only one suffering here.

"We had a—" Dylan frowned. How to explain the BFF break-up? That wouldn't be girly. Not at *all*. He cleared his throat before going on. "We had a bit of a disagreement. But I'm here to fix that."

And if Dylan was absolutely honest with himself—something he'd avoided more aggressively than usual of late—part of him wondered if Tyler was the reason Alec didn't want to be Dylan's friend anymore. Because reconciling with his ex would be tough with the backup boyfriend turned one-night-stand hanging around.

Dylan's frown grew deeper.

"Are you sure fixing the relationship is wise?" Tyler asked.

No, he wasn't fucking sure of anything, except that none of this was any of Tyler's business. "Yeah," Dylan said. "I'm thinking it's a brilliant plan."

"I think you have the potential to really hurt him," Tyler said.

Dylan let out a snort of...something. Annoyance, maybe, at Alec's ex. Or maybe the sound reflected general confusion directed at himself. "That's a surprising claim coming from the man whose leaving made Alec so miserable."

Tyler didn't flinch, and Dylan met his gaze out of sheer stubbornness.

"You can't possibly understand why I really left. In fact"—a chill entered Tyler's tone, matching that infernal, unflappable gaze—"neither would Alec."

What the heck did that mean?

And after a sharp nod of goodbye, Tyler headed out the front door, clearly done with this uncomfortable conversation. Another ten minutes passed as Dylan waited. Should he leave? Where was Alec? Maybe he didn't want to see Dylan, and this was a passive-aggressive way of telling him to get lost.

Growing antsy, he picked up a *People* magazine and flipped aimlessly through the pages. Voices drifted from up the hallway. In khakis and a pullover, Alec rounded the corner, holding a little girl's hand, a tired-looking, middle-aged woman at his side. The sight sent Dylan's eyebrows climbing.

Alec's gaze met Dylan's, and Alec sent him a slight nod. But his full attention remained on the small family. The kid bounced on her feet, occasionally swinging on Alec's arm. But he calmly kept talking to the mother, completely unconcerned he was being used as a swing set.

Finally, Alec shook the woman's hand goodbye and ruffled the kid's head. The little girl giggled in response, and Dylan noticed the pleased crinkles around Alec's eyes. The same crinkles he'd gotten every time he'd fired up the Harley.

Dylan's chest gave a ridiculous twitch at the memory.

After showing his patients out, Alec approached Dylan. "Martha said my boyfriend was here to see me."

For the life of him, Dylan couldn't remember why he'd thought seeing the Dragon Lady's reaction took priority over fearing the clingy girlfriend label with Alec.

"Uh, yeah." Dylan dropped the magazine to the table, trying to decide if the moment was awkward or not. "About that..."

"She didn't seem to believe your claim."

The amused crinkles around Alec's eyes reappeared, and Dylan relaxed a bit.

"Man, everyone sees right through me." Dylan smiled. "Guess I make a lousy backup boyfriend."

A light laugh escaped Alec. "You had your moments."

This time the pause was definitely uncomfortable. The memories of those moments crowded into the empty spaces between them, soaking up all the oxygen from the empty waiting room. Memories of Alec kneeling at Dylan's feet, Dylan on all fours in front of Alec...

Jesus, this wasn't helping with the awkward vibe.

Alec tucked his hair behind his ears. "What brings you here?"

Tell him the truth. Tell him you want to fix where they went wrong.

Dylan opened his mouth, but at the last moment, he lost his nerve and took the coward's way out. "Noah's driving me friggin' nuts."

A single eyebrow on Alec's face rose higher.

Dylan stood, pacing a few steps away in hopes of easing the tension. "He's changing the poker run all around."

"Okay," Alec said, drawing out the vowels. "But he *is* in charge this year."

Plowing a hand through his hair, Dylan said, "I know." He turned to face Alec and dropped his arm to his side. "But now he wants to run the whole thing in *teams*. Which is a ridiculously dumb idea. And the food he's serving at each stop is friggin' weird."

Gaze intense, Alec said, "Dylan, why are you really here?"

Dylan stuck his hands in the back pocket of his jeans, running through his response in his mind. As the fifth anniversary of the poker run slowly drew near, the antsier Dylan grew. Five years without his best friend felt like a milestone—a really depressing milestone. The dark thoughts left him biting back the real answer to Alec's question and the words that were filling Dylan's chest, itching to get out.

Because I wanted to see you again.

Because I've missed your company.

Because I need you as a friend.

Fuck, the creepy melancholy was seriously mucking with his brain.

All Dylan could come up with was pretty lame. "I came because I hoped to talk you into being the fifth on my team for the poker run."

"Dylan." Alec blew out a breath. "I think—"

"Hands to myself." Dylan held up his arms, palms facing Alec, as if taking a two-handed solemn pledge. "I promise. Besides, you don't want to miss out on all of Noah's hard work, do you?"

Dylan wasn't sure why getting Alec to ride along felt so important. More important than work. More important than even the poker run itself.

"Come on, Alec." Despite the urgency pounding its way through Dylan's brain, he sent Alec an easy smile, hoping to take the edge out of the moment. "You got something better to do next weekend?"

Alec's lips quirked. "Not really."

"Good," Dylan said, pouncing on the admission as though Alec had said yes. Best just to keep moving forward. "I'll plan on meeting you at the starting point."

Alec hesitated, looking if he was about to protest, so Dylan quickly went on. "Trust me, you don't want to miss Noah wearing his hot pink T-shirt with the words *Drama Queen In Charge*."

Alec laughed, his eyes crinkling in the corners, and Dylan smiled his first *real* smile since landing at the Front Street Clinic.

Dragon Lady appeared from around the corner, a large tote slung over her shoulders. "Good night, Alec."

"'Night, Martha," Alec said. "See you Monday."

When the woman narrowed her eyes at Dylan, he smiled. "Careful you don't trip over that motorcycle parked on the walkway," Dylan said, enjoying the visual daggers she lobbed in his direction. "And thanks for all your help."

Martha let out a snort as she passed by and pushed her way out the front door.

"Good employees are hard to fine," Alec said with a wry twist of his lips. "Next time you drop in to say hello, I'd be most appreciative if you wouldn't piss off my staff."

The words *next time* echoed in Dylan's head, feeling almost like a victory and easing the two-week-old tightness in his chest. "Sure thing, man. Whatever you say."

Alec hesitated. "There's a football game tonight."

Instead of interrupting, this time Dylan knew to keep his mouth shut, feeling hopeful as Alec went on.

"Ole Miss versus Vanderbilt," Alec said. "Should be good. You want to go grab some dinner and watch the game?"

Dylan grinned at Alec, the victory officially real. "Absolutely."

~~~***~~~

The day of the Fifth Annual Vintage Memorial Poker Run began with a glorious sunrise and the *buzz, buzz, buzz* of Alec's cellular against his nightstand. He barely stifled the moan. No need to check the number to see who was calling.

"Mom." Alec's pillow muffled his voice as he answered. "It's five o'clock in the morning."

During the pause that followed, Alec pictured her blank face, the subtext in his comment completely lost on his mother.

He tried again. "And it's a *Saturday*."

The added information didn't seem to help.

Alec shifted to a more comfortable position in bed. "Why are you up so early?"

"I'm working on an article I'm writing for the *Journal of Nanoscience and Nanotechnology.*"

As usual, a stab of guilt followed. He couldn't fault his mother for being, well, *her.* Like his father, she was a brilliant researcher and the ultimate geek, but loving in her own odd way. She hadn't batted an eye when, at the age of sixteen, Alec had announced he was gay. He'd spent months working up the courage to come out to his family, and their reaction had been awfully anticlimactic. Suddenly he couldn't turn around without being inundated with supportive pamphlets and facts and figures about gay teens, all courtesy of his mother.

She'd applied the same energy to overturning DOMA and Proposition 8.

"What are you and dad doing tonight?" Alec asked.

"Preparing our presentation for the Nano Fundamentals and Applications Conference next month."

"Anything else? Like something that doesn't involve work?"

Two second ticked by before she answered. "Getting Chinese takeout."

"Sounds..." *Remarkably like eating dinner.* "Nice."

How his parents had found their way out of their respective labs, much less met and married, Alec would never know. Fortunately, he and his brother had been spared their awkward social skills.

And then Alec remembered how he'd gone mute in front of Tyler that day in his garage. And how Dylan's proximity at the party had rendered Alec a babbling fool.

Okay, so maybe he'd avoided *most* of his mother's awkward social skills.

"I was calling about the awards ceremony," she said. "Since you and Tyler are the winners, your father and I are taking the time off that Saturday to drive up and attend."

"It will be good to see you both," Alec said.

"We were hoping to have drinks with you and Tyler beforehand."

Alec stifled a groan as he propped his elbows on the mattress and rubbed the sleep from his eyes. A visit from his parents was rare, but not unwelcome. Every few months or so, Alec and Tyler had climbed into the car and made the five-hour trip down to Los Angeles to see them. Having them here would be a nice change.

Except for the small detail that he and Tyler weren't a couple anymore.

"Mom, you know Tyler and I broke up."

And telling his mother about the split had been one of the most difficult things he'd ever done. He'd hated disappointing her.

"You said yourself, Alec. There's always hope."

Hope.

As his mother rambled on about statistics regarding breakups and reconciliation—and Christ, where did she find all her data?—Alec glanced out his bedroom window as dawn claimed the sky, the fiery sphere slowly dominating the horizon.

A week ago Friday, he'd started the day in a foul mood, missing Dylan more than he'd ever imagined. Still, he'd been convinced walking away had been the right decision. Dealing with Tyler and the strained atmosphere at work had provided a daily reminder of just how much relationships could muck with your   mind.   And   theirs   had   been   fairly straightforward, not the messed-up version like Alec and Dylan's. So Alec had remained firm in his resolve to stay away from the man.

When Dylan had strolled into the clinic looking as fine as ever, Alec hadn't been prepared for the hopeful look on Dylan's face. The expression left Alec believing Dylan had missed him too and was dying to have him back as a friend.

And Alec had caved.

Since then they'd fallen back into the familiar rhythm of talk about bikes and repairs and football, general discussions that meant nothing, yet, at the same time, meant *everything*. Alec steered clear of any conversations that involved the physical aspect of their relationship. He was careful not to accidentally touch Dylan, and if the occasional memory reared its persistent head, Alec pushed the image aside. The situation wasn't perfect but beat the misery of the two weeks alone. And Alec looked forward to spending this weekend with Dylan.

Probably more than he should.

"Alec?"

He forced his attention back to his mother.

"Are you and Tyler working things out?" she went on.

Shit. He dragged a hand down his face. His mother adored Tyler. How could Alec tell her the man had a new boyfriend? How could Alec tell her that he couldn't stop thinking about *someone else*?

He wasn't up for disappointing his mother again, especially after everything she'd done for him.

"Not really," he said vaguely. "But I'd love to have you and Dad over before the ceremony."

He needed to be more prepared before he shared the news about Tyler. About Dylan. About *himself.* Hell, he needed to figure out the truth before he could explain the facts to anyone else.

~~~***~~~

Two hours later Alec stood in the massive parking lot and tuned out the chatter of motorcyclists in various stages of preparedness, silently reciting the reasons he needed to maintain a casual attitude around Dylan. Despite the sunshine, the early morning temperatures still clung to the air, and he zipped his slim-fitting racing jacket against the chill. But he needn't have bothered because Dylan pulled up beside him and parked. The resulting thrum of pleasure created a shimmer of heat that left Alec feeling supercharged, his skin electric.

Damn.

"You ready?" Dylan pulled off his helmet, the soft spikes of his hair looking especially rebellious today.

Alec longed to smooth out the strands, so he fisted his hand at his side. Dylan appeared completely relaxed and unaffected by Alec's presence. The easy attitude brought to mind Dylan's words in Alec's kitchen that fateful morning...

"...just pretend the night never happened."

"You can do that?"

"Absolutely."

Alec swallowed hard, pushing the memory aside. "Ready as I'll ever be. What are the rules for today's run?"

"Each team member collects a playing card at the designated points along the way. The team with the best hand at each stop wins a free round of drinks tonight. There are two stops up to today's final destination and two stops on the way back tomorrow. But the weekend is really all about the bikes."

Alec eyed Dylan's cherry-red Ducati Monster, a motorcycle that looked as if two-hundred-mile-an-hour speeds were not only possible but inevitable. "How many do you own anyway?"

"Seven," Dylan said. "But I've been looking at various Triumph TR5 Trophys for sale. Always wanted a bike like James Dean. You should come with me some time to check one out."

Amused, Alec said, "Have you ever considered therapy for your obsession?"

Dylan's smile nearly did Alec in. "Absolutely not."

Fifteen minutes and several internal pep talks later, Alec followed Dylan to meet up with their three teammates at the starting line. With almost a hundred and fifty participants, the motorcycles took off in groups, the roar of the engines creating an impressive rumble. When their time came, Alec followed Dylan out onto the highway, enjoying the feel of his Harley. The motor purred like a contented lion since the tune-up. They quickly settled into a rhythm on the road, Dylan's five-man team sticking close together.

Charlie, a redheaded, middle-aged fireman from Sacramento, took the lead. Following him was his brother Rob, a younger, slimmer, less hairy version of Charlie. After Rob came James, an accountant from Redlands who looked like...well, an accountant. He wore wire-framed glasses, and his personality was less boisterous than Charlie and his brother.

Dylan and Alec brought up the rear, riding side by side, the position comfortable. By now they'd learned each other's habits well enough to anticipate the reactions of the other.

And despite Alec's conflicted feelings, being back on the road with Dylan felt right.

By the time they arrived at the first stop of the day, the chilly temperature had dissipated, the sun glinting off the rows of parked motorcycles. In the center of a large field, a huge tent had been erected and filled with tables.

They parked, and Alec followed Dylan toward the makeshift rest area. The time spent on the road must have whittled away at Alec's willpower because he couldn't tear his gaze from Dylan's ass. Surely Jacob Davis and Levi Strauss had specifically pictured Dylan's form when they'd created blue jeans.

Mercifully, a voice pulled Alec from his traitorous thoughts.

"There you two are."

Among the sea of leather and boots and riding chaps, along with those in racing apparel, Noah approached in a neon pink T-shirt. Dylan hadn't been exaggerating. The words *Drama Queen In Charge* were plastered across Noah's chest.

Noah gestured at the swarm of motorcyclists enjoying themselves. "What do you think?"

At one end of the large tent, a woman in an evening gown stepped up onto a small stage, picked up the microphone, and began to talk. The voice was definitely masculine.

Dylan stared at the drag queen. "I think—"

Piano music filled the air, and the performer began belting out "I Will Survive" by Gloria Gaynor. Five music-filled seconds passed before Dylan looked recovered enough to speak.

"Jesus, Noah," Dylan rasped out.

Which, apparently, tapped Dylan's ability to form words. So Alec responded to the overly innocent *What?* expression on Noah's face.

"It's a little much for a Saturday morning in the middle of nowhere," Alec said.

The singer hit an earsplitting high note, and Dylan finally recovered from his apoplectic state. "There isn't even any beer to dull the senses."

"You know the rules," Noah said. "You made them. No drinking during the run. And Destiny's Bitch is one of the Bay Area's hottest attractions."

Dylan shot Noah a skeptical look.

But then Destiny's Bitch hit another high note, and Alec silently thanked Noah for settling for plastic cups over glass. A server wearing a matching neon pink T-shirt and the words *Little Minion* passed by with a platter of appetizers delicately arranged. Noah reached out and snagged two.

Dylan's dismayed look was almost comical. "What *is* that?"

"Today's refreshment, donated by my favorite restaurant, is a thin slice of green apple topped with prosciutto and goat cheese and drizzled with honey." Noah popped one into his mouth and held the other out to Dylan. "Try one. They're delicious."

Dylan stared at the offering with a hint of horror. "I gotta go talk to...to... someone."

"You do that, handsome," Noah said before turning to Alec. "Alec and I will catch up."

Although the words were benign, the tone in Noah's voice created a fist of tension in Alec's gut. Fortunately, Noah remained silent as Dylan headed off, threading his way through the crowd. *Un*fortunately, Alec didn't tear his gaze away from Dylan's ass fast enough.

Noah stared at Alec without saying a word, and, despite the cool breeze, heat crawled up Alec's back. He forced himself to remain calm and stuck his hands into the pocket of his jeans.

"Dylan asked me to make a fifth for the team. So in a way," Alec said, "it's your fault I'm here."

Noah simply shot him a look that screamed *bullshit*.

"We're just friends, Noah."

Noah's expression didn't budge.

Alec tried again. "Nothing else."

Noah finally let out a scoff. "There isn't a gay man in the world who wouldn't want more than that from Dylan Booth. Probably a few straight ones too."

Alec tipped his head, a thought suddenly occurring to him. All this time he'd assumed Noah's chastising words were in response to the potential for Alec getting hurt. Now he wondered who, exactly, Noah worried about the most.

"Does that include you?" Alec asked.

"Oh my God." Noah tipped back his head and let out a loud laugh, nixing Alec's previous thoughts. "Are you jealous?"

"No," Alec said, although a part of him considered the possibility. The two men were clearly tight. And Alec wasn't so delusional as to deny his burning curiosity about Dylan Booth. Alec suspected Noah knew more about Dylan than he let on. "I'm not jealous. But I thought maybe you were."

Noah huffed out a breath. "I'm too familiar with Dylan to set myself up for that kind of heartache."

Heartache.

Before Alec could process his thoughts, Dylan wandered back in their direction, looking a bit more relaxed now that Destiny's Bitch was taking a break. Alec stared vacantly into the crowd and half-heartedly listened as Dylan began to discuss tomorrow's route.

Was Dylan hoping for more between the two of them? So far he'd stayed true to his promise, keeping his hands to himself. In fact, he looked so *un*affected that Alec had begun to reconsider Noah's morning-after speech. Had Alec been "the hand," a convenient way for Dylan to get off? Maybe Dylan had simply had a moment of bi-curiosity.

An ache set up camp behind Alec's heart. He watched Dylan take a swig from his plastic bottle, a drop of water sliding down Dylan's neck and settling into the dip at the base of his throat. A perfect fit for Alec's tongue. He shook his head to rouse himself out of his stupor.

What was wrong with him? Dylan didn't appear to want him anymore. Alec wasn't supposed to want Dylan.

Christ, why had he agreed to come today?

Redheaded Rob sidled up to Dylan's side with an appetizer in hand. "Anyone know where can I get more of these apple thingys?"

Noah eyed Rob up and down before sending the man a brilliant smile. "I'd be happy to show you."

"Fantastic," Rob said with a grin.

Alec watched Noah escort the man away and forced his gaze to remain on the two men, despite Dylan's disturbing proximity.

"Should we warn Rob that Noah will probably hit on him?" Alec said, finally risking a glance at Dylan.

"Nah." Grinning, Dylan studied the two men as they disappeared into the crowd. "Why ruin the surprise?" With barely a glimpse in Alec's direction, he went on. "Let's go get our playing card."

And, as he followed Dylan, Alec focused on the crowd around him. He needed to stop searching for the return of The Look. He needed to stop wondering if it would reappear in Dylan's eyes.

More importantly, Alec needed to figure out what he'd do if it did.

Chapter Nine

Turns out, Alec had no reason to worry how he'd respond to the return of a Dylan who stared at Alec with that familiar heat in his gaze. The day ended much like the start, with a fiery sun lingering just over the horizon and nothing resembling desire appearing in Dylan's eyes.

In fact, he'd almost disengaged completely.

The restaurant patio brimmed with bikers, and chatter and laughter and the clatter of cutlery filled the air. Alec had laughed when Dylan pretended to weep with relief when they smelled barbecue being served to the participants—the fleeting sign of humor from Dylan the first since the morning.

Their five-man team had eaten dinner while debating the day's best bike sighting. Oddly, Dylan stayed out of the friendly argument, silently focusing on his food instead. And there was something obscene about the way Dylan wolfed down his barbeque. Watching Dylan lick the sauce from his lips and fingers constituted a form of torture. Fortunately, with the dinner dishes mostly cleared, they all sat around the table sipping their beers while Dylan's friends told stories about past poker runs. The conversation was a welcome distraction from the finger porn and the almost withdrawn look on Dylan's face.

"Alec," Charlie said, the middle-aged man startling Alec out of his stupor. "You ever think of buying a real bike?"

Being the newbie, Alec had borne the brunt of the group's good-natured ribbing all day. Each man had his favorite brand of motorcycle. Alec had quickly learned their preferences as the men tossed about their favorite insults along the way, insults such as "foreign piece of shit," "BMW stands for big money waster," and "Harleys are for people who think professional wrestling is real."

"A better question, Charlie"—Alec met the redhead's gaze with a lazy hike of an eyebrow—"is when are you going to grow a real beard?"

The burst of laughter from the table was loud, but Dylan simply gazed out across the patio deck, not even a hint of a smile on his face.

When his chuckle died away, Charles rubbed the patchy hair covering his cheeks. "How long you been riding, anyway?"

"A little over a month," Alec said.

"Holy smokes, you *are* a neophyte," Charlie said.

Dylan suddenly leaned forward in interest. "But the man's got a mind like a friggin' steel trap. I think he's got a photographic memory." He turned to Alec—

And good God, Alec should have been embarrassed by the wave of pleasure caused by the simple attention.

"What year did Honda introduce the CB750 to the US market?" Dylan asked.

"1969," Alec replied.

"How many years did Harley Davidson make the Knucklehead engine?"

"Eleven."

"When did Indian produce its first V-twin?" Charlie fired off.

"1907," Alec said. "But there is some debate about the date."

Charlie's brother, Rob, let out a whistle. "He's like a walking Wikipedia."

"Maybe," Alec said with a laugh. "Just don't ask me to help you with a tune-up."

Dylan tilted his head in Alec's direction. "It's true," he said. "He doesn't know the difference between a Phillips and a flat-head screwdriver."

Rob barked out, "You gotta be kidding me?" at the same time several incredulous groans came from rest of the men. Alec grinned, amused the friendly ribbing now extended to his abysmal mechanical skills, but mostly relieved because Dylan *not* teasing Alec had felt so wrong.

"Time for the traditional birthday toast." Rob lifted his beer. "To Rick Adams."

With a general murmur of agreement, the small band of men raised their mugs, and Alec glanced at Dylan. The subdued mood suddenly clicked, and Alec mentally kicked himself in the ass.

Christ, how could he have been so *blind*?

Alec slowly set his drink down. Today was Rick's birthday, the friend Dylan had spent every year honoring by organizing a massive fundraising event. The one who the proceeds were donated in honor of. The name splayed on the side of Dylan's garage.

Catching his eye, Dylan sent him a small smile, but his usual twinkle of good humor was gone.

The table began to discuss tomorrow's route, and Alec leaned closer to Dylan, his voice low. "You okay?"

Slouched in his chair, legs spread in a relaxed position, Dylan shrugged. "As well as can be expected."

For the first time in weeks, Dylan held his gaze too long, lingering beyond a respectable time frame. And what started out as a worried feeling on Alec's part took a long, slow slide into something else...

Several seconds ticked by during which Alec knew he needed to shift his attention somewhere else. *Anywhere* else. But Dylan sabotaged the attempt when his eyes dropped to Alec's mouth and turned a darker green. A shade Alec was very familiar with.

It was the look a small part of him had been hoping to see all day.

Despite the cool breeze, heat flushed up Alec's neck. He sipped his beer and shifted in his seat. Unfortunately, repositioning himself in his chair brought his knee up against Dylan's, the contact sending a jolt through Alec's body.

His throat suddenly felt twice baked and lacking in moisture. He carefully set his mug down, licking the foam from his lips and very aware Dylan watched the procedure with intense interest.

Shit.

Now that his beer sat on the table, Alec didn't know what to do with his hands, so he tucked his hair behind his ears. Dylan's gaze seemed to follow his every movement, and Alec's pulse picked up speed, the conversation around them fading.

The time had come to stop pretending. Nothing was the same since they'd resumed their friendship. Right now the seemingly innocent contact of knee against knee distracted Alec to the point where he couldn't follow the conversation, not when Dylan's gaze kept crash-landing back into Alec's. Asking questions Alec couldn't answer.

Making dark promises Alec shouldn't want Dylan to keep.

Dylan's expression stuck with Alec as they settled the bill and made their way back to the hotel with the rest of the group. When Alec entered his room, alone, he tossed his keys onto the dresser, restless. Sweeping his gaze across the boring beige décor and the king-sized bed made Alec feel...lonely.

And he was so tired of being alone.

Alec was standing in the same spot contemplating a shower when a sharp knock at the door made him jump. The sound echoed in the hotel room and, no doubt, down the hallway. For a moment, Alec stared at the door, a deep-seated feeling of anticipation and dread and inevitability welling in his chest. He knew who stood on the other side.

He knew what Dylan wanted.

But did Dylan really want Alec, or was this just a convenient way for Dylan to deal with a difficult day?

As soon as the thought popped into Alec's head, he tensed.

A second knock came. Mind reeling, Alec crossed the carpet and opened the door, still wondering what to do when he saw the man. Dylan stood with his hands on his hips, T-shirt tight across his shoulders, bare feet poking out from the bottom of his frayed jeans. For some reason, Dylan looked angry.

Three thudding heartbeats later, Alec said, "Dylan, don't you think—?"

Like a brake released on a bike revved to full throttle, Dylan fisted his hands in Alec's T-shirt and crowded him up against the doorjamb. Alec struggled to finish his question, confused, but Dylan's intentions became clear when his lips landed on Alec's.

Dylan pressed Alec's mouth open wide. Several damp, *hungry* kisses followed that left Alec little room for thought. Somewhere in the back of his brain, he realized this was their first real kiss. One that hadn't started out fake or been dulled by the effects of alcohol.

Dylan tipped his head to take more. His tongue stroked Alec's and sent a spike of pure pleasure straight to his groin, and every rational thought in Alec's brain went on permanent sabbatical.

~~~***~~~

Dylan couldn't remember the last time, if ever, the need to be inside someone tore through him with such intensity.

But as they'd sat at the restaurant, Dylan in the middle of a self-pitying sulk—and, *Jesus*, shouldn't he have recovered from the loss of Rick by now?—Alec had tucked his hair behind his ear, exposing the line of his jaw. Dylan had been momentarily transfixed, imagining his tongue tracing the angle and his lips on the pulse at his neck. He longed to mark Alec's skin. Dylan had spent the day trying to keep his hands off as promised, but he was suddenly struck by the insatiable desire to bury himself inside Alec and not come up for air.

The need was all consuming. Crushing. Driving him insane.

And right now felt too friggin' far from what he had, which was fucking fabulous, to all that he wanted, which was *everything*. All of Alec splayed on his back, ankles over his head with Dylan buried deep in his ass. In an attempt to bring him closer, Dylan hooked his fingers in Alec's jeans and maneuvered their bodies inside the room, trapping Alec against the wall.

Two hard cocks now pressed together through several frustrating layers of denim and cotton briefs.

"I need..." Dylan groaned against Alec's mouth as he kicked the door closed. "You can't—"

Leave me like you did before.

Dylan dove in for another soul-drugging kiss before trying again. But the mental image of the two of them folded together like a pretzel was too much, mucking with his ability to speak. "I...*damn*—"

Just like that day at the clinic, the words tumbled chaotically in his mind. He struggled to arrange them in the correct sequence, but they escaped without consulting his brain. A rambling mess of "need" and "can't" and "now" randomly slipped from his mouth between hot, messy kisses, in no particular order and with no particular meaning.

In a fumble of hands and flying fingers, Dylan worked on Alec's clothes because he wanted them gone, gone, *gone.* Hips still trapping Alec against the wall, Dylan shoved Alec's T-shirt over his head, static leaving a few wayward strands of hair sticking up in all directions. Dylan tossed the fabric aside and reached for Alec's jeans.

Dylan got the button undone and grunted in victory, only to have things briefly deteriorate when Alec tried to help with Dylan's shirt. Fingers skimming up Dylan's chest, Alec hampered Dylan's efforts, slowing him down. And when Alec reached Dylan's nipples... Shit, now Dylan could barely see straight.

He batted Alec's hands away. "Stop helping."

Impatient, he wanted Alec naked *now,* because this wasn't just about getting off. An orgasm wasn't Dylan's only intent. He wanted to be *inside* Alec when he came and to watch Alec's face as he did. He wanted to see the color rise on his cheeks and the dark, I'm-so-close look in those blue eyes. He needed to feel Alec's cum spill on his skin.

Dylan wrestled the front of Alec's jeans into submission, flicking open the zipper before plunging his hand down the front. Two frustrating seconds passed as Dylan searched for the waistband of the briefs beneath.

Holy hell, he'd never felt so clumsy during sex before. His fingers finally tunneled inside and stroked the fully erect cock, hard, yet covered in the softest skin. Dylan circled Alec's slit with this thumb, smearing the precum, and Alec choked back a sound that resembled something like a sob. And Dylan?

Dylan remained silent, so grateful to have Alec back in his arms he could barely breathe.

"Off," Dylan grunted out.

Alec complied, pushing his jeans to the floor and kicking them aside. Dylan spun them both around and backed a gloriously naked Alec toward the center of the room. His mouth consuming soft lips, Dylan detected a hint of barbeque smoke and fresh air clinging to Alec's hair as he steered with one destination in mind. One purpose.

One goal.

When they hit the bed, Dylan kept moving forward, and they both tumbled down, bouncing on the mattress.

Dylan landed on top of all that bare skin and let out a satisfied hiss. "Yes."

One arm braced beside Alec's head, Dylan bent forward, straining to unfasten his own jeans and still keep their lips sealed. The open-mouthed kisses turned downright filthy. Alec met him turn for turn, his tongue stroking Dylan's, but his hands remained wrapped around Dylan's biceps. Whether Alec was holding on because of the insane pace or because he refused to interfere again, Dylan wasn't sure. With a grunt of satisfaction, Dylan finally got his jeans unzipped.

He only got as far as unfastening the front before he pulled out his dick and lowered himself down, too eager to take the time to remove his clothes. Their cocks lined up side by side as though they'd been waiting for the two men to get over themselves and get with the program, and Dylan let out a long, slow moan.

Because he so fucking agreed with the sentiment.

It dawned on him that he hadn't asked Alec if this was okay, if Dylan was allowed to be here like this, stretched on top of him. But when Alec groaned and thrust his hips in search of friction, Dylan figured, at this point, asking the question would be pretty damn stupid.

"Lube," Alec gasped, followed by, "condom."

And, yeah, asking for permission now would be about ten steps in the wrong direction.

Dylan reached into his back pocket and pulled out a packet of lube and a condom. When he'd stomped over to Alec's room there'd been no question in his mind that they would end up here, that the two of them would fix where they'd been seriously derailed by Noah and his dumbass opinions—

Alec tipped his hips and spread his thighs in invitation, granting Dylan full access.

"Shit," Dylan said with a shaky breath.

He made quick work of the condom and the lube, fumbling only for a moment, thankyouverymuch. Dylan worked Alec open, progressing from one to two and then three fingers, barely taking the time to process the response of one before adding another. He knew he was going too fast, but Alec simply dug his blunt nails into Dylan's arms and worked his hips in begging counter-circles. He offered no resistance, only demanded more. Alec shifted his legs higher and settled them around Dylan's back as if to hurry him up. But Dylan craved better friction. More contact. Hell, he needed *leverage.*

Dylan hooked an arm under Alec. "Hold on."

He hauled him down the bed until Alec's ass reached the edge and Dylan could plant his feet firmly on the carpet. Not a second thought entered his mind as he lined up his cock with Alec's hole and pushed, bottoming out in one long stroke.

The tight heat enveloped his cock, and Dylan let out a hiss and froze, his limbs tense. Fine tremors wracked his every muscle. He fought the urge to move as the words racing around his head since Alec had ended things—the words itching to get out when Dylan had hunted him down at the clinic—finally escaped.

"This isn't over," Dylan rasped out.

The feeling had been churning inside Dylan since Alec had put their friendship, or relationship, or what-the-fuck-ever this was on hold. Dylan pulled his hips back before thrusting again, and Alec arched his back to meet Dylan.

"I know," Alec murmured.

Somehow, the admission felt horrifically inadequate. Dylan pressed his forehead against Alec's and repeated the process, near full withdrawal followed by a hard drive forward, burying himself to the hilt.

The harsh words sandblasted Dylan's throat. "We're not through."

"I *know.*"

This time Alec's confession rumbled out like a perfectly tuned Harley, and there was no fucking way Dylan could work up the proper amount of fear he knew his declaration—and Alec's response —should generate.

Shoving the thought aside, Dylan began a demanding pace he hoped like hell he could maintain. Time blurred. The bed creaked.

Until Dylan's breath came in shuddering pants.

And because pounding Alec's ass and breathing weren't complicated enough, Dylan felt the need to maintain control of Alec's lips as well. So he pushed Alec's legs higher. With his elbows pressed against the bed, Dylan jammed his fingers into the man's hair, holding his head still so he could devour Alec's mouth in time with his hips.

Alec murmured incoherently, nonsense sounds intermixed with mewling noises as Dylan slammed into him relentlessly. Fingers buried in Alec's hair, Dylan pinned Alec to the bed, afraid he'd suddenly change his mind about wanting this, about wanting Dylan. But Alec seemed incapable of anything beyond spreading himself wider and begging Dylan to take more. Even better, Alec tilted into Dylan's hips every time Dylan's cock hammered inside.

The movements turned greedy and hot and hard, and now Dylan barely pulled out before thrusting back in. "*Alec.*"

In response, Alec's fingers bit into Dylan's arms, no doubt leaving marks by now. But Dylan didn't mind. Sweat dampened Dylan's shirt, his back steaming, but he didn't care about that either, not while he was busy laying claim to Alec. With so much to see, Dylan grappled with what he preferred most. Alec's slack mouth or his eyes rolled back in pleasure? The desperate expression or the ruddy color of his cheeks? But, Jesus...

The sight of Alec's naked ass with Dylan fully clothed made the moment better, hotter, more urgent.

Alec sucked in a breath. "Please—"

Pleasure swelled from the inside out, clenching Dylan tighter, every sensation sharp. The cold teeth of Dylan's zipper pressed against his cock and the rough rub of denim chaffed his skin. Inhaling enough oxygen became a real challenge. But still he wanted Alec closer, needed more.

And the weight of that want was fucking terrible.

Alec sounded broken. "*Dylan.*"

Dylan glanced down at Alec's blood-red cock, swollen and glistening at the tip. The vision sent the mother of all whammies slamming through him.

Desperation made Dylan's voice hoarse. "Touch yourself."

"But I'll—"

"Do it *now.*"

Alec reached between them and gave several tugs in time with Dylan's thrusts. Precariously close to spontaneous combustion, Dylan groaned as his hips stuttered, losing the rhythm. Alec arched his neck, his spine stiff as thick, white streaks of cum shot up his chest, and Dylan almost sobbed with relief. He dug his toes into the carpet and gave one final push, pleasure incinerating every cell. All the air punched from his lungs, and Dylan's eyes rolled back, his vision going black.

~~~***~~~

When Alec finally managed to corral his mind and body back into the same room, he slowly became aware of a crushing pressure. Dylan had collapsed on top of him. Alec shifted, trying to ease the burden currently preventing him from breathing.

Christ, the man consisted of nothing but solid muscle.

Alec managed to wheeze out, "Dylan."

"Sorry," he mumbled, shifting off.

They scooted higher on the bed, and Dylan plastered himself against Alec's side, his arm over Alec's chest. After several seconds, Dylan hooked his leg across the top of Alec's. Whether to prevent him from escaping or to touch more skin, Alec didn't know. The lighter weight felt pleasant and the heat reassured him that Dylan was still *here*. Peace washed over Alec, and everything—the worry and the doubt and the fear of the future—got pushed aside.

Well, everything except the curiosity.

Their breaths slowed as their bodies cooled, and Alec traced the largest scar on Dylan's back. "Tell me about Rick."

The pause that followed lasted several beats before filling with the sound of motorcycles pulling into the parking lot outside the window. The roar of the engines was replaced with the laughter of several poker-run participants retiring for the day. Alec waited patiently as the scuffle of footsteps and voices passed outside the hotel door and faded as they headed up the hallway.

Would Dylan respond? Or would he simply ignore the request? After the energy he'd just exerted, pretending to have fallen asleep was a believable option.

"He was..." Dylan paused, as if searching for the right words. "A lamb among wolves."

Alec remained silent, waiting for Dylan to go on.

"Funny. Kind. Almost sweet." Dylan tipped his head to look up at Alec. "A lot like you, in some ways." Alec's lips quirked until Dylan went on. "Even though his parents had kicked him out because he was gay, he remained an optimist. I was the teen who took out my frustrations by constantly looking for a fight." He let out a soft snort, his breath tickling Alec's skin. "And there was no shortage of people willing to take me up on my offer."

Alec swallowed against the knot in his chest and smoothed his fingers over Dylan's scar.

"I used to get so pissed at Rick," Dylan said. "Some asshole would heckle him, calling him a cocksucker or whatever, and Rick never did a thing. He wasn't a big guy, so it wasn't like I expected him to fight physically. But he wouldn't say a word. Just forced a smile and kept on walking."

Alec's lips curled up at the ends. "I'm guessing you responded for him."

"Hell yeah," he said. "Angry teen pissed at the world? Let me at 'em." Alec felt Dylan grin against his skin. "Rick used to say the only reason we were friends was because it gave me an excuse to kick the shit out of people if they got rough with him."

Alec smiled. Picturing Dylan as a cocky adolescent spoiling for a fight came easy.

"Eventually I figured out Rick was on to something," Dylan said. "He always claimed people hated being ignored more." He shrugged before going on. "I dunno. Maybe he was right. Me, I was just happy for the excuse to vent my frustrations."

Vent my frustrations.

Asking about those frustrations weighed heavily on Alec's mind. But before he could take the risk and question Dylan about his childhood, Dylan went on.

"Rick was so happy the day we finally scraped together enough money for the first and last month's rent for an apartment. The place was a dump, a real shithole."

Dylan let out a laugh. "Rick was always trying to brighten the place up, using stuff he found, posters and junk to tack up on the walls. As if covering the holes somehow made the place more appealing."

Alec could practically hear the roll of Dylan's eyes. All traces of sarcasm disappeared as he continued.

"But it felt so fucking good to have a place to just *be*," Dylan said. "People used to think we were boyfriends. But, hell, I was so happy to have a roof over my head I didn't care."

Which explained a lot about Dylan's willingness to pretend to be with Alec at Noah's party. If Dylan had had any qualms about being seen as gay, the concerns had been exorcised out of his system long ago.

"We were just starting to get our feet on the ground," Dylan said. "Noah had come into our lives, and Rick was happy, ya know? But then he started getting sicker."

Nothing Alec could say would make the words any easier, so he simply waited for Dylan to go on.

"If we'd had the money, could have afforded to take Rick to a doctor sooner, he might still be around today. That's what sucks so much."

Dylan lifted his head to look at Alec again. "That's why I think what you and Tyler are doing is so friggin' awesome. I wish we'd looked for a place like your clinic when Rick first got sick."

In Dylan's gaze, Alec saw admiration, respect, and enough regret to load a landfill.

"It's not your fault," Alec said.

"I know. It wasn't his fault either. Rick wasn't stupid." Dylan tucked his head underneath Alec's chin. "He was careful. He knew the risks. But, in the beginning, when he was really hurting for cash, he'd let a guy fuck him bareback because the money was good."

Christ.

Alec closed his eyes, his chest aching.

Dylan cleared his throat. "Today would have been his thirtieth birthday." Though delivered matter-of-factly, sadness infused the spaces between the words. "Fuck, man," he went on wearily. "I don't want to discuss this anymore."

Alec tightened his grip on Dylan's back. "I'm sorry—"

Rolling on top of Alec, Dylan stretched that hard body between Alec's thighs and buried his fingers in Alec's hair, his voice rough. "No more talking."

As if to ensure Alec followed through, Dylan took Alec's mouth in a kiss that clearly signaled the beginning of more.

Chapter Ten

Monday after work, Alec rode the elevator up to Noah's condo, eyes gritty from a lack of sleep. He clutched his latte gratefully. After spending the week since the poker run either at work or in bed with Dylan, Alec needed the end-of-the-day caffeine infusion. Especially in light of what he'd have to endure before he could meet Dylan back at home for takeout.

His phone beeped, and Alec glanced at the text.

I'm on the way to your place with Kung Pao chicken, wonton soup, and a sex swing.

Alec's chuckle got lost in the sound of the elevator doors sliding open. But, as he headed up the hallway leading to Noah's condo, the smile slipped from his face.

During last month's discussion about the Front Street Clinic Residential Fund, the plan to meet Tyler and Noah here had seemed reasonable. In general, Noah supplied the refreshments and sarcastic comments while Noah and Tyler went over the next phase of their plans. But with recent events, namely Alec's decision to ignore Noah's initial advice about sleeping with Dylan, the location now proved tricky. Not only was Alec through listening to Noah's lectures, he'd spent a good part of the week ignoring the man's fundraiser-related texts as well.

Alec used to drop everything when something needed to be done in regards to fighting Proposition 8 or supporting the housing fund. In retrospect, he realized his schedule had been kind of pathetic. Now that he'd gotten a taste of enjoying his motorcycle and Dylan—and *life*—he felt less eager to be so blindly available.

He texted Dylan back.

B there ASAP.

As he approached Noah's door, Alec cracked his neck to relieve the tension, every muscle sore in a way only a week's worth of sexual activities could produce. A few bruises in the form of fingerprints marked Alec's wrists. The rug burn on his ass chafed beneath his briefs and left him questioning his brand of fabric softener. But Alec enjoyed the reminders of Dylan's ruggedly raw...enthusiasm.

Two Sundays ago, Alec had spent all of five seconds considering calling things off again and giving himself hell for landing back in bed with Dylan.

While Alec had no doubt Dylan's actions that Saturday night had been partially fueled by a fit of melancholy, the man's attitude afterward had been reassuring. The ride back down to San Francisco had been spectacular, with nothing but clear skies and friendly company. Dylan had returned to his usual easy, relaxed state. He'd continued a hands-off attitude in public, but his behavior and his occasional reassuring wink reaffirmed that the two of them were definitely on more solid ground.

After that, ending things had felt impossible.

As a friend, Dylan made Alec happy. They had sex. Brain-meltingly hot sex. A bonus with the potential for serious complications for sure. Maybe the decision to stick with Dylan made no sense. Maybe Alec was setting himself up for an even bigger fall than before. Because who knew where this crazy relationship would wind up? For once in his life, he'd made a firm decision not to care.

Alec came to a halt in front of the condo and rang the doorbell. Gearing up for the upcoming encounters, he squared his shoulders and gave himself a swift mental kick in the ass.

He heard footsteps and tugged his sleeves to cover the marks on his wrist. Get in. Discuss the next fundraiser. Get out.

Should be simple.

Noah opened the door. "*There* you are."

Well, simple except for two things. He had to endure the tension between him and Tyler and deal with Noah, the one who couldn't seem to comprehend that Alec had finally gone out and found a life.

Refusing to feel guilty, Alec gripped his coffee cup more firmly. "Of course I'm here." Alec passed his friend and entered the foyer.

"You've been avoiding me all week," Noah said. "And you were supposed to call last night to discuss this meeting."

Mind searching for a believable excuse, Alec could feel Noah's eyes on him as he entered the living room done in muted gold and russet, the furniture and decor reflecting his friend's expensive tastes. Tyler sat on an overstuffed couch in front of the floor-to-ceiling windows overlooking San Francisco Bay. Alec headed for the matching loveseat.

No sense lying because he sucked at it. "I was busy, Noah."

Busy learning that Dylan did indeed like sex. Lots of sex.

Alec dropped onto the cushion and a stab of pain shot up his ass, a reminder to be careful. He went to shift into a more comfortable position and then noticed Tyler watching, his eyes narrowed. So

Alec made a show of placing his latte on the coffee table next to a platter with crackers and cheese.

Focusing on the reason for the meeting seemed Alec's best hope of getting out of here in a reasonable time frame. "How much do we have in the building fund anyway?"

Tyler reached for his computer, powering up his laptop. "I can tell you in a second."

"Correct me if I'm wrong." Noah leaned against the doorjamb, eyes on Alec. "But I believe you agreed to print out a financial report *before* this meeting."

"I forgot," Alec said. "I do have a life outside of work and this project of ours, Noah."

Skeptical lines bracketed Noah's eyes. "Since when?"

"Since DOMA died and Alec and I broke up," Tyler said.

Alec tried, but failed, to ascertain if his ex's statement held any subtext or not. Since the party, they'd generally tried to avoid each other. The constant, low-grade tension was beginning to wear Alec out.

Noah stared at Alec. "Which doesn't explain why you didn't return my message yesterday."

"Which one of the eight messages are you referring to?" Alec said drily.

"Eight in one day?" Tyler looked up from his laptop. "Sounds like it's time to have Noah's number blocked."

Alec couldn't be sure, but the crack from Tyler felt like support.

Noah tossed Tyler a tolerant look, finally crossing into the living room. "I purchased these crackers just for you, Tyler, despite the fact they appear to have been made out of birdseed. Don't make me toss them out the window."

Tyler concentrated on his computer. "You know you love me, Noah."

"Don't flatter yourself, vegan man."

"Vegetarian," Tyler said. "Not vegan."

Noah dismissed the distinction with a wave of his hand. "Whatever." Apparently he'd finally realized Alec refused to apologize for being unavailable, because Noah sent them both a grin. "But you two are going to love *me* even *more* when I share the news about our fundraising efforts."

Finally. Now that the meeting had officially started, the tension in Alec's shoulders eased, and Alec reached for a cracker and took a bite. Alec's phone beeped again, and he discreetly checked the message.

Climbing in shower. Don't make me get started without you.

A seed got caught in Alec's throat, and he coughed, taking a sip of his latte.

"God, Tyler," Alec said, trying to recover from the mental image of Dylan jacking off while washing away a day's worth of sweat and dirt. "I forgot how dry these crackers are."

"I thought you liked them," Tyler said.

"Alec lied to spare your feelings because he's too nice." Noah dropped onto the couch. "No offense, Tyler, but your strict, healthy diet is horrendously dull."

"I'll keep that in mind when I'm adjusting the insulin drip treating your red-meat-induced diabetes, Noah," Tyler said.

A chuckle escaped Alec, and Noah shot him a look.

"Back to our funding issue," Noah said, his expression turning serious. "Remember Jack Davis from my party, the moody bastard who sits on the board at Charity Regional Hospital? Anyway, I got a call from him today. He and his wife, Sylvia, have a proposition for us."

Alec sat up higher in his seat. Maybe this discussion would be over even sooner than he'd hoped.

"They want us to throw a charity bachelor bid," Noah said.

Tyler stared at Noah, obviously unimpressed, and Alec sank back against the couch, his optimism for a quick meeting slipping away.

"A bachelor auction?" Alec said.

The way Noah had spoken, Alec had thought the couple planned to hand over enough to meet their goals. Problem solved. Back to Dylan. A pipe dream, clearly, but a nice one nonetheless.

"Please tell me you're kidding," Tyler said. "An event like that is a waste of time."

"You haven't heard the rest of the proposition. If we throw a bachelor bid and raise forty-thousand dollars, then they'll donate the rest to meet our funding goals." Noah cleared his throat and picked up a seed from his pants. "With the condition that we include their nephew in the event," he mumbled.

"We can't raise that kind of money with a charity auction unless we're selling sex along with the dates," Tyler said. "And wait..." He glanced back at Noah. "Who is their nephew?"

"Probably some loser in desperate need of a social life," Noah said with an indifferent shrug. "But their reasons don't matter. Except that, lately, Charity Regional has gotten a lot of flak in the news for their lack of community involvement. Jack wants the hospital to team up with us on this and the bachelors to be volunteers from their employees."

Tyler looked less than convinced, but Alec couldn't think of a valid reason for continuing to argue against the idea.

"Look," Noah said, "the hundred grand we're getting for the humanitarian award is significant. And we could continue to slowly eke forward and eventually meet our goals to secure financing for housing. But we also need to think long term."

Times like these reminded Alec why he and Tyler had chosen to include Noah in their plans. The man's fierce dedication and boundless energy were an asset.

Except when applied to Alec's personal life.

"Starting a popular annual event will provide us funds for future projects," Noah went on. "I think a bachelor bid has the potential to be a regular draw *and* pull that kind of figure off, provided we generate a good amount of buzz."

"How?" Alec asked.

"First," Noah said, "we sign on someone famous and film a couple of creative commercials."

Alec barely restrained the groan. Christ, he'd never get home to Dylan with this kind of delusional thinking on Noah's part. Not without a massive supply of antipsychotics.

"Oh?" Alec knew he sounded as weary as he felt. "Is that all?"

Noah looked unconcerned. "Between the three of us and the six degrees of Kevin Bacon thing, I'm sure there is a famous acquaintance in our midst."

Alec tipped his head. "One of Tyler's exes fits the bill."

The snap of Tyler's gaze to Alec spoke volumes, and guilt stabbed him.

Never one to let the chance for a well-aimed dig slip by, Noah said, "Tyler has a lot of exes, including you." He popped another Gouda-topped cracker into this mouth. "Which one?"

Alec bit back the name, considering his options. The look on Tyler's face made his feelings clear. He didn't want the stunt man involved. Alec had two choices. He could out Tyler, and watch his ex suffer Noah's relentless hounding, or he could truly put the past behind him and support his ex. All middle school feelings aside, the time had come to move past the residual resentment and anger.

"No one special," Alec said, avoiding Noah's eyes. The need to lie made the words feel pressured. "Just a guy Tyler dated in med school who is now some big wig at Stanford. He went on to host a morning talk show on a small local cable channel." Shit, now what? His mind spun, searching for something that would make the made-up ex sound unappealing to Noah. "He's...uh, super smart and probably knows more about the rates of sexually transmitted diseases in this county than anyone else."

Noah stared at Alec for a moment before responding. "Are you on drugs? We need sex *appeal*," Noah went on. "Not a STD expert." Noah shook his head in defeat. "Never mind. I'll find someone myself."

Relieved, Alec quietly blew out a breath. His stomach grumbled, and he tried hard not to think of the Chinese food waiting at home and Dylan, naked, in the shower...

Distracted, Alec reached out to slice a piece of cheese— "Hey!"

Noah gripped Alec's wrist, and Alec almost dropped the knife.

"For chrissakes, Alec," Noah said, staring down at the faint bruises on Alec's skin.

Fuck.

Time ticked by in painful increments. Alec waited a moment before releasing the knife and pulling his arm from Noah's grasp. Face burning, he tugged his sleeve down to cover the marks while the two men stared at him.

Noah looked shocked, but Tyler was studying him as if seeing Alec in a new light.

Tyler had been serious when he'd claimed Alec didn't have a sex swing. Their sexual relationship had been satisfying, but nothing like the headboard-banging, mind-melting ride with Dylan.

Alec knew Dylan had only been kidding in his earlier text—ninety percent sure anyway. But their sex life had left Alec feeling high for days. Dylan couldn't seem to decide which he liked more, being the top or the bottom. So far he'd exerted a considerable amount of energy testing the two positions while trying to make up his mind, with Alec happily encouraging the comparison process.

"Are you and Dylan a thing now?" Noah asked.

The answer rolled easily off Alec's tongue. "That's none of your business."

Two seconds later, Noah turned to Tyler. "Will you grab the second package of crackers on the counter in the kitchen?"

No one commented on Noah's request for more birdseed. After a last glance in Alec's direction, Tyler silently headed into the kitchen.

Noah turned to Alec. "Has Dylan decided he's bisexual?"

The question shot through Alec's brain and ricocheted around his skull, and he glanced at the kitchen doorway. For reasons he couldn't explain, especially to himself, he didn't want Tyler to know the truth just yet. Mostly because he wouldn't survive another person giving him shit about his choices. Noah's doubts were bad enough, and Alec's were tenuously held at bay by the sexual fog Dylan induced.

But Alec had made a decision.

"I'm not just the hand, Noah," Alec said.

As soon as he'd spoken the words, Alec sat up higher in his seat. Noah's original claim that Dylan had only slept with Alec out of convenience still burned in ways Alec hadn't recovered from.

Noah looked confused, so Alec went on. "I'm not just the most accessible means for Dylan to get off," Alec said. "He *is* attracted to me."

Alec felt that simple truth in Dylan's every glance. He didn't have to touch Alec or say anything suggestive because every time Dylan looked at him there was no doubt the man felt the same pull. It was The Look from that first night at Danny's Suds and Sports. The attraction had most definitely been mutual then. Dylan had just needed a little time to sort the realization out.

"Yes, I suppose you're right," Noah said. But before Alec could celebrate his victory, Noah's voice dropped an octave. "But I'm not sure that protects you much, Alec."

Shit. Noah always went for the jugular.

Alec fought the need to close his eyes and ignored the misgivings howling in his brain.

He shoved his hair back from his face. "Look, I hear what you're saying," Alec said. The more of Dylan he unraveled, the bigger the remaining puzzle pieces grew. "I won't argue with you about the risks. But—"

Tyler reentered the living room and set the second package of crackers on the coffee table. Alec went on, despite his ex's presence.

"Right now I'm choosing to be with Dylan." Alec steadily met Noah's gaze, refusing to look away first. "And I don't need any more lectures from you."

Alec sent his friend a small smile to ease the sharp edge to his words.

With a sigh that bordered on melodramatic, Noah reached for the cheese board. "Fine," he said, slicing a piece of Gouda. "But when it all goes to hell in an overpriced messenger bag, I'm going to find new and creative ways to say I-told-you-so. On a daily basis. For the rest of your life."

Noah's gaze remained firm. "Which means every morning you'll be subjected to a wakeup call from me as I deliver a long-winded reminder of why you should follow your friends' advice."

"Another good reason to have Noah's number blocked," Tyler said.

Alec shot his ex a small smile, grateful for the loss of hostility and what appeared to be a return to their supportive, collegial relationship. With any luck they could relearn how to be friends. Standing firm in the face of Noah's well-intentioned meddling felt like a major accomplishment too.

Alec had no idea how long Dylan would continue with a status quo that consisted of easy companionship, great sex, and zero talk about what the situation meant.

For now, Alec intended to sit back and let Dylan set the pace.

Chapter Eleven

"You'll never find another one like her, Mr. Booth."

Standing on the driveway, Dylan kept his eyes on the Triumph TR5 Trophy and bit back his disagreement with the owner's claim, acutely aware of Alec's gaze on his back.

"Mmm hmm," Dylan murmured, sure he sounded as unconvinced as he felt.

Dylan had already taken the bike for a quick spin around the block, and seriously, the girl ran rougher than some of the neighborhoods Dylan had grown up in. Weird to now be standing with Alec in front of a middle-class home located in middle-class suburbia, the warm breeze smelling of freshly cut grass. A place so squeaky clean and sweet the sight made Dylan slightly sick to his stomach, like he'd overdosed on cotton candy and been sentenced to Stepford neighborhood hell.

"Why are you selling her?" Dylan asked.

"Between my new job and the family, I don't have much time for riding anymore," the owner answered.

The twenty-something man bouncing a drooling, barefoot baby in his arms was watching Dylan eagerly, clearly committed to making the sale. Dylan was inspecting the bike. And Alec...

Well, Alec appeared to be checking Dylan out.

The heat crawling up Dylan's back and sweat dotting his neck had nothing to do with the late afternoon sun and everything to do with that appreciative gaze. To cover his partial hard-on, he knelt to study the front tire.

Today's plan appeared to be working. Alec always looked turned on whenever Dylan and motorcycles got within ten yards of each other. Dylan figured the bike that James Dean drove would add some extra sex appeal.

A couple of days ago, Dylan had been kneeling in Alec's garage, fixing the clutch on the Ducati, when Alec had come home from work. The flash of lust in Alec's expression would have brought Dylan to his knees if he hadn't been there already. But Dylan's grease-stained hands and sweaty T-shirt must have been more than Alec could stomach. The man had headed directly into the kitchen to make dinner.

Undaunted, Dylan had dragged Alec along today. He hoped to generate a little more of that motorcycle-induced lust because, two weeks after they'd first landed back in bed together, Dylan had only one complaint.

Why did he always have to instigate the touching first?

Dylan hated the thoughts now plaguing his brain, like maybe Alec didn't want him as much as he wanted Alec. Or maybe the sex wasn't as good as Dylan thought. But, damn it, he knew better. Alec might not start their marathon sessions, but he damn well enjoyed them. It seemed more likely that Dylan represented a convenient source of sex until Alec got over his ex.

Crap. Where had that thought come from? As Alec and the owner chatted behind him, Dylan squeezed the tire in frustration, a lame-ass attempt to pretend to check the pressure.

In the beginning the situation hadn't bothered him because he was still busy adjusting to the concept of sleeping with the same person for more than two nights in a row. And he wasn't even gonna touch on the fact that the person was a dude.

He wanted Alec, case closed. He wanted Alec on him, under him, or any other way he could have him. Dylan refused to waste time wringing his hands and weeping in his morning coffee or moaning *why*, like a teen who turns everything into an emotional nuclear event.

So he'd moved on to the more pressing concern of Alec's behavior.

Dylan believed Alec's assertiveness the night of Noah's party had either been an anomaly due to alcohol or something was holding Alec back in bed, a fact Dylan hadn't been able to overcome by trying new positions and unusual ways to make Alec come.

Except for blowjobs. Dylan couldn't stomach the thought of sucking a guy off, a dick in his mouth. Not again.

Fuck.

Dylan closed his eyes and fought the memory of a bruising grip on his head, the brick alley wall pressing against his back as he choked, unable to escape. Unable to breathe. Drowning. *Drowning*...

With herculean effort, Dylan sucked in a lungful of oxygen.

That was years ago. Quit being such a pansy-assed wuss.

Concentrate. Just...concentrate. Overpriced bike. Sale. Alec. Baby drool.

Struggling to control his rapid breathing, Dylan fingered the worn tread on the tire and forced himself to take stock of the Triumph's condition. Due to the rust, the frame required sanding, and a new paintjob ought to be a priority. The headlight needed replacing, but that was an easy fix—

"You want to take her for a longer ride?" the owner asked.

Jesus, couldn't the man see Dylan was in the middle of talking himself back from the ledge?

"Looks like she hasn't been ridden much lately," Dylan said, willing himself to friggin' calm down and wiping black grease on his shirt. And then he looked at his arms, realizing they were smeared with oil from when he'd checked the level on the Triumph.

Damn, he was a mess again. This wasn't the lead up to sexy times Dylan had been hoping for.

"It's hard to get away with a toddler and a four-month-old in the house," the owner said.

Dylan's concentration didn't break as he stood, his eyes roaming the bike. Overpriced, but still salvageable. "She's a beauty."

"Thanks. Her name is Chloe."

"Uh…" Dylan lifted his gaze to the infant. "Yeah, her too."

The proud father glanced down at the baby, who was attempting to shove her entire fist into her mouth. The drool now made an impressive trail down her arm.

"The bike comes with the original owner's manual," the man said. "Here, I'll show you."

He held out his daughter in Dylan's direction, and Dylan's oh-*hell*-no expression obviously didn't register with the dad. Stunned, Dylan automatically gripped the baby under the arms, Chloe dangling like a puppy in a toddler's grasp as she stared up at Dylan with wide, blue eyes and a river of drool.

Whoa. Nothing like a baby to kill those sexy thoughts. And what about his plans for Alec? Dylan had already accumulated enough grease and sweat to turn Alec off. Now he'd added saliva to boot.

Alec's lips twisted in suppressed humor as he stepped forward to, thank *God*, rescue Dylan by scooping up the infant.

"I'll hold her." Alec settled Chloe expertly into the crook of his elbow.

Dylan would have kissed the man if his arms hadn't been full of a slobbery infant.

The father fumbled to unlatch the saddlebag, yet another item that didn't function right. Dylan stared at a well-dressed, *clean* Alec holding the baby with a sizeable line of drool now hanging from her mouth, dangling in the air. Seriously, someone needed to shut the main water line off and fix that horrific leakage problem.

But Alec? He seemed totally unconcerned. In truth, he appeared content, for lack of a better word. And right after Dylan sent a frustrated look at the mood-killer of a tiny human with massive blue eyes, Dylan's mind registered just how natural Alec looked holding the baby. Clearly, somewhere in the acquisition of all those letters after his name—BS, MD, MPH—Alec had actually spent time handling kids.

The scene was kinda cute. Almost...adorable.

Dylan blinked, the word rolling around in his head. Adorable. *Adorable*? Shit, next he'd be buying a fucking minivan.

"I also have the maintenance record and two spare keys," the owner said.

The man finally pulled out the manual and tried to pass it to Dylan. But Dylan couldn't focus, too caught up in just how far his thoughts had wandered from getting Alec to jump him.

"Impressive," Alec said to the owner, discreetly shooting Dylan a get-with-the-program look.

Dylan cleared his throat and took the manual. "Yeah. Impressive." He flipped through the pages of instructions, not seeing a thing. "Cool that you still have the original. Too bad you have to let her go," he said, returning the handbook to the saddlebag.

"I don't mind. Besides, I could use the extra money," the man said.

"Well, she's a sweet ride." Or she could be, with a lot of work. "But I've got a couple more I want to check out before I make any decisions."

"No problem," the man said, taking his daughter back from Alec. "Just give me a call if you decide it's the one for you."

"You bet," Dylan said.

Dylan headed up the driveway toward his motorcycle parked on the street. Alec followed along, his car parked just behind Dylan's bike. Because of the timing and the location in relation to Alec's work, they'd had to meet here instead of riding together. Fate was a bitch, and she'd been determined to screw up Dylan's plan to tempt Alec into seducing him.

And, Jesus, he'd never recover from the brief thought that Alec holding a baby was cute.

"That was the grossest thing I've ever seen, man," Dylan said to Alec.

Alec raised a brow in question.

"Baby slobber," Dylan said.

Alec grinned as they parted, and he rounded his car before stopping at the door. "This coming from the man covered in grease."

Dylan mentally winced. So, yeah, Alec found the mess a total turn-off. "But that's not nearly as gross," Dylan said in protest. He covered the awkward feeling with a teasing grin. "And now we got that slobber on our *hands*."

"Do I have to shower before you'll touch me?"

Dylan's heart stopped in his chest. Maybe he could salvage this outing yet. He'd have to, cuz right now he itched to be climbing into the car. Dylan hated that he couldn't get his hands on Alec during the trip back. Nothing Dylan could do about that now though, especially while covered in grease and sweat and baby drool.

Brilliant. Derailed by a 1955 Triumph and a malfunctioning four-month-old.

"No. But you gotta at least wash your hands first. Or..." Dylan tossed Alec a wicked smile as he headed toward his bike. "I'll be happy to touch you *in* the shower."

Alec chuckled, and Dylan threw his leg over his motorcycle. Tonight Alec's Harley would just have to do as a replacement to the Triumph. The new saddlebags for Alec's bike had arrived several days ago, which provided the perfect excuse.

Eager to get back to Alec's house and salvage his plan, he looked back at Alec. "I need to pick up the Allen wrenches at my house so we can replace the bags on your bike."

Alec's hand paused on the door handle. "You want me to follow you there?"

The words *not necessary* formed on Dylan's lips, but he bit them back. He'd fallen into the comfortable routine of spending about three out of every four nights at Alec's place. Not once had Dylan invited Alec to his home. Of course, Alec's house was a hell of a lot nicer than Dylan's apartment, so the setup only made sense.

But maybe Alec would loosen up a little after seeing where Dylan lived. It wasn't like viewing his apartment meant they were attached at the hip or something stupid like that. Of course, other than their discussion about Rick the night of the poker run, the conversations had been kept well away from anything personal. Oh, there'd been some indirect attempts for sure, but Alec's subtle tries to gain more information had been ignored by Dylan.

Taking a shower was easy. Changing clothes? A no-brainer. Cracking open his chest so more of the crap he kept inside could spill out? Oh, *hell* no.

But Alec had asked and refusing would be rude, even for Dylan.

"Sure." Dylan let the dregs of his resistance go. "I'll be careful not to lose you."

The crinkles around Alec's eyes were reassuring. "As if you could."

Twenty minutes later they pulled into the driveway of his landlord's well-kept home of concrete block and stucco, the white offset by blue shutters. Brightly colored flowers lined the front walkway, and trees dotted the front yard. Dylan found the scene soothing, despite the fact the main house looked as if fucking Mary Poppins was about to land on the roof.

Alec parked behind Dylan and exited the car. "Is that the sex swing you keep referring to?" Alec asked with a nod at the front porch swing.

Unfortunately, Alec's comment held more humor than heat. In fact, the lack of heat in Alec's look was disappointing.

Dylan let out an amused grunt. "Hardly."

He tried hard not to think about how much he longed to tease the fire back into Alec's eyes as they made their way around back, up the stairs, and into his garage apartment. The sparse living room and bathroom were functional. His bedroom on the other hand? Definitely a contender for the Worst Bachelor Pad Ever award. The kitchen was almost none existent, but he didn't cook anyway. Dylan had never cared before, so why did he feel awkward and anxious now?

He just needed to grab his tools and get them both back to Alec's place, where everything felt more...normal.

Alec's gaze swept over the furniture pieces that looked exactly like what they were, a starter set for a college student who'd used the shit out of them and then paid Dylan to haul the stuff away.

"Homey," Alec said.

As a teasing comment, the words fell flat. Mostly because Alec no longer looked relaxed; he looked distracted. And not in a good way.

Dylan rolled his eyes. "You're as bad as Noah," he said. "The rent is good and includes the garage beneath."

Before Alec could comment further, Dylan escaped into his bedroom. Yep, good plan. Get some clean clothes and then get the heck out of here. In the meantime, he wracked his brains to come up with something to fill the strained silence. Anything to get them back to more familiar ground.

"Have you and Tyler decided on a fundraiser yet?" Dylan called out.

"Maybe. Jack Davis sits on the board at Charity Regional Hospital. He's invited us to a Tigers' game to tempt us into teaming up for a bachelor bid, with Noah in charge."

Dylan gripped the doorway of his bedroom and leaned around to stare at Alec. "Are you friggin' kidding me?"

The pained look on Alec's face was almost comical. "I wish."

"Man, I shudder at the thought of Noah acting as MC at a bachelor auction."

Alec chuckled, and Dylan grinned at the laugh lines around Alec's eyes. Dylan's grip eased on the wood trim. Good, awkwardness gone. Finally, *progress*.

"Are you going to put yourself up for bid?" Dylan asked.

The look on Alec's face sent Dylan's stomach into a tailspin.

Damn, what a way to shine a spotlight on the ticking time bomb between them.

Referencing Alec's bachelor status had been a moronic move on Dylan's part. The oblique reference to their dead-end relationship went over like gut-splitting laughter at a funeral. Dylan totally owned the blame for this one. He should have known that, to Alec, a commitment took priority over a good time. Otherwise, he wouldn't have spent two years trying to make things work with Tyler. He held babies as if he liked them, for fuck's sake. But, for some reason, Alec had decided being with Dylan for a while was worth putting his significant-other goals on hold.

Making Alec unhappy sucked. In fact, the look on Alec's face now was kind of crushing.

Shit.

Dylan pushed the turbulent thoughts aside and escaped into his bedroom, blindly rifling through his dresser. His fingers fumbled as he randomly selected a clean shirt and jeans. No getting out of his plans gracefully now.

"I'll shower at your place after I work on the Harley. Next stop"—he avoided Alec's gaze as he exited the bedroom and swiped his keys from the kitchen counter—"the garage and my tools."

Though at this point, why bother? The universe had mucked with his plans from the beginning, and Dylan had sabotaged the rest with his dumb mouth.

Jesus, Alec was right about him.

He really didn't know when to shut the fuck up.

~~~***~~~

Still numb from Dylan's question, Alec trailed behind the man as they headed outside and down the stairs, the sun almost an afterthought in the late-afternoon sky.

And where in the grand scheme of things had he thought he could sleep with Dylan and keep everything simple? If Dylan didn't mind Alec selling himself for a date to the highest bidder, then why bother sticking around?

Christ, Alec. You're being as melodramatic as Noah.

Dylan had asked him about participating in a charity bid, not signing up for a dating service. Alec shoved his hair behind his ears. He needed a major attitude adjustment, feeling completely off kilter.

Because the moment he'd entered the apartment, his heart had suffered a strange kick.

He ached at the thought of Dylan coming home to such a stark environment. Tan walls, threadbare carpet. The furniture looked like rejects from a second-hand store. There'd been no attempt to decorate. No color. Nothing personal. The kitchen didn't even look used except for the motorcycle part sitting on the scarred dinette table.

Frowning at the disturbing memory, Alec followed Dylan into the garage through a side door. And then Alec stopped short, too stunned to move as he stared at the scene.

While the no-frills apartment clearly bordered on depressing, this space, however, was a thing of beauty. Tools filled two of the four walls, as well organized as Dylan's shop. Seven motorcycles were lined up along the middle of the room, each carefully covered. The eighth had the chain removed, now lying on the drop cloth beneath the bike. Colorful license plates filled the free walls in an artistic design. One side of the garage contained a table with a small TV and a patio lounge chair—more comfortable looking and certainly newer than any of the furniture upstairs. There was even a mini refrigerator.

Not only did Dylan work in a garage, he practically lived in one as well.

The years Dylan had spent on the streets had left a bigger hole than Alec had first thought. No wonder the idea of a real relationship wigged Dylan out. He barely knew how to live in a home.

Alec couldn't decide which hurt worse, his head or his chest.

Hoping to recover from the turmoil, he headed for a rack of what looked like memorabilia. Antique helmets, saddlebags, and a few things Alec couldn't identify lined the shelves.

"Looks like you spend most of your time at home down here," Alec said.

Dylan stopped at a shelf and picked up a small set of tools shaped like tiny crowbars, all easily fitting into his palm. "Most of my waking hours anyway."

Alec mulled this over as he ran his hand over an old helmet.

Dylan glanced at Alec and stuck the tools in his back pocket. "That belonged to my dad."

Surprised at the share, Alec said, "Your dad was into motorcycles?"

"Yep. But he was into the booze more. Spent the majority of his time passed out drunk." He paused and shifted on his feet awkwardly before crossing to pick up the chain on the drop cloth. "I preferred passed out over awake though. Didn't have to dodge his fists then."

Alec's heart caught, and he had to fight the urge to press his forehead to Dylan's back, to wrap his arms around him. Not for sex, but to hold on to Dylan and simply *be*.

But Alec knew that kind of touching wasn't welcome. "I'm sorry."

"Happens," Dylan said with a shrug

"Not much of a home life."

The bark of laughter held less bitterness than Alec would have thought. "Growing up," Dylan said, "I made sure to spend most of my time elsewhere. When things finally got bad enough, living on the streets became the better option."

Alec waited, but Dylan didn't go on. In light of Dylan's closed-lip behavior so far, Alec knew he wouldn't get this opportunity again. He hated bringing the subject up, but he plowed ahead anyway.

"Do you know where your mother is?" Alec asked

"Nope." Dylan absently fingered the motorcycle chain dangling in his hands. "And I don't know whether my old man's drinking caused my mother to leave or was triggered by her departure. Guess I'll never know."

Though the words were far from cheerful, they lacked the starkness present when he talked about Rick. Obviously losing his friend had affected him the most, which only made Alec's heart hurt more.

"Doesn't really matter," Dylan said, placing the chain on a worktable. "Gone is gone."

Gone is gone.

Alec had been curious about Dylan's past since learning about the three years he'd spent on the streets. Now that Alec knew more, he hardly felt better. Their seriously nontraditional relationship didn't help matters either. Although Dylan did the buddies thing well, he avoided anything truly personal. And Alec had no idea how to negotiate a relationship based on two fractured pieces: easygoing friend and sexual partner.

How could he offer comfort when he wasn't allowed to touch outside of sex? And how was he supposed to initiate sex with someone he wasn't allowed to show affection for?

The nonstop merry-go-round in his head left him dizzy. Fortunately, in the bedroom, Alec's awkwardness didn't matter because the man was on Alec every chance he got. In that sense, letting Dylan set the pace had worked out well. Sadly, Dylan seemed obsessed with taking showers, which made Alec's fantasy of garage sex with a dirty, sweaty Dylan unlikely.

Alec gazed at Dylan, the sweat-dampened T-shirt plastered to the broad back, muscles shifting with every change of Dylan's posture. Given the end-of-the-day, stuffy temperature in the garage, the additional surge of heat nearly did Alec in.

From the first moment he'd laid eyes on Dylan, he'd found the man thrilling. He adored the brash attitude and rough edges and finely honed physique. Three days ago Alec had come home and found Dylan working on his motorcycle built for speed, looking like a fantasy incarnate. Alec had almost choked on his own tongue. But, as usual, he kept his hands to himself and waited for Dylan to make the first move.

His decision to let Dylan set the pace had worked so far. What Alec had today was so much better than Dylan's absence, and Alec feared upsetting the status quo. Besides, by now he'd figured out that this relationship would proceed one small step at a time. He was willing to be patient. But the bachelor bid comment still ate away at his confidence, reminding Alec of the massive question that constituted their future.

Suddenly, those small steps forward felt grossly inadequate. What if Dylan got skittish? What if tomorrow he woke up and declared their lopsided relationship over? Alec had known from the beginning their time was limited.

Damn, this was *limited*.

Alec scraped his hair back from his face, willing his pulse to quit freaking out. Before he'd wanted to push Dylan away to protect himself, now all Alec wanted was to pull him close and hold on tight.

Dylan eyed Alec with concern. "I should open the garage door," Dylan said, passing by Alec. "Let in a cool breeze."

Alec's arm shot out, stopping Dylan in his tracks. "Don't," Alec ground out. "I need..."

Chapter Twelve

Dylan's confused expression sent an awkward wave of heat up Alec's face, and he briefly lost the ability to speak. He couldn't wait anymore. Just like the discussion about Dylan's parents, Alec might never get this chance again.

He gripped Dylan's wrist tight and managed to croak out five more words. "Just don't open the door."

Because how could he take advantage of Dylan if he knew the neighbors might see? Dylan now looked more worried than confused.

He probably thought Alec was suffering from heat stroke. And, as usual, Alec failed to get his ridiculous tongue to work. But, thank *God*, this was a time for showing not telling. He placed his hands on Dylan's chest, turned them both, and then pushed Dylan backward. Alec tried hard to forget that the last time he'd behaved this way he'd been flying high on alcohol. Shit, maybe he should drink more often.

On the third step back, Dylan bumped into the shelf behind him. Tools rattled, and comprehension lit his eyes.

"I'm all dirty, man," Dylan said.

"Just how I like you."

Dylan let out a bark of skeptical laughter. "You like me sweaty?"

How could the man be so dense? Alec traced the sweat-dampened hollow below Dylan's rib cage, the ripples of abdominal muscles, and an embarrassingly loud sigh of contentment escaped Alec's mouth. But, damn, he just couldn't afford to care about keeping his feelings to himself anymore.

"Yes," Alec said. "I like you sweaty."

Dylan looked doubtful. "But I'm covered in grease from that rustbucket of a Triumph."

Alec pushed Dylan's T-shirt up, his palms sliding over Dylan's nipples, and Dylan sucked in a breath. Apparently his concerns about hygiene were beginning to waver because he grabbed Alec's hips and yanked him closer.

"Man." Dylan's voice sounded rough. "You have the smoothest hands. But I'm getting you all messy. Now your khakis have stains—"

"God, yes," Alec groaned.

Alec glanced down and admired the black fingerprints smudged on his pants, courtesy of Dylan handling the bike chain. Oddly proud of the marks, Alec pushed Dylan's shirt off with more force than necessary, tossing the fabric aside before burying his nose at Dylan's neck. Alec inhaled the scent of motor oil, hot man, and musk, giving the moment the time it deserved. So perfect. So right. Except for one thing.

"Clothes," Alec said as he slid his knuckles down the hard cock beneath Dylan's jeans.

An encouraging sound scraped from Dylan's throat, and he gripped Alec's waist for balance, toeing off his work boots. Suddenly clumsy in his eagerness, Dylan shucked the right one easily enough but took two tries to finish the left. Alec scrambled to unfasten Dylan's zipper and push the denim, along with the briefs, down. Once they were around his ankles, Dylan kicked the clothing aside and shed his socks.

Since the beginning, Alec had been fantasizing about Dylan streaked with grease and sweat. The day had come to stop being patient and *do* something about fulfilling the mental image keeping Alec up at night. Why had he waited so long? Now, he had every intention of seeing this through to the logical conclusion: Dylan...filthy and compliant, bared skin and muscle on display.

So when Dylan reached for Alec's clothes, he caught Dylan's wrist, stopping the attempt. Alec loved topping the hell out of Dylan, and they'd spent two weeks going at each other like crazy. But right now Alec needed more.

Eyebrows raised in question, Dylan stared at Alec. "What's wrong?"

How to explain? This was all about being greedy and selfish, putting Alec's need for more than just a fantastic fuck before everything else. For once he wanted to slow this wild roller-coaster ride down and simply enjoy Dylan's body.

"Absolutely nothing," Alec replied.

In a fit of inspiration, he turned Dylan until he faced the shelf. Alec lifted the man's arms until they extended straight out, angled slightly above the level of his shoulders.

"Whatever happens," Alec said as he threaded Dylan's grease-stained fingers through the bars of the stainless steel shelf, "don't move unless I say so."

Alec placed his foot at Dylan's instep and pushed out until Dylan complied, widening his stance. The spread-eagle position displayed his naked body in all of its beautifully-proportioned glory.

"Okay." With a smug tone, Dylan tipped his ass back in invitation. "I know what you want."

Alec ignored the smirk in Dylan's voice.

"No," Alec said softly. "I don't think you do."

You don't know the half of what I want.

Two muggy seconds ticked by. Dylan waited, maybe patiently, although Alec couldn't be sure. Dylan's submissive posture tempted Alec to do exactly what Dylan expected, what the man no doubt *wanted*.

For Alec to bury his cock in Dylan's ass.

Desire crawled up Alec's spine, and he closed his eyes, imagining the sweet, tight heat, the pressure and the glorious *friction*. But Alec wanted something less frantic, less primal and more...personal.

And during all their activities in bed together, not once had Dylan sucked Alec off. Alec had thought Dylan was immune to sexual hang-ups. As time went by, Alec realized he might have been wrong.

He pushed the thought aside. "Leonardo Da Vinci's drawing of the Vitruvian Man was on the cover of my anatomy textbook in medical school," Alec said, admiring the tanned skin and the toned muscles. "He dedicated himself to studying the proportions of the human body."

And, dear God, Dylan's form deserved that kind of dedication.

Over his shoulder, Dylan stared at Alec as if he'd lost his mind. "Is this really the time to regurgitate the facts from one of your research hunts?"

Alec ignored him and went on. "Most of his drawings were of the male form. In his essay about Da Vinci, Sigmund Freud claimed Leonardo was gay." He caught the *who the hell cares?* look Dylan tossed him but went on anyway. "I think Freud blamed Da Vinci's mother."

"Yeah," Dylan said with a roll of his eyes. "Now there was a dude with issues."

Alec suppressed the smile. "You are now arranged just like Leonardo's anatomical drawing."

He placed an appreciative hand on the wide expanse of Dylan's back. "His interest in perfect proportions could have been inspired by you."

Dylan snorted, no doubt an attempt to cover the flush of embarrassment staining his cheeks. Despite his cocky attitude, Dylan always looked uncomfortable when someone praised his looks.

Feeling lucky as hell, Alec slid his gaze from the top of Dylan's hair, matted and damp at the temples, down past the black smudges on his arms to the back that glistened with sweat. The muscular legs and enticing ass were so tight they looked carved from stone. They also looked entirely too clean. Alec scanned the shelf beyond Dylan's head, his gaze landing on a small container labeled wheel-bearing grease.

"There'll eventually be touching during this seduction scene, won't there?" Dylan asked.

"Of course there'll be touching." He met Dylan's amused gaze. "You're just not dirty enough yet."

Alec grabbed the can, pried off the plastic lid, and scooped a small amount of the amber-colored goo in his fingers. The humor in Dylan's eyes died, turning to pure lust.

"Jesus, Alec. That's hot." He blinked. "But I'm, um, not sure that's safe to use as lube."

"I'm not going to," Alec said. "In fact, we won't need lube at all."

The flash of confusion in Dylan's eyes almost did Alec in. Dylan looked...lost, most likely thrown by the thought of anything other than anal or a hand job. Oddly enough, that made Alec's heart hurt the most.

All this time he'd assumed Dylan's no-holds-barred sexual energy stemmed from his research of top versus bottom. He'd never considered Dylan might be unable to comprehend anything less frenzied and more personal, more *intimate*. His private life was as stark as the apartment he lived in.

Concentrating on the endless expanse of naked skin, Alec placed his slick palms on Dylan's shoulders. He slowly slid them toward Dylan's outstretched hands, enjoying the peaks and valleys of sinew and muscle, leaving streaks of grease trailing behind.

Perfect.

"The length of the spread arms is roughly equal to the height of a man," Alec recited.

He skimmed his fingers back to the shoulder blades and then traced circles around each vertebral body as he headed down Dylan's back.

Alec slid his palms around Dylan's torso toward the front, leaning close to murmur in Dylan's ear. "According to Da Vinci, in your current position"— Alec splayed his hands low across Dylan's stomach, his thumbs dipping into Dylan's belly button—"the center of the extended limbs will be the navel."

Alec grinned at the sight of Dylan's pulse pounding at his neck and the goose bumps popping up along his arms. After rubbing axle grease over Dylan's washboard abdominal muscles, tracing every narrow groove, Alec made his way down the front of Dylan's thighs, slowly dragging his thumbs along the thatch of hair at Dylan's groin, close to his cock.

"And creates a space between the legs consistent with an equilateral triangle," Alec finished.

"This is the messiest, geekiest kink ever." Dylan's voice held a hint of awe. "Why the hell is this a total turn-on?"

Alec squeezed Dylan's hard quadriceps. "Because I'm making you wait."

"I'm not much for patience."

"I've noticed." Alec skimmed his fingertips across the top of Dylan's crack.

Dylan sucked in a breath, and his muscles grew taut. Alec's dick attempted to punch through his pants to hurry the process along. He pulled open his fly to provide a little relief from the pressure, and the sound of the zipper triggered a hungry look on Dylan's face. A shot of adrenalin left Alec's fingers fumbling as he freed his cock, fighting to maintain control. He hadn't waited this long only to give up on his goals now.

No matter how aroused.

With Dylan's widened stance, they were almost the same size. Alec slotted his erection along the length of Dylan's ass, the head now just above the top of Dylan's cleft. Dylan groaned and tipped his hips back, embedding Alec deeper between the cheeks. A pulse of hot pleasure shot from Alec's cock outward, and his stomach muscles tensed.

"Remember." Alec managed to keep his voice firm. "You're not allowed to move."

"Who knew you were such a tease?"

"Who's teasing? This is serious."

Alec began to thrust his hips, slowly sliding his cock along Dylan's crack. Sweat slicked the way, and Dylan's hard ass provided incredible friction. Alec's erection brushed by the puckered hole hidden beneath, up and down, and he longed to pop through that tight ring of muscle. Dylan began to pant, his breathing labored even as the rest of his body remained still, buttocks in just the right position. Alec gritted his teeth, wanting...

He pressed his mouth against Dylan's hot, salty skin. "The root of the penis is at half the height of man," Alec murmured.

"Da Vinci measured that?"

"Yes."

"If he wasn't gay"—the underside of Alec's shaft directly skimmed Dylan's hole, and Dylan groaned, his ass relaxing as if in submission—"he should have been."

As he continued to thrust, pleasure gripped Alec. Sparks flickered before his eyes and his balls grew tight. He dug his fingers into Dylan's hips, no doubt leaving bruises as he fought the need to grasp Dylan's shoulders and plant himself deep inside, lack of condom be damned.

Dear God, what the hell was he thinking?

Alec forced himself to focus and take a step back.

Dylan's head whipped around. "Wait," Dylan said, pupils dilated. "Where the heck are you going? You gotta do *something*."

Ignoring his thumping pulse, Alec pried Dylan's fingers from the rack, turned him so he faced Alec, and then repositioned Dylan's grip on the shelf. "I am." He used his foot to fix Dylan's stance.

Dylan spread eagle while facing Alec was worlds better because Dylan's hard cock curved and strained upward, precum gleaming at the tip.

"Preferably something *more*." Dylan's voice sounded strained.

Alec began to regain a bit of control. "According to Da Vinci, the distance from below the knee to the root of the penis is one quarter of a man's height."

"Dude was totally gay."

"If he wasn't," Alec said, repeating Dylan's earlier words, "he should have been."

Dylan let out a harsh laugh until Alec palmed Dylan's ass and dropped to his knees. Alec concentrated on keeping his gaze on Dylan's hip so he wouldn't get distracted. He cupped the back of Dylan's legs.

"Jesus," Dylan rasped out.

No doubt Dylan thought he had a blowjob in store, and Alec certainly craved the taste of the bead of precum at Dylan's slit. Instead, he kissed his way up the hard thigh, careful to avoid the axle-grease-covered spots. He stood, mouth continuing higher until he reached his neck, kneading Dylan's butt the entire way. But, still, Alec kept a decent amount of space between their hips. He licked the pounding pulse at Dylan's throat as he traced his hands up Dylan's flanks, across his shoulders, and along his biceps.

"For someone so caught up in measurements and distance"—Dylan's voice sounded strained—"you seem to be headed in the wrong direction."

Alec dropped his hand to brush his fingers along the coarse hair at Dylan's groin, and the man let out a hiss. Dylan's cock, hard and blood red, curved upward, as if in a silent scream for Alec's attention.

"Touching me now would be good," Dylan said, his voice raw. "Two minutes ago would've been *great*."

Alec lazily drew circles on Dylan's abdomen, tracing the muscles.

"Jesus, Alec." Dylan rasped out. "Are you trying to kill me here?"

In response, Alec gripped the juncture between Dylan's ass and his legs and pulled him close, slotting his dick in the natural groove alongside Dylan's. Alec began to rock his hips and closed his eyes with a groan relief.

"Can I move now?" Dylan said.

"Yes, you may."

"Finally," Dylan growled, and he eagerly joined in on the rhythm.

The sweet, *sweet* friction of two hard cocks was almost too much, and Alec scraped his teeth across a nipple. Dylan arched his back, mouth slack, silently thrusting his hips. Although his body screamed to finish, Alec refused to hurry.

"I've wanted this for so long," Alec murmured.

"To fuck against a tool shelf?"

Alec kissed Dylan hard, tasting him with his tongue before answering. "No."

"To smear me with axle grease?"

"Take the initiative."

After another hungry kiss bordering on a bite, Alec rocked his hips faster. Precum joined the sweat and grease on Dylan's stomach, and the hem of Alec's shirt grew damp.

"Seriously," Dylan moaned, "I thought you'd never put the moves on me."

Stunned, Alec drew his head back to stare at Dylan.

"You've been waiting for me to?" Alec said.

"Hell, yeah." Dylan frowned and leaned in, going for Alec's lips. "Now, can we—"

Alec blocked Dylan's attempt to kiss him. "Why didn't you say anything?"

"I thought..."

A flash of emotion came and went in Dylan's eyes, something resembling a vulnerable look.

"I thought maybe you didn't want me as much as I wanted you," Dylan said.

Alec didn't know whether to let out a hysterical laugh or a scream of frustration. He chose to press his lips to Dylan's shoulder, cutting off both.

Dylan said, "Maybe—"

Need shivered through Alec, and he bit Dylan.

Voice hoarse, Dylan went on. "Maybe we should work on our communication skills."

Holy Mother of God, yes.

Desperate, Alec increased the force of his thrusts. The sound of skin slicking against skin filled the air, and tools rattled as the steel shelves rocked slightly against the wall. A wrench, or a screwdriver—Alec wasn't sure which—hit the floor with a *thunk* and rolled across the concrete.

Cheeks ruddy, lids at half-mast, Dylan looked sucked up in a sexual vortex. His forearms strained against their self-imposed confinement, knuckles white against the steel rack. His thighs trembled as he met Alec's hips with thrusts of his own. Alec nipped along Dylan's jaw before moving down to his throat.

Damn, he wanted to drag this moment out forever. Despite the crushing need to finish, he hoped to delay the inevitable. When would he get Dylan naked in his garage again? When would he have the chance to enjoy the sight of Dylan slick and filthy and covered in a day's worth of grease?

Alec whimpered. With another hard thrust and no warning, he came, his cum shooting upward and coating Dylan's skin. Alec fought the post-orgasmic stupor and opened his eyes. Dylan was biting his lip, his hips moving desperately against Alec.

Christ. He'd never tire of the dazed look on Dylan's face and that beautiful body spread before him, streaked with the evidence of his orgasm. Large, white drops clung to Dylan's pectoral muscle. Inspired by the sight, Alec leaned in and sucked a salty splotch into his mouth. Dylan moaned and twisted his fingers on the shelf rack, arching his back.

Lips slick with cum, Alec threaded his fingers through Dylan's hair. This would either go well...or crash and burn.

"Kiss me," Alec said.

Dylan stared at Alec's mouth, hesitating for two beats. Alec was just about to tell him not to bother when Dylan leaned close and took a tentative taste. His tongue touched Alec's bottom lip experimentally, and a hot jolt shot through Alec, frying his nervous system.

Ridiculous really, after all they'd done to date.

Another split second passed, their breath clashing as Dylan continued to grind his cock against Alec. And then Dylan rubbed his mouth against Alec's, smearing the cum before sucking some from the lower lip. With a groan, he pressed Alec's lips open and proceeded to lick Alec's mouth clean.

The taste must have pushed Dylan over the edge, his moan of relief filling the garage as he pulled Alec's torso against his own and came. Alec gripped Dylan's hips, guiding the now jerky movements as hot, thick liquid pulsed between them. When Dylan's body finally grew quiet, Alec kissed Dylan's jaw for good measure.

"Goddamn," Dylan said, lids closed and chest heaving. "You should take the initiative more often."

When Alec didn't respond, Dylan opened his eyes. Alec pressed their mouths together but kept his gaze on Dylan, enjoying the heavy-lidded, sated look while waiting for Dylan to recover. Or at least be present enough to hear what Alec had to say.

"From here on out"—Alec tightened his grip on Dylan—"every once in a while, I want to slow down and not be the rabbits strung out on Viagra, okay?"

"What can I say? I tend to chug my beer too."

"There's nothing wrong with that. In fact, I'm *definitely* a fan. But sometimes I like to sip my wine and savor the flavor. And..." Alec attempted to relay the importance of his words with his gaze, afraid to hear Dylan's response. "And I get to touch you whenever I want. Even if it isn't for sex."

Dylan narrowed his lids, as if he couldn't figure out why anyone would want to do such a thing. His green eyes grew serious as he pursed his lips in thought.

"Just not in public, okay?" Dylan grimaced. "I don't care who you're fucking, guys, girls, or friggin' aliens, that shit should be kept private. Otherwise, I'm fine with the idea."

Relieved, Alec nodded in agreement as he absently rubbed a smudge that had wound up on Dylan's cheek. Dylan reached back and grabbed the can of grease from the shelf, handing the container to Alec.

Eyes lit with humor, Dylan said, "We need to find out if this stuff is safe to use for lube during a jack-off session."

"And how do you propose we do that?"

"Call the poison control center?" Dylan suggested with a shrug.

Alec's lips twitched. "I am *so* not making that call."

~~~***~~~

One Week Later

From his sky-box seat on the fifty yard line, Dylan leaned back in his comfy leather chair, feeling out of sorts and wondering why the hell Jack Davis came to the Tigers' football game if he preferred to chat with his guests. Enclosed in glass, the air-conditioned room comfortably held two dozen people and protected them from the elements—or, as Dylan suspected, from the unwashed masses busy screaming for their team. Three big screen TVs hung on the surrounding walls and broadcasted the game, just in case anybody wanted to actually watch the activity taking place on the field below.

Noah utilized his time working the crowd of rich guests as they enjoyed the hospitality of the even richer Jack Davis. Most likely Noah intended to secure more donations for the Front Street Housing Fund. Dylan was watching the game, enjoying a mug of beer and a plate of cheese sticks with marinara sauce. Alec sat to Dylan's left, talking to Tyler.

His *ex-boyfriend*.

Dylan wrestled the resentful frown into submission as he watched the two from the corner of his eye, hoping his overly attentive scrutiny managed to go unnoticed. But he could barely spell discreet, much less pull the act off.

A hand clapped his shoulder from behind, and Dylan tensed as if punched.

Busted.

Palm on Dylan's back, Noah leaned in to address Tyler and Alec. "Tell me again who I'm supposed to be rooting for, the blue guys or the red?"

Dylan let out a silent breath. "Jesus, Noah." Dylan forced his muscles to relax, grateful the overwhelming task of keeping two teams straight had rendered his sharp-eyed friend unusually oblivious to the subject of Dylan's scrutiny. "The ones with the Tigers on their helmets."

Despite the first-class environment of the sky box, Dylan preferred Danny's Suds and Sports for watching football games. Since the start of football season, he and Alec had fallen into the habit of spending one night a week at the sports bar watching the game. On the other nights, Alec cooked, and Dylan cleaned up.

Dylan had existed on takeout for more years than he could remember. As far as he was concerned, the food pyramid should be constructed of Styrofoam containers. Lately, though, Dylan had grown fond of a home-cooked meal. He also preferred the comfort of Alec's house, which had excellent food and Alec for company. The cooking process provided a whole new variety of ways for Dylan to get his hands on the man while he couldn't defend himself. Better yet, groping was not only welcome it was actively encouraged. And so what if the touching sometimes held zero sexual intent? Dylan was learning to be okay with that too.

But, right now, what thrilled Dylan the most about their time at home was the absence of Alec's ex.

"Tigers? Is that what's pictured on their helmets?" Noah squinted at one of the TVs on the far wall. "No wonder they lose. The cute little cartoon tiger is hardly a kick-ass kind of image."

Tyler smiled, Alec laughed, and Dylan knew he should too.

He just...couldn't.

"Tell me again why we're here?" Dylan asked. "You don't even like football, Noah."

"I will always be in favor of a sport with men called eligible receivers or tight ends. *Especially* when a play involves those men piling on top of one another." He swiped a lock of brown hair from his forehead. "Though the Catholic in me objects to the term Hail Mary pass."

Alec stared at Noah as if seeing him in a new light. "You're Catholic?"

Tyler tossed his ex a look. "Only when the label suits him, which—"

"Is never," Alec said, completing the thought.

Damn, bad enough the two had decided to become friends again, but did they really need to finish each other's sentences? Frowning, Dylan concentrated on the football players crashing into each other below.

After two years together— Shit, Tyler and Alec had lived together for *two years*.

Dylan had never been bothered by that fact before. Why now? Most likely the whole tag-team conversation thing represented a habit more than anything else. But still...

Feeling cranky sucked, and Dylan knew he was being an unreasonable bastard. Technically, he and Alec weren't even dating. They were just...two friends enjoying some primo benefits.

Dylan chose not to hurt himself dwelling on the thought for long.

Instead, he pretended to be interested in the cheerleaders down below. Women in unbelievable short shorts and what could only generously be called tank tops, doing intriguingly bendy things. He appreciated the view. That definitely hadn't changed. He just wished he could work up a little more enthusiasm for following through.

"All of this is fascinating," Dylan said dryly. "But how did we wind up *here*?"

Noah dropped into the seat beside Dylan. "A shameless bribe by Jack Davis. Of course, what he *really* wants is to capitalize on the award Tyler and Alec are set to receive next weekend."

"I meant to ask you earlier," Tyler said to Alec. "Are your parents coming to the ceremony?"

Alec hesitated. "Probably."

Tyler's gray eyes studied Alec, and something passed between the two. "Sorry."

"Me too," Alec said quietly.

What the hell was that all about? Dylan gripped the armrest of his seat, his thoughts interrupted by Noah.

"This is Jack's way of persuading us to team up with his hospital for an annual fundraiser." Noah eyed Tyler. "But *some* people are being stubborn."

Tyler looked at Noah, his voice firm but calm. "I said no." He rose to his feet.

"We'd be fools to pass on his proposition." Noah looked up at Tyler. "It's like throwing money away, for chrissakes."

Ignoring Noah, Tyler went on. "I'm going to get a drink. Anybody need anything while I'm up?"

Dylan needed for the man to be gone. He needed for Alec to quit talking to his ex as if they'd been friggin' boyfriends for years. Most importantly, Dylan needed to understand why he needed those things.

When Alec murmured no, Tyler headed toward the bar. Noah leaped up to follow, and a concerned expression crossed Alec's face as he watched the two cross the room.

"Tyler's perfectly capable of handling Noah," Dylan said.

"I've never seen Tyler so ruffled before."

Dylan studied the two men at the bar. Tyler relaxed against the counter as he shook his head in refusal while Noah gestured in that melodramatic way of his.

"He doesn't look ruffled to me," Dylan said.

"I can tell."

Yeah, because they'd lived together for *two fucking years*. Dylan couldn't commit to a cell phone service for that length of time.

"I think we've got a disaster in the making on our hands," Alec said.

Dylan cocked his head. "A ran-out-of-gas kind of disaster? Or a Titanic disaster?

Alec ticked his gaze to Dylan and smiled, resting his hand on Dylan's thigh and leaning closer. For a moment Dylan thought Alec was going to kiss him, and Dylan's muscles grew rigid. Alec must have felt him tense, because, at the last second, he reached across Dylan's lap and picked up a cheese stick from his plate. Dylan relaxed.

Kissing was good. Kissing *Alec* was great, but Dylan didn't do public displays of affection.

He hoped the grin he sent somehow compensated for his stupid hang-up. "Or maybe a Destiny's Bitch kind of disaster."

Alec let out a huff of humor. "Much worse than a drag queen show at a poker run." He dipped his cheese stick in the marinara sauce and sat back in his chair. "Noah has managed to convince a camera guy and a director to volunteer to film advertisements for the bachelor bid."

"Did he seduce them? Or harass them until it was either surrender or throw themselves off the Golden Gate to end the agony?"

"I don't know. Either way, if we agree to Jack Davis' plan, we need a celebrity to shoot the ads. Unfortunately for Tyler, he used to date Memphis Haines."

Dylan watched Alec take a bite of his cheese stick. "Isn't he some stunt guy?"

Alec swallowed and wiped his mouth with a napkin. "That's the one," he said. "But mostly he's known for his Fifth and Taylor advertisements." When Dylan's brow bunched as he tried to place the name of the store, Alec continued. "The designer underwear ads."

Dylan's eyelids stretched wide. "The nearly naked dude on the billboards?"

"The very one."

"How did Noah find out?"

"I...uh..."

A sheepish Alec looked kinda cute, and it was doing strange things to Dylan's chest.

Alec grimaced and went on. "I accidentally mentioned that Tyler had a famous ex-boyfriend. When Tyler shot me down with his gaze, I had to make something up to cover."

"Dude," Dylan said with a laugh, his first since Tyler had arrived on the scene today. "You're a terrible liar."

Alec frowned, but his heart wasn't in it. "I'm going to take that as a compliment." He blew out a breath. "Anyway, somehow Noah sniffed out the truth. And now he's harassing Tyler to ask Memphis to star in our ads. Tyler is refusing. Noah says he'll just visit Memphis himself, using Tyler's name."

"Sounds like your usual Noah fuckup waiting to happen."

"Don't remind me."

Alec tucked his hair behind his ear. The thick waves appeared to have been through the wringer, as though he'd spent the day shoving his fingers through the strands in frustration. Dylan wasn't sure if the frustration stemmed from the friction between Tyler and Noah or Alec's worries about raising the matching grant money.

"What do you think of the Bachelor Bid plan?" Dylan asked.

Dylan studied Alec carefully as the man glanced at his ex. Another worried look crossed Alec's face, and Dylan felt the emotion all the way to his goddamn work boots.

"I think the plan is sound," Alec said. "But it's not worth risking Tyler's peace of mind."

Alec still cared about Tyler.

Okay, maybe not in an I-want-you-back kind of way, but he clearly didn't hate the man. Normally Dylan didn't encourage hostility between people—peace and good will and all that bullshit worked just fine for him.

But...damn.

"I'm sure the clinic will raise enough money to match the grant in time," Dylan said.

"If we don't, our plans for housing will be seriously delayed."

Alec stared blankly at the field below, obviously lost in thought and totally unconcerned as the Tigers attempted a first down and missed. Dylan hiked his ankle up to rest on his knee and wished he could fix the funding problem for Alec. No one knew better than Dylan that providing housing for their most vulnerable patients was vitally important. Expecting Alec to stay away from Tyler bordered on being one of the most selfish ideas Dylan had ever had.

And he'd had some doozies, for sure.

The two men ran a clinic together. They provided a crucial service. Of course they needed to get along, but a hint of lingering tension would be nice. A residual resentment would be awesome. But maybe Alec missed having a full-time partner in his home. Maybe he wanted someone who actually liked to touch in public.

Or maybe Alec simply missed blowjobs.

Dylan's stomach took a Screamin' Demon nosedive for the floor.

Fuck, what a stupid thought. Dylan slumped in his seat and watched the Tigers rally on the fourth down and gain fifteen yards on a spectacular pass. The fans below jumped to their feet, their screams and catcalls and fog horns muted by the thick glass.

Dylan briefly pressed his lids closed, his mind spinning.

Communication. After the hot, Da Vinci-inspired moment in Dylan's garage, he'd promised to work a little on his communication skills. 'Course, at the time, he'd meant it in regards to sex, but maybe he should follow through on that promise in another way.

"So..." Dylan cleared his throat, keeping his voice low and hoping he didn't sound as moronic as he felt. "At one point in my sordid past, I gave blowjobs in exchange for money."

Chapter Thirteen

Alec's breath whooshed from his lungs, and his stomach contracted with a sickening lurch. Christ, he felt as if he'd been tackled from behind. The need to pull Dylan into his arms and hold him was overwhelming. He knew Dylan would hate the response, so he gripped his chair and forced himself to focus on the activity below. The opposing team blocked a field goal, the chorus of groans from the crowd filling the silence between them as Alec struggled for something to say.

Dylan kept his eyes on the game, his posture relaxed as he reached for the beer sitting on the side table. Even the fingers wrapped around his mug looked loose. The absence of a white-knuckled appearance threw Alec off kilter. How could Dylan drop such a bombshell and act so nonchalant?

Three seconds ticked by before the muscles around Dylan's mouth tensed, betraying his emotions.

Dylan still refused to meet his gaze. "Aren't you going to say anything?"

Alec tried to swallow, but his throat felt too tight. "I think you're one of the most amazing men I've ever met."

The scoff that ripped from Dylan held a fair amount of skeptical amusement. "You're too goddamn nice, Alec. We gotta work on that."

But Alec didn't buy any of the garbage that sprang from Dylan's mouth, especially now. The moment felt huge. Pivotal. And Alec felt inadequate. Unfit for the conversation ahead. All those stupid letters after his name, all those degrees he'd earned, and not one of them had helped prepare him for this task.

He struggled for the right words as he stared at Dylan's profile. "Don't tell me you feel ashamed... because you shouldn't."

The thought actually hurt. Dylan lived his life wide open, not giving a damn what other people thought about him. And that was all well and good.

But what did he think of himself?

Dylan paused long enough to blink twice. "No shame here," he said, finally meeting Alec's gaze. "I did what I did to survive on the streets, and I don't regret a thing. Regret's a useless emotion anyway. But..."

His lips twisted wryly. Alec waited, not moving a muscle. Any reaction on his part could be misconstrued as judgment or pity. And Dylan clearly tolerated neither.

Dylan heaved out a breath. "I'm just sorry it's ruined things for you."

"For me? What are you talking about?"

"I can't"—he rolled his hand as if to help the words along—"you know."

"My God, Dylan," Alec said, leaning closer. "Do you really think I care about that?"

Dylan scowled, his expression obviously stemming from confusion, not anger. "Shouldn't you?"

The question was horrendous, heartbreaking, and so perfectly, perfectly Dylan.

Dylan chewed on his lower lip and turned his attention back to the field. Alec used the time to scan Dylan's profile and the puzzled look on his face. Apparently, Dylan couldn't understand Alec's lack of concern about a sexual hang-up that affected him directly. After the weeks they'd spent together, is that still all Dylan felt the two of them were good for? A great fuck?

Pressure built in Alec's chest, a pressure so great Alec's heart rate dropped in response. Time slowed. The sound of the crowd faded. His field of vision narrowed to Dylan as awareness buzzed through him, skirting the edges of something so big, so monumental, the magnitude rendered him unable to move. And then the truth hit with a ruthless force.

He loved Dylan.

The knowledge was sharp, brutal, and unforgiving. Dylan had started this relationship on a lark, and Alec had fallen in love. Alec's lips twisted wryly, biting back the hysterical laughter threatening to bubble to the surface. Noah had been right all along.

Damn, there'd be no living with his friend when he learned the truth.

The words from Dylan and Alec's first time in bed came back.

It's just sex. It doesn't mean anything.

It doesn't mean anything.

Alec tried to wrestle the growing fear into submission, feeling about two seconds away from a mental meltdown. He loved a man who had yet to define his sexual orientation, a man who called himself Alec's backup boyfriend because, as far as Alec had been able to ascertain, he'd never even been in a serious relationship with a woman. Ever.

Jesus, Alec couldn't even touch him in public.

Good God. Panic appeared to be the only viable option.

The throb at Alec's temple felt powerful enough to burst a blood vessel. But of all the choices he had, coming unglued wasn't one of them, not when Dylan had shared such an important part of his past. And, as Alec struggled to find the right words, Dylan finally went on.

"The last time I turned a trick, I just wanted enough money to buy a hamburger." Dylan let out a bitter bark of laughter. "And not just any hamburger. I wanted the deluxe double cheeseburger from Swanson's Diner." He shook his head and looked at Alec. "Isn't that the stupidest thing you've ever heard?"

"No."

Dylan ignored Alec and kept on talking. "But the shithead was big, and he got rough, and I couldn't breathe. I felt like I was choking."

Alec's eyes burned, and his words came out hoarse. "How old were you?"

"Fifteen."

Christ.

Alec gripped Dylan's shoulder, but Dylan shifted until he was just out of reach, and Alec's hand dropped to his lap. Any physical act of support wouldn't be welcomed by Dylan, especially not in public, no matter how much Alec hurt for the boy Dylan had been. The reminder of the one-sidedness of their relationship left Alec feeling drained.

"I friggin' lost control over my mouth and throat, no coordination at all," Dylan went on. "So when he came, I thought I was drowning."

Pulse pounding now, Alec struggled to keep the pain and the fury on Dylan's behalf from showing.

"Anyway," Dylan said with a shrug, "it turned out fine in the long run."

"How the hell can you say that?"

Dylan sent Alec a small smile. "Cuz I stopped selling blowjobs after that. And a few hours later, I'd mentally recovered enough to hunt the SOB down. I found him getting rough with Rick."

"The night you two met."

"Yep," Dylan said. "Gave me an even better reason to punch him. 'Course, the coward got me with the broken bottle in the back." A grin crept up his face. "But the fight was fun while it lasted. Afterward, Rick patched me up, and I bought him dinner at Swanson's Diner."

At fifteen, Dylan had dealt with a horrendous experience by saving a stranger from an abusive john, making a new friend, and eating a deluxe double cheeseburger.

"I said so before, and I'll say so again," Alec said, slowly shaking his head. "You are an amazing person, Dylan Booth."

"And don't you forget it."

Despite everything, the return of the cocky light in Dylan's eyes made Alec smile, the mix of self-confidence and embarrassment in Dylan's expression overwhelmingly endearing. A familiar flutter under Alec's breastbone made him painfully aware of his predicament. And, as he tried to wrap his mind around all that had been shared, only one question remained.

How to survive loving Dylan without losing his mind.

~~~***~~~

The Wednesday after the Tigers game, Dylan entered the combination into the keyless entry on Alec's front door and let out a sigh.

Man, what a sucky day.

His air compressor had finally taken its last gasp, and the replacement he'd purchased had been missing vital parts. He'd assumed the brand-new one would come complete with a regulator as stated on the box. He'd assumed wrong. By the time he'd made his way back to the hardware store and returned to the garage, missing regulator in hand, Dylan had been about three hours behind on an already busy hump day. The rest of the afternoon he'd scrambled to catch up, a feat he never quite accomplished.

Fortunately, everything was about to take a turn for the better.

With a prolonged beep, the lock released, and Dylan entered the house, inhaling the scent of garlic, herbs, and tomatoes. Alec's afternoon off usually meant dinner would be especially delicious and sometimes included dessert. Today proved no exception. From the smell, Dylan guessed the oven contained his favorite: eggplant Parmesan.

How in the hell he'd wound up loving a meatless recipe Dylan would never know. He supposed he owed Tyler for the friggin' fantastic variety of meals Alec loved to cook, half of which contained no meat. But neither an extraordinarily crappy day nor the thought of the ex could ruin Dylan's mood.

Dylan tugged at his laces and toed off his boots before padding down the hallway toward the kitchen. He paused in the doorway and took in the familiar scene. Alec stood at the center island chopping vegetables for a salad, his back to Dylan. Studying Alec's economy of movements, his efficiency in the kitchen, Dylan crossed his arms, a smile tugging at the edges of his mouth.

Used to be when Dylan looked at Alec, he saw the lean body of an academic. Then he began to appreciate the nicely formed ass and thick, dark hair great for burying fingers in during sex. Alec's blue eyes broadcasted his every emotion—whether he was confident, babbling nervously, or completely mute— and Dylan found them totally compelling.

He especially loved to watch Alec's eyes as he came.

There was no doubt the man enjoyed the sex too, but he also liked every other aspect of having a companion in his home. Alec oozed domesticity, enjoying simple activities like cooking for two or talking about his day over dinner. Despite Dylan's protests, Alec even insisted on helping with the cleanup, preferring the company in the kitchen to relaxing in the living room alone. He always waited for Dylan to settle in front of the TV before picking up whatever reading material he chose for the evening. After years of living by himself, Dylan should have needed time to adjust.

Odd how comfortable he felt here. Over time, his spare tools had slowly made their way to Alec's garage. Dylan had purchased a utility bench, setting the stainless steel table up in the corner. Dylan had claimed a rack along the wall and was now well on his way to filling the shelves. Alec had made a comment about breaking the sucker in, and Dylan had rolled his eyes, secretly pleased.

Sex with Alec defined the word awesome.

And now Dylan could choose between that quick, sharp hit of pleasure he craved or a long, slow burn that left him dying for more until he came. The relief of release was almost as thrilling as the orgasm itself.

Several days had passed since his confession, and Dylan felt lighter, freer, and more comfortable with Alec than he'd ever been with another person. He'd never shared that part of his past with anyone. Not even Rick.

Dylan braced himself for the crushing pain that always followed thoughts of his friend, but today the sensation resembled more of a dull ache. The gaping hole felt smaller and less sharply defined—about bloody time after five years.

Alec turned to reach for a red pepper and saw Dylan. "Hey. You're home."

Home.

Dylan's lips quirked. "I got behind today, so I skipped changing the oil on the Ducati as planned." No need to share he'd rescheduled the task, choosing to come home early because he knew Alec would already be here.

"Does she really need it?" Alec asked.

"Nothing but the best for my babies."

Alec smiled, crinkles appearing at the corner of his eyes. "So I've gathered. What's on your agenda for tonight?"

"You."

Alec laughed, and a familiar light lit his gaze.

"Good," Alec said. "I want to discuss something with you."

The words plowed into Dylan like a speeding bus.

Shit. He recognized that look on Alec's face, and it had nothing to do with sex. Dylan had seen the same expression on Alec several times since the football game. Dylan couldn't be sure, but he had a feeling the things Alec wanted to talk about involved the future.

His chest grew tight, and Dylan cleared his throat, forcing a light tone. "You want to discuss switching to a new brand of lube?"

"No." Alec nervously tucked his hair behind his ears. "I'm hoping you can pry your mind out of the gutter for five minutes because there's something I want to ask you."

Fuck. He hated being right.

Needing time to regroup, Dylan said, "We can talk over dinner. I'll just snag a beer and go wash up before we eat." He pulled open the refrigerator door and grabbed a bottle, escaping into the garage.

"I'll finish the salad," Alec called after him.

Heart hammering at a stupid rate, Dylan stood and stared blankly at his wall of tools, wondering how he'd gotten himself into this predicament. Questions clogged his thoughts and left him unsure what to do next.

As far as Dylan could figure, Alec had wanted to have this discussion for several days. Dylan, being the friggin' coward he was, had never encouraged Alec to share his thoughts. Only one possibility made sense. The man was going to ask him to move in, for them to live together like a *couple*.

Jesus.

Dylan didn't know which to do first, laugh at the absurdity of his situation, panic, or give the idea serious consideration. The thought of laying claim to half of Alec's bed held a definite appeal, and for more than just the obvious advantages.

Dylan took an insanely embarrassing amount of pleasure in sleeping next to Alec. In fact, Dylan had come to hate waking alone. He craved the heat and loved the feel of skin on skin. Wrapping himself around Alec, or vice versa, came as naturally as breathing.

But he sure as hell didn't want to be someone's significant other.

He pushed the conflicting feelings aside and headed for his Indian Blackhawk parked next to the workbench, which had tools spread out across the top. He picked up an Allen wrench and absently rubbed his thumb along the metal tool, his head swirling.

"Thirty more minutes till dinner," Alec said as he entered the garage. "Maybe we should talk now."

Dylan tensed, still unprepared for the possible discussion.

The look returned to Alec's face, and he stepped closer. "Dylan—"

"My old air compressor finally died today." Heart wedged in his throat, Dylan turned and knelt at the motorcycle, running his finger along the chain as if testing the tension. He should have bolted for home, like *ten minutes ago*. "I had to buy a new one."

There was a two-second pause before Alec responded. "From what you've said, the event was well overdue." He sounded hesitant now, almost guarded.

Dylan fought to remain calm, at least on the outside.

"Yep," Dylan said. "It got to the point where fixing the sucker cost more than purchasing a new one."

"Dylan," Alec said. "I—"

"I meant to ask you earlier. How's Tyler?"

Dylan kept his eyes on the bike. Clearly he'd gone off the deep end if he was asking about the ex to dodge the conversation. Dylan suppressed the scoff threatening to escape. Next he'd be calling and inviting Tyler over to share their meal, just to delay the inevitable.

"He's fine," Alec said. "Noah's still giving him shit. And he's bummed Logan can't make it to awards ceremony." He cleared his throat. "Which reminds me, there's something I want to ask—"

Alec's cellular rang, and Dylan gripped the chain and closed his eyes, grateful for the delay, his mind scrambling. How would he avoid the discussion without pushing Alec away? Dylan glanced at Alec from the corner of his eye as Alec answered with a hello.

Immediately Alec's expression fell. "Hi, Mom." He turned, his profile facing Dylan as he went on. "I told you, that's not necessary."

Dylan could just make out a female voice droning over the phone, and he pretended he wasn't straining to hear the words. Now he was sorry they'd been interrupted because, while he might be a complete chicken shit about discussions involving the future, he hated seeing Alec upset.

Alec's lips grew tight. "I know, it's just—"

The words died as his mother's voice continued, and Alec stepped away from the table—away from Dylan—and began to pace. Dylan watched Alec walk back and forth. A few more minutes passed as the telephone conversation continued, and the tension in Alec's shoulders never eased. Unfortunately, Alec's mumbled one-word answers gave no clue as to the topic.

Alec finally said goodbye and slipped his phone into the pocket of his khakis, heading back to Dylan. "My mother."

"Yeah," Dylan said with a small smile, hoping to cheer Alec up. "The 'hi, Mom' was kind of a giveaway."

Alec didn't go on, and Dylan gnawed on his lip. Should he let the moment pass? Employ an evasive maneuver and bolt for home, as planned? Or should he ask Alec about the phone conversation? In the end, Dylan couldn't ignore the dejected look on Alec's face, the eyes bleeding vulnerability.

Not when the expression made Dylan's chest ache.

"What's up?" Dylan asked.

Alec met his gaze. "My parents are still planning on coming to the awards ceremony."

"Well, hey, that's good, right?"

Alec rubbed his forehead with both hands as if to scrub away his worries. He seemed unsure of his answer.

"Or not," Dylan went on softly.

Tyler knew why having the parents attend the reception was a problem, but not Dylan. The ex knew, and Dylan didn't have a fucking clue. The realization annoyed the hell out of him. And the fault clearly belonged to Dylan.

Alec dropped his hands to his side. "I purchased a new mirror for my bike. I'll go get it from my car."

He disappeared out the side door leading to the driveway, and Dylan stared after him. He could spot the evasive maneuver from a mile away, especially since his personal superpower was Avoidance. Dylan was still debating what to do about Alec when he returned to the garage, a rearview mirror in his hand.

"You want some help?" Dylan asked.

"No," Alec said. "I can handle this."

From his squatting position in front of his motorcycle, Dylan watched Alec push his Harley closer to Dylan and the workbench. And while he wasn't the handiest person with tools, he'd definitely gotten better with a little instruction. He could do simple things now and replacing the mirror was definitely one of them.

Alec's accomplishment left Dylan feeling so friggin' satisfied it was ridiculous, and the last thing he wanted was to ruin the mood with a heavy discussion.

At the thought, Dylan's throat grew tight enough to choke him.

But ignoring Alec's mood hardly seemed fair. Talking about Rick the day of his birthday had gone a long way toward keeping Dylan from losing his mind. Fucking the life out of Alec had helped as well. Alec deserved some sort of outlet too, and words appeared to be his tool of choice.

"The award is a big deal," Dylan said.

"I know."

When Alec didn't go on, Dylan prompted him again. "You should be proud."

"I am."

Alec's response was followed by a minute of silence.

With a sigh, Dylan rested his arm on his knee. "Then why don't you want your family here?"

Alec unscrewed the clamp that held the cracked mirror with more attention than the process required. "My mother adored—*adores*—Tyler." His hand stilled as he met Dylan's gaze. "And she's...uh...having a hard time letting go."

"She'll have to figure out how on her own. You can't do it for her."

Alec's hand paused briefly before going on with his task, his breath escaping in a rush. "I wish the issue was that simple."

Clamp now loose, Alec removed the old mirror. Dylan waited patiently for Alec to continue as he screwed the new one in place. Just when Dylan thought Alec had decided the discussion was over, the man went on.

Alec checked the stability of the mirror. "She attended just about every protest in three counties, hoping to end Proposition 8. Worked harder than anyone I know to gain me and Tyler the right to marry." He stared at the handlebar, and then, with a small huff, he tossed the screwdriver back onto the utility table. "And now, of course, that's not going to happen."

"Dude, she'll adjust."

"I owe her a lot."

"You don't owe her your personal life."

Alec briefly pressed his eyes closed. "Being a teenager sucks. Being a gay teen makes the phase a million times worse." Hands on his waist, Alec scanned his motorcycle as if looking for something else to fix. "I was in a dark place when I came out to my parents."

The statement settled in Dylan's gut, leaving him sick at the thought of a depressed Alec. Dylan stood and settled his hip against the workbench, searching for the right thing to say. As usual, words failed him.

"My mom's not your typical mother," Alec went on with a wry smile. "She finds showing affection...difficult. But every afternoon when I came home from school, she'd prop a new piece of literature or a pamphlet on my desk. Usually something about adolescent gays." Blue eyes ticked back to Dylan's, and Alec's smile faded. "For a while, those handouts and her wordless support were the only things standing between me and succumbing to the self-loathing."

The desolate words triggered another painful twitch in Dylan's chest.

"I owe her more than I can ever repay," Alec said.

Dylan should be working out how to escape the upcoming talk about their "future." He should be leaving, but anything that interfered with Alec's smile and the resulting crinkles had to be shut down.

And *pronto*. The longer he spent looking at Alec's expression, the harder Dylan's heart hurt, and the more he felt the need to fix the situation.

Sadly, the only way he knew was to replace Alec's defeated look with one of desire.

Jesus, Dylan, you really are a pathetic bastard.

Dylan stepped forward, placing his hand on Alec's torso. The turbulent look in Alec's gaze slowly eased as Dylan slid his palm down to cup Alec's dick.

"What are you doing?" Alec said.

"If you have to ask, I'm not doing it right."

Dylan rubbed his thumb across the head, and the air around them grew heavy as Alec's cock slowly grew stiff. Outside the stroke of Dylan's fingers, neither of them moved.

Alec's gaze now dark, he said, "What did you have in mind?"

"You'll have to be patient and see."

This Dylan could handle. Sex was preferable to talking and a damn sight better than a miserable look on Alec's face. Dylan would do anything, even leap off the nearest bridge to cheer Alec up. Of course, he preferred sex to jumping.

"Unzip your pants," Dylan murmured.

Brow furrowed in question, Alec said, "Should we move to the bedroom?"

"Nope."

Alec glanced doubtfully at the shelf with its assortment of petroleum products and hiked an eyebrow dryly. "But what about lube?"

"We won't be needing lube."

Alec's eyebrows rose, and there was a short pause before he did as previously instructed, unsnapping his pants and lowering the zipper. "Far be it from me to—"

Dylan sank to his knees, and Alec froze, a stunned look on his face. Clearly this wasn't what he'd been expecting. A bit surprised himself, Dylan ignored the disturbing thoughts in his head and pulled Alec's cock out through his briefs.

So, yeah, in the beginning, a blowjob had been completely out of the question, the thought stirring ugly memories he'd worked damned hard to *forget*, thankyouverymuch. But this was for Alec. A gift, of sorts—though that seemed an incredibly lame use for the word. Regardless, another hand job felt...inadequate. How hard could giving head be? Dylan knew what felt good and what pulled a guy out of the moment.

Alec pressed a hand to Dylan's shoulder, concern on his face. "You don't have to do this."

"Jesus, man. I know that," Dylan said. "I want to."

"Why not go with an activity we can both enjoy?"

Because I need to do this.

"Because I want to do something just for you," Dylan said.

Alec murmured a protest, which got cut short when Dylan buried his nose in the thick patch of hair, giving himself an internal pep talk as he stroked Alec's dick. He'd given Alec plenty of hand jobs, but the sight of his cock so close, right in Dylan's line of vision, was new. And while a small part of him expressed doubt, grumbling at the sensation of another man's junk in his face for the first time in fifteen years, another part of Dylan was definitely turned on.

Hunh. He hadn't factored that reaction into the equation.

But this was Alec, and everything with Alec turned out good.

Intent on experimenting first, Dylan touched his tongue to the head. A sharp hiss broke from Alec's mouth. Encouraged, Dylan closed his lips over the tip, marveling at how something so hard could feel so silky and soft. He tested the feel in his mouth, checking out the size before going farther. When he began to suck harder, Alec let out a whine and twisted his fingers in the shirt at Dylan's shoulder. The grip grew tighter and tighter the longer Dylan's mouth worked and the more of Alec he took in. After a minute Dylan glanced up.

Lips parted, Alec panted, his breaths audible. Despite his obvious arousal, Alec cupped Dylan's jaw. His thumb rasped gently across the stubble as if to smooth away any doubts. The gesture was a symbol of reassurance, letting Dylan know what he already knew, that he could trust Alec.

Dylan wrapped his hand around the base and began to bob his head, taking as much of Alec into his mouth as possible. Time ticked by with little incident, and Dylan's confidence grew. Saliva pooled on his tongue, slicking the way. He enjoyed the smooth, salty skin and the weight of Alec's cock stretching his mouth, the action erotic as hell.

But then the faint tang of precum hit, and he panicked, the memories surging forward. He couldn't breathe.

Couldn't breathe.

Dylan slammed his eyes shut and pulled back a fraction. Hoping to cover his reaction, he took his time circling the tip of Alec's head with his tongue as he continued to stroke Alec with his hand. Concentrating on slow, easy breaths.

In and out through the nose.

In and out through the nose.

And as the suffocating sensation slowly passed, Dylan's heart rate recovered. Mouthing Alec's head, he glanced up and focused on the blissed-out look on Alec's face, the sex noises escaping his lips. Finally, Dylan became aware of the salty tang on his tongue again.

But this time he remembered licking Alec's cum from his mouth during that fantastically hot moment in the garage.

Dylan's dick twitched, very much interested in taking things further. He pressed his mouth to Alec's slit and sucked, seeking more of the flavor. Alec dug his fingers into Dylan's shoulder and let out a long groan. If the strength of his grip was anything to go by, he was definitely enjoying Dylan's efforts.

Alec started to thrust his hips forward and then stopped.

"'S'okay, man," Dylan said. Need totally surpassed any lingering traces of fear now. Dylan trailed his tongue up the engorged vein along the base of Alec's cock, around the flared crown, and then licked a glistening drop of precum from the tip. "Do what you gotta do," he murmured and swallowed Alec down.

Alec let out something resembling a sob and rocked his hips, sliding deeper into Dylan's mouth. Several visions punched Dylan in the libido at once. Dylan on all fours, Alec pumping into him from behind. Alec on top, spreading Dylan's knees wide as he targeted Dylan's prostate with unerring accuracy. Dylan still couldn't decide which he liked better. Fucking Alec was awesome, but getting fucked by Alec was like awesome squared multiplied by a thousand.

And Alec using Dylan's mouth in a similar fashion was a total turn-on.

Dylan moaned, his cock growing hard. He didn't have Alec's coordination. He couldn't jerk himself off while in the midst of a blowjob—maybe next time or after a bit more practice. But, for now, the moment was perfect.

Today revolved around Alec and making *Alec* happy.

Besides, if Dylan got caught up in himself, he'd miss the little things like Alec's hand now fisted in the hair at the back of Dylan's head. The desperate clutch of his fingers on Dylan's shoulder. The arch of Alec's hips and the slow slide of his cock in and out of Dylan's mouth.

He liked hearing the noises wrenched from Alec's throat. Sucking Alec off wasn't quite as good as being on the receiving end. But, *Jesus*, it came pretty damn close.

"Dylan," Alec whimpered in warning, his thrusts growing faster. "I'm going to—"

Dylan didn't pull back. Instead, he gripped Alec's ass and shoved him deeper. Alec cried out as cum hit the back of Dylan's throat. He swallowed eagerly around Alec as the man continued to pump his hips, riding out his orgasm, the warm ejaculate pulsing and pulsing and pulsing...

Despite his attempts, Dylan couldn't keep up with it all. When Alec finally crumpled forward a bit, spent, hand on Dylan's shoulder for support, Dylan released Alec's cock. Cum dribbled down his chin.

No longer feeling victimized by a hellacious memory, Dylan grinned up at Alec, wearing the drops proudly. As far as he was concerned, they were a goddamned mark of honor.

"What do you think?" Dylan asked.

Okay, maybe he shouldn't be gloating so much about the stupefied look on Alec's face. Seriously, how needy could a guy get? He shouldn't be seeking approval from someone who currently looked incapable of blinking, much less speaking coherently.

Words slurred, Alec murmured, "I loved every moment." Dazed and glassy eyed, he sent a gut-punching wave of need through Dylan when he smoothed his finger across the slick spot on Dylan's chin. "I love *you*."

Jesusfuckingchrist.

Chapter Fourteen

The deer-sighted-in-the-hunter's-scope look on Dylan's face jarred Alec out of his loose-lipped, post-orgasmic stupor. Oh God, what the hell had he done? A buzzing sound droned on and on in the background, and he blinked hard, trying to make sense of it all. Unfortunately, he was still reeling from his premature words to Dylan when the noise finally connected in his brain.

The timer.

Oven.

Eggplant Parmesan.

The buzzing sound stopped as if by my magic.

"Dinner is ready." Dylan looked all kinds of awkward, making Alec feel the same. And then the man let out a nervous laugh. "You should, uh, be careful of those words triggered by great sex and endorphins."

With that, Dylan shot to his feet and strode for the kitchen. Alec stared at the door Dylan had disappeared through and tried to breathe against the thick mud filling his chest.

Damn.

For the last three days he'd been working up the courage to ask Dylan to attend the awards ceremony as his date. An actual date, not a fake one. As an actual boyfriend, not the backup. Alec was dying to inch this relationship closer to where he needed them to be, declared outright for all to see. Authentic. Genuine.

Real.

What the hell had he been thinking? A declaration of love during sex? Good God, why couldn't he have been struck mute?

I love you...

Fingers shaking, Alec adjusted his clothes, making himself presentable. Avoiding Dylan would only make matters worse. So he smoothed down his shirt with a resigned sigh and headed inside, the scent of spicy tomato sauce in the air. The eggplant Parmesan sat on a counter in an empty kitchen. Had Dylan left the house? Had he run away because he'd freaked about the blowjob?

Alec knew better. He'd seen the front of Dylan's pants and the raging hard-on beneath. And, although massively pleased for Dylan that he'd overcome his fear of sucking someone off, Alec knew the discovery hardly helped when the man had escaped, perhaps never to come back...

All because of Alec's big. Rambling. Mouth.

Fear settled deep, oozing out his pores. He'd wigged Dylan out but good, and Alec had two choices. He could pretend he hadn't meant the words or explain that he *did*, which had a 99.9% likelihood of pushing Dylan away.

Neither option felt possible.

Mind churning, Alec gradually became aware of voices coming from just beyond the kitchen. And only one person would drop by unannounced.

Alec pushed aside the churning thoughts and picked up the eggplant Parmesan—Christ, as if dinner could be used as a shield—and headed into the dining room. He spied Noah, drink in hand, leaning against the wall chatting with Dylan.

Noah caught sight of Alec. "I saved dinner from burning, so I should be allowed to join you in reward for my impeccable timing."

Alec murmured an agreement as he set the dish on the table, too caught up in the way Dylan avoided his gaze to tell Noah the timing couldn't have been any worse. Dylan distributed napkins to the three place settings as though the furniture would explode if not done just right.

This from a man who'd just as soon wipe his mouth on his sleeve.

Because he lacked anything brilliant to say, Alec nodded at Noah's glass. "What's the beverage of the day?"

"Mojitos." With a huge smile, Noah lifted his drink of lime, mint, and citron vodka in a toast. "I just booked my tickets to South Beach for the Winter Party Festival. You should come with, Dylan."

"I don't know, Noah," Dylan said as he began to place silverware on the table. "I prefer something a little dressier than running around in nothing but a speedo and a dog collar."

Noah took a seat at the dining room table. "So says the man who thinks a black tie event refers to the color of the shoelaces in his work boots."

"Parties aren't my thing," Dylan said.

Dylan turned to squat in front of the china cabinet, gathering plates. Damn it, he still hadn't looked Alec in the eyes. But Alec *had* to ask.

"I was hoping you'd come to the awards ceremony," Alec said, addressing Dylan's back.

Dylan didn't turn around. "'Course I'll be there. What kind of guy misses out on his friend's big day?"

The knot in Alec's stomach grew larger. The use of the word *friend* hardly made him feel better, Dylan's manner too evasive for comfort. Clearly he'd gone with option A: ignore Alec had confessed he'd fallen for Dylan in a big way.

"I was hoping you'd attend as more than just as a friend," Alec added.

Breath stuck in his throat, he waited for Dylan's response.

Dylan paused in the task of stacking plates, looking over his shoulder with a frown. "You need another pretend date?"

All the blood in Alec's head drained to his toes. He dropped into a seat at the table before his legs gave way. Several seconds passed in what could only be describe as stunned silence. Noah finally swiveled his confused gaze from Dylan's broad back to where Alec sat. Clearly his friend was wondering what the hell was going on, blissfully ignorant of Dylan's reluctance to discuss what their situation meant.

And totally unaware of the "I love you" that might kill this thing before even being declared a relationship.

"I'm confused," Noah said with a puzzled tone. "Aren't you two—?"

Alec shook his head slightly, insisting with his eyes that Noah not. Go.

There.

Noah opened his mouth, apparently to go there anyway, and Alec hurried to speak first. "My parents are coming to the award ceremony, and Logan will be out of town."

"What's that got to do with me pretending we're dating?" Dylan asked.

Alec fought back the bitter bark of laughter. They'd eaten dinner together every evening since the poker run. Dylan had spent seven of the past seven nights in Alec's bed. At this point the only thing missing was Dylan's name on Alec's mailbox.

"Without someone running interference, my mother will spend the night trying to convince me and Tyler to get back together," Alec said. "She's pretty clueless in social situations." *Completely* clueless would be a better description. "But if you're there as my date, she'll know enough not to push."

Without comment, Dylan rose to his feet, set the plates on the table, and slid into the chair beside Noah.

Alec knew he shouldn't let the choice bother him. He knew he should let the seating arrangement roll off his back, but the position rankled. Dylan purposely chose to place them at a distance when other people were around, even in front of Noah—a man well aware that Dylan had sex with Alec every chance he got. Worse, Dylan steadfastly chose to play dumb about Alec's moment of weakness when he'd confessed all.

Mud filled Alec's chest again.

"Seems like a whole lot of effort to avoid a simple conversation," Dylan said.

"You don't know my mother." Alec's lips gave a wry quirk. "It's just to make the night easier."

"Last I checked"—Dylan hiked a brow—"life was rarely *easy*."

The mud in Alec's chest grew thicker, and each breath seemed to meet resistance.

"Your parents already know you're gay." Dylan crossed his arms, lips pursed in thought. He looked disturbed. "So what kind of closet are you hiding in now?"

Heat flushed up Alec's neck. "Not funny, Dylan."

Dylan stared at Alec. "Who's laughing?"

The tension in the room climbed several hundred degrees, and the mud in Alec's chest turned to concrete.

"Do you have a problem with the idea?" Alec asked.

"I'm not thrilled about lying to your parents," Dylan said.

"You didn't have a problem with lying before."

"You're ex was acting like an asshole. I've never even *met* your parents."

Guilt simmered in Alec's veins. Dylan, as his significant other, would definitely take the pressure off. But, God help him, Alec longed for the situation to be true. He craved some sort of sign that, with time, Dylan would come around. But Dylan appeared to be happy with continuing as is.

And while Alec had originally mustered the patience required to give Dylan time to adjust, suddenly Alec's ability had run out.

"I'm asking you as a favor, Dylan," Alec said.

"Fine," Dylan said with a nod. "I'll play the boyfriend again." He settled back in his chair with a smirk any other time Alec would find sexy. "Though I think I should be getting something in return."

"I thought you were getting some on a regular basis," Noah said.

Face hot, Alec fought the urge to close his eyes, disregarding Noah and addressing Dylan instead. "Something in return? Like what?"

"Something sexual," Noah murmured.

Christ. Where was the muzzle when you needed one?

Dylan picked up on Alec's agenda, also ignoring Noah. "A home-cooked dinner that includes *meat*, every night for the next two weeks."

Noah's amused gaze darted between Dylan and Alec. "How domestic."

This time Dylan shot Noah a look before reaching for the serving spoon.

Dylan dished up eggplant Parmesan onto three plates before addressing Alec. "But we need to get the PDA clarified up front."

Confused, Alec tipped his head.

"I can do an arm around the shoulders." Dylan placed food in front of Noah and Alec. "But only while seated at a table." He cocked a brow at Alec. "And ass grabbing is out of the question."

"Someone should be writing this down." Noah pulled his phone from his pocket, his fingers flying across the tiny keyboard. "Is kissing acceptable?"

Dylan frowned in concentration as he served himself food. "Depends."

"Tongue?" Noah asked.

"Hell no. And handholding is out." Dylan pointed his plate Alec. "I do *not* hold hands." He set his food down.

"Footsies?" Noah asked.

Dylan's mouth quirked. "Footsies will be extra."

"How much extra?" A spark glimmered in Noah's eyes.

Alec bit his tongue, dying to tell his friend to quit encouraging the ridiculous discussion. Dylan pursed his lips in thought again—lips that, less than an hour ago, had been wrapped around Alec, pulling the most obscene noises from his mouth. Like a stupid fool, Alec had ended with the words *I love you*.

Dear God, he couldn't breathe.

Dylan dug his fork into his food. "Like lemon-meringue-pie extra."

Watching Dylan attack dinner with his usual gusto was satisfying and felt comfortable, familiar and strangely reassuring. Alec concentrated on the fact that Dylan hadn't run off. He was still *here*, in Alec's house.

Which meant Alec still had a fighting chance.

"Lemon meringue pie it is," Alec said.

"Perfect. I'll send you both a copy of the agreement." Noah's lips quirked in amusement. "Just so we're all on the same page."

Alec narrowed his eyes at the man. He should have poisoned Noah's food when he had the chance.

"And for the record..." Dylan pointed his fork in Alec's direction. "I will not discuss linens or patterns or whatthefuckever domestic issues with your mother."

"Trust me, Dylan," Noah said dryly as he set down his phone and picked up his drink, "you'd be better served brushing up on your nanotechnology."

Dylan's eyebrows scrunched together. "Nano-fucking-whatology?"

Alec closed his eyes. Christ, this was going to be a disaster.

~~~***~~~

The night of the awards ceremony, Dylan stood beside Alec's mother and tried to decide whether to be amused or alarmed.

Eventually he settled on both.

He'd been so sure this backup-boyfriend gig would be easier the second time around. But, for some reason, Dr. Emily Johnson, sure to be the next brainiac cast on *The Big Bang Theory*, had decided to attach herself to Dylan for the night.

"Essentially we're developing tools for early detection of ovarian cancers via in vitro diagnostics and in vivo molecular imaging," Emily Johnson said.

She stared up at Dylan with big blue eyes, the spitting image of Alec's, completely unaware that Dylan had no fucking clue what she was talking about. She continued to ramble on with barely a pause to breathe.

Like mother, like son.

Fortunately—or unfortunately, depending on one's perspective—the conversation didn't require Dylan's participation. He half listened as he scanned the crowd milling about the reception, searching for Alec.

Nearly one hundred and fifty people filled the spacious hall, the chatter bouncing off the high, ornate ceilings and polished wood floors—Brazilian cherry, Noah had whispered, as if Dylan actually cared. Lined with bay windows overlooking the city, the site represented some primo San Francisco real estate.

"These include adoptive T cell immunotherapies and small interfering RNA molecules," Emily droned on, tucking her brown, chin-length hair behind her ears.

Clutching his beer, Dylan remembered to smile. "Fascinating."

She blinked up at Dylan in what he'd begun to recognize as a sign of approval.

As promised, Alec had served his parents drinks and appetizers at his house before the event. Noah, of course, had invited himself along. And thank God too because, from the moment Emily Johnson arrived, she'd sat next to Dylan and proceeded to ask him about his work. In great detail. Then she'd proceeded to share random, statistical facts about small businesses until Dylan's head swam with numbers. Noah provided a much-needed buffer, and Dylan had been relieved when the time came to make their way to the event.

Nobody argued when Dylan suggested they take two cars.

Whether her intellectual ramblings were a nervous habit or standard operating procedure, Dylan wasn't sure. After several hours in her presence, Dylan finally understood Alec's tendency to babble when stressed. His father, currently listening to Noah chat about plans for the clinic, was tall, black-haired, and blissfully quiet. Or maybe he simply lacked opportunity.

Dylan had noticed the pride and adoration in the man's eyes as his son accepted the plaque and a check for one hundred thousand dollars for the Front Street Clinic. Alec had clearly inherited his father's tendency to wear his heart on his sleeve.

"Most people don't realize homosexuality occurs in the animal kingdom," Emily Johnson said.

Whoa, he'd really tuned out for a moment. When had the topic changed? To cover his confusion, he lifted his beer to his mouth.

"Animals masturbate too," Emily went on. "And some primates have been known to use sticks for genital stimulation."

Mid sip, Dylan coughed on his drink. Fortunately, Alec had inherited only a fraction of his mother's questionable social skills. But the subject of discussion had taken an interesting turn, and the woman was really starting to grow on Dylan.

He bit back a grin, racking his brain for an appropriate response—if one even existed—as she went on.

"Homosexuality is quite common among the species *Cygnus atratus*," Emily said. "And male-male pairings can last a lifetime."

A lifetime... Wait, *what*? Jesus, was this Emily's way of asking about Dylan's intentions toward her son?

A vise clamped around his chest. Hell, he could barely wrap his mind around Alec's *I love you*. In fact, Dylan had been studiously ignoring the memory.

Love.

Seriously, how was he supposed to respond to that? He'd been worried Alec would ask him to move in, and then the man had lobbed the L bomb instead. Dylan figured, *hoped*, the words had simply been triggered by his fabulous technique while sucking Alec off.

Maybe Emily was fishing because Alec had told her how he felt about Dylan.

And what if Alec started to push? What if he began to expect more? When Dylan told him no, Alec might end things again. Not that Dylan could blame him. Alec thrived in a domestic setting, and he *certainly* deserved more than Dylan could ever give. Fiddling with his motorcycle at Alec's was easy. With Alec there, the company was easy too, filling a long-standing void Dylan hadn't even known existed.

The thought of returning to his lonely garage left him feeling empty and depressed. He could feel a mother of a melancholy mood looming in his future.

But every day after work he headed to Alec's because he chose to, not because he *had* to.

Alec weaved his way through the crowd and came to a halt at Dylan's side. "You two okay?"

"We were just discussing the sexual practices of *Cygnus atratus*," Emily said.

Alec tossed Dylan an I'm-sorry look, and Dylan sent a small shrug back.

Oblivious, Emily went on. "Alec, have you seen Tyler? I had a few things I wanted to discuss with him."

Dylan thought he heard Alec sigh.

"Mom," Alec said, "you have to let go."

"Let go?"

"Grieve," Alec said. "Move on with your life."

"Who says I need to grieve?"

"I do," Alec said. "Tyler's here to accept the award and enjoy himself, not be cornered by the mother of the man he *used* to live with."

"I just..." Emily Johnson blinked owlishly at her son. "I just expected to see you happily married by now, Alec."

The air around them grew thin, as if pulling enough oxygen from the atmosphere took more of an effort. Alec's shoulders sagged as he shifted his gaze elsewhere, a little bit of misery and a whole lot of guilt in his expression, and the painful catch in Dylan's chest made breathing that much more difficult.

All Dylan wanted was to offer him a little comfort. Standing by Alec's side, Dylan had no trouble discreetly reaching out to link their fingers together. Alec sent him a wistful smile, squeezing Dylan's hand in a clear message of appreciation and sidetracking Dylan with smooth skin and the heat of his palm. Even more distracting was the way the fingers curled around Dylan's so easily.

Half listening to Alec's mother ramble on, Dylan realized the handholding represented the most intimate act he'd ever engaged in, which was a friggin' ridiculous notion, really. They'd spent countless hours wrapped around each other, Dylan's front pressed to Alec's back or vice versa as they'd driven each other higher.

Reassured by the hot memories, Dylan squeezed Alec's fingers back. Alec visibly relaxed. And when he smiled and those blue eyes crinkled in response, the wave of relief nearly bowled Dylan over.

Jesus, maybe this *was* more than friendship.

A suffocating feeling started in his chest and spiraled outward. Panic rising, Dylan dropped his gaze to Alec's nails—clean and well-trimmed and lacking any of the stains Dylan constantly found on his own—and a memory of the only other time he'd held a man's hand slowly seeped into his consciousness.

As the morphine pump whirred softly in the background, Dylan stared down at the hospital bed sheets and the fingers threaded through his. The fingers were too pale and too thin, and Rick far was too young to be so weak.

"You're gonna be fine, kiddo," Dylan said, squeezing his hand.

He'd used the nickname intentionally, hoping to get a response, and he waited for Rick's laughing protest. The one-year gap in their ages had always felt more like a hundred. Rick had been born optimistic and kind while Dylan was convinced he'd dropped from the womb bitter and angry. His nickname for his friend was more a reflection of their personalities than their ages.

But Rick didn't comment on Dylan's use of the name.

"Fine?" Rick said.

He didn't open his eyes, and Dylan wondered if he was now too weak to lift his lids. Panic crowded the back of Dylan's throat, cutting off his air.

"You're king of the bullshitters," Rick muttered, his lips curving at the corners.

Dylan smiled, so friggin' grateful his friend could still speak that, for a moment, the simple joy bubbled up and spread, infusing him with a warmth that had been hard to find lately. Learning to appreciate the little things was new for him, something Rick had always been ragging on Dylan to do. But, as Rick's condition grew worse, and the end closer, those little moments were the only thing that got Dylan through the day.

And they were becoming harder and harder to find.

"King of BS? That's totally me. Until my last breath," Dylan said, squeezing Rick's hand again and regretting the words that were a reminder of Rick's current condition.

Rick murmured something Dylan couldn't make out, and he leaned closer to catch the words on his second try.

"Hopefully your last breath won't be for a long time."

Dylan tightened his fingers around Rick's because, Jesus, pushing forward hardly felt doable right now. They'd spent years holding each other's spirits up, refusing to let the crappy weather, the rain, or a cold night spent in a back alley get them down. But right now it took all of Dylan's energy not to scream and rant and bang his fists against the wall.

Because life was so fucking unfair...

"Dylan?"

Dylan blinked, bringing his focus back to Emily Johnson as she continued talking. Dylan was very aware that Alec was looking at him with concern.

"Sorry," Dylan murmured, a heated flush of embarrassment creeping up his neck.

"Four to five percent of geese and duck pairings are homosexual," Emily said. "I've heard females will lay eggs in a homosexual pair's nest. Some say they're better at raising the young than the heterosexual

couples." She turned to address Dylan. "Do you plan
on getting married and having kids?"

The words landed like a swivel kick to the chest.
Married? *Kids*?

"Christ, Mom," Alec said at the same time Dylan
blurted out, "*Hell* no."

The suffocating feeling reached its zenith. Five
heartbeats pounded painfully by as two sets of
identical blue eyes—Emily's a blank, blinking stare
and Alec's more of a horrified gaze—remained
firmly fixed on Dylan. He finally succumbed to the
desperate need to bolt.

"Excuse me," Dylan said hoarsely and pivoted on
his heel, taking off in search of air.

~~~***~~~

"Mom, I've got to go," Alec said.

"But—"

Alec ignored whatever she'd been about to say,
heading for the French doors as he followed Dylan's
path. Once outside, he paused on the brick patio.

The evening was beautiful, crisp and clear. The
lights of the city spread out below, headlights
streaming by like ribbons of light. He spotted Dylan
standing in the corner between the wall and the
metal railing that provided protection from the
considerable height, his hands pressed against the
top bar.

Alec came to a stop and crossed his arms against
the pressure beneath his sternum, fighting not to fall
apart. There was so much riding on the next few
minutes. His future. Dylan's future. Their *happiness*.
Alec knew Dylan played the part convincingly, but
prior to their relationship, he hadn't been happy.

"Your mother is really something," Dylan said.

"I know," Alec said softly, but this wasn't the conversation they were about to have.

The cool, nighttime breeze smelled of recent rain and ruffled Dylan's hair as Alec waited.

Dylan still didn't look at him. "At least I'm more convincing as the backup boyfriend this go-around."

If Alec heard that term one more time he'd puke.

"Christ, Dylan. We've spent every night together for the past three weeks. We've tried every sexual position in my repertoire, and a few that were new to me—"

"Really?"

For some inexplicable reason, Dylan looked pleased, as if succeeding at sex was a mission to be accomplished. Nothing wrong with admirable goals and all, but *seriously*.

"Yes," Alec said. "But that's not the point. The point is you're still hell bent on pretending this relationship isn't real."

"Whoa." Dylan threw up a hand as if to stop traffic, eyes wide with shock. "Nobody said *anything* about a relationship—"

"Bullshit."

Alec watched Dylan's mouth work, jaw clenching and unclenching as he scanned Alec's gaze. And then Dylan shifted his focus to the door beyond. Hoping for an interruption? Looking for an escape route?

The pain beneath Alec's ribs made every breath hurt.

"Because I don't know about you," Alec went on, "but this began to feel real a long time ago."

Dylan looked as if he couldn't decide whether he wanted to run screaming from the building or throw himself over the rail.

"Dude, I'm not..." Dylan plowed a hand through his hair. "We don't..." He dropped his hands and began to pace along the low brick wall. "I am *not* your boyfriend."

Alec inhaled, trying to rein in his frustration. And his pain. He watched Dylan stride to the end of the small patio and return, waiting until Dylan was close enough to hear the words that came out low.

"Do you enjoy spending time with me?" Alec asked.

Dylan frowned. "'Course I do."

"Do you, or do you not, enjoy having sex with me?"

"Dude." Dylan whirled, his frown bigger as he strode closer, coming to a stop in front of Alec. "I am not gonna dignify that with a response. But that's just friendship with...with..." He rolled his hand in the air, as if the motion would help him find the right word. "Extras."

"Benefits."

He threw his hands up. "Whatthefuckever, man. Does it really matter what it's called? The bottom line is, I don't want to be labeled as anybody's boyfriend."

Alec forced himself to steadily meet the turbulent green gaze, debating his next move. He could say no. He could go on pretending it didn't matter. At least he had Dylan in his life. But he was tired of Dylan referring to himself as the fake boyfriend.

And Alec couldn't live in limbo anymore.

"And what if Tyler claimed he wanted me back?" Alec asked, and Dylan's features froze. But the man said nothing, so Alec pushed forward. "What if I told you I was going back to him?"

"Fuck a duck," Dylan said, scowling as he moved closer. "Is that true?"

Alec held his gaze and refused to step back. Or back down. "Does it matter?"

"Oh, heck yeah, it matters."

"So what would you say?"

Dylan's chest rose and fell with every aggressive breath. "I'd say you don't belong with him."

Hope flared bright, almost consuming the pain. "Then who do I belong with, Dylan?"

Me, Alec wanted to hear him say. *Me.*

Instead, Dylan said, "How the heck should I know?"

The clamp around his chest grew tighter, and Alec pretended to remain calm. "You're not the first man who's struggled with his sexual orientation."

"My orientation is irrelevant to this conversation."

"I think it's very relevant. I think you're afraid to admit you're bisexual."

"What does that even mean?" Agitated, Dylan strode a few steps away before turning to pace back. "Fifty percent gay? Fifty percent straight? Can I be ninety percent of one? Ten percent of another? I'm not part this or part that. I'm just me." He came to a halt in front of Alec. "A hundred percent *whole* me."

Which all sounded to Alec like denial wrapped up in pretty protests.

"You couldn't admit it with Rick, and you can't admit it now," Alec said.

"I told you." Dylan's voice was harsh. "That's not what this is about."

"Then what is it about, Dylan?"

"Rick—" He snapped his mouth closed.

Alec held his breath and then let it all out in a rush. "You loved him."

"'Course I did," Dylan shot back.

Oh God. Acid burned Alec's stomach, crawled up his esophagus, and reached the back of his throat...

Don't vomit. Don't vomit.

The first time he'd asked Dylan if he loved Rick, Alec had wanted him to say *yes*. A Dylan who'd loved Rick would have been gay or bi, and either one would have been infinitely more available. Now Alec didn't know what to believe. With Dylan, Alec was learning nothing was set in stone.

"But I didn't love him like that," Dylan said. "Jesus, I told you before. Rick was a brother, not a boyfriend."

"So why—"

"Because he died on me, goddamn it!" Dylan blurted. "Everyone always leaves. And I have such a huge fucking hole in my chest—" Dylan clamped his lips together. "Shit." He turned away, his shoulders rising and falling as if fighting every necessary breath. He braced a hand against the brick wall of the building and closed his eyes, slowly shaking his head. His words no longer held any punch. "Why did he have to leave?"

He sounded so...lost.

And maybe that was what this was all about, a loss that Dylan would never recover from. One too many for him to adjust. He'd lost his mother, his father, and even his childhood. And, if that hadn't been enough, he'd gone and attached himself to Rick. And then lost him too.

Like a self-protective mechanism of an animal forced to shed a tail to survive, Dylan had sacrificed a piece of himself at every devastating turn.

Until not enough of him remained to recover.

Eyes burning, Alec stepped forward, hoping his voice remained steady. "*I'm* not leaving, Dylan," he said, laying a hand on Dylan's back.

"Don't." Dylan spun away from his touch. "Don't touch me."

Stung, Alec dropped his arm to his side.

Dylan's eyes flashed a shade of green Alec had never seen. "You just had to push, didn't you?"

Dylan might be lost, but he was also pissed as hell. Or maybe furious fit the description better. Whether Dylan was furious at Alec, at Rick, or the world in general, Alec didn't know. At this point the recipient of all that anger hardly mattered because the emotion took up so much space there wasn't room for anything else.

Like Alec.

"You're so friggin' set on a committed relationship that you can't see what's right under your nose," Dylan went on.

"That's not true."

"I'll admit Noah's party was my idea, but you were the one who wanted to keep up this charade in hopes of avoiding a confrontation with your mother." Dylan's gaze refused to budge, boring into Alec's. "Face it, you're too fucking scared to be honest with your own family."

Alec opened his mouth, hoping to produce a decent protest. But none came.

"I've had enough of this black tie affair," Dylan said.

Dylan turned and headed toward the door, and this time, Alec didn't bother following.

Chapter Fifteen

Dylan drove his car home and then spent the next two hours on his Indian Blackhawk, riding aimlessly around town with no particular destination or plan in mind. Thinking about the end of his friendship with Alec made Dylan feel slim, spread thin. Like not enough jam trying to cover too much toast.

No surprise this charade had finally caught up with him.

He passed through neighborhoods Alec liked to cruise and wound up parking at Alec's favorite sports bar. The destination reeked of a stupid idea, but Dylan couldn't help himself. So he parked his bike and found a table inside, ordering a beer. He never, ever drank while driving, but tonight seemed like a good time to start.

He jerked open the top button of his dress shirt, pissed he hadn't taken the time to change before he'd left on his motorcycle. But being revved up and ready to burst at the seams meant movement was the only way to remain sane.

Speeding down the highway hadn't helped.

Settling back against the booth, he tuned out the sound of the patrons who had gathered to watch a football game. From the occasional cheers, the crowd seemed pleased with the score. He remembered how Alec had looked every time they'd wound up here and got caught up in a college game. Or the fucking beautiful smile on his face when he first started getting his Harley to start. But Dylan didn't want to dwell on how he felt with Alec around cuz that wasn't going to happen anymore.

The thought twisted Dylan's heart in ways he'd never experienced before. Grumpy as hell, he slumped deeper into the seat.

Four beers later and Dylan's head spun, his stomach churned, and his chest didn't feel any less likely to detonate at any moment. And why did walking out on Alec hurt so badly? Not that how he felt right now held a candle to Rick dying, but in some ways, the feeling *was* similar.

Loss was loss, whether through situation or death.

Dylan clutched the handle of his mug. "Why'd you have to die, you son of a bitch?"

"Handsome, you are going to regret this in the morning."

Dylan blinked, and for one bizarre moment, he wondered if Rick was speaking to him. But Rick never called him handsome. That was Noah's job. And when Dylan looked up, he spied Noah, who was peering around as if he'd just entered a meat market and was dying for a prime rib.

"Mmm," Noah murmured, eyeing the men in suits enjoying end-of-the-day beers at a table nearby. "Wall Street movers and shakers."

Despite the headache, Dylan rolled his eyes and then winced when the dizziness grew stronger. "How did you find me?"

Noah cocked an eyebrow. "You drunk texted me."

"Oh." Dylan frowned. He didn't remember doing that.

"I'm kidding." Noah slid into the booth beside him. "If you believed that, you must be worse off than I thought. Alec called, worried you were so angry you'd crash your car on your way home from the ceremony. When you didn't answer your cell phone, I said I'd go look for you."

Well, damn. That was a relief. Maybe he wasn't as drunk as his whirling brain suggested. He blinked hard, trying to clear his vision, and spied four empty mugs.

Okay, maybe he was.

"When I got to your apartment, your car was there, but you weren't," Noah said. "So I called Alec to report back, but he was still worried. Said I had to go find you."

"San Francisco's a pretty big city."

"He told me which routes you two liked to take when out for a ride. He also mentioned Danny's Suds and Sports. From the number of mugs on the table, clearly I'll need to drive you home." He picked up a napkin and wiped the table, clearing a spot for his elbows. "Why were you angry?"

Dylan scowled into his current beer but didn't say a word.

"Alec was very tight lipped about the whole thing," Noah went on.

During the silence that followed, a waitress wandered by, and Noah ordered a sparkling water. When she was gone, Noah hooked his arm around Dylan's shoulders.

"Come on. Tell your Auntie Noah."

Dylan sent his friend a frown, though his heart wasn't in it. "You gonna try and take advantage of me again?"

"Please," Noah said with a loud bark of laughter that made Dylan's head hurt worse.

The waitress returned with his Perrier, which, fortunately, meant Noah had to remove his arm from Dylan's shoulder to take a sip of his drink.

"Just because you've discovered you like dick doesn't mean I want yours," Noah said.

"I don't like dick." And then Dylan frowned, hating the taste of the words in his mouth. "Not most of 'em anyway."

"You like Alec's."

Dylan kept his mouth clamped tight and tried hard not to think about how Alec would be surprised to learn that he *could* shut the fuck up. Several seconds ticked by, and Noah's silent, speculative gaze finally did Dylan in.

"There's something very neat and orderly about sleeping with your friend." Proud he'd made so much sense while buzzed beyond belief, Dylan went on. "You know, like a two for the price of one kind of thing."

Even after the words left his mouth, he knew they didn't fit any better. Noah lifted his eyes heavenward, calling Dylan out on the lie. Maybe he should try something a little closer to the truth.

"I'm pissed off," Dylan said.

"I can tell."

"Alec shouldn't have pushed," Dylan said, growing angry all over again. "He wants me to make some kind of goddamn commitment. Just because he said he loves me—"

"He said that?" Noah looked positively stunned.

"What? Is that so hard to imagine?"

"To be perfectly blunt, yes. You wouldn't be an easy man to love." Noah crossed his arms, regarding Dylan calmly. "In fact, you might never get this chance again."

"Be serious."

"I am."

Dylan ignored Noah and finally shared his greatest fear, the one that had been nipping at his heels for weeks. "But how do I know Alec won't suddenly decide he wants Tyler back?"

Dylan's chest ached, as if set to split wide open. That was the trouble with voicing his thoughts instead of keeping them safely tucked in his head. They sounded so much worse when spoken out loud.

Noah, as usual, wasn't helpful. "You don't."

Dylan scowled, and the memory of his response to Alec's question punched hard.

Who do I belong with?

How the hell should I know?

The desire to push back with everything he had returned. Scream profanities. Punch through a wooden door. Kick a brick wall.

"He could go back to Tyler at any second," Noah went on. "He *is* the safer choice, being a confirmed gay and all."

"If you're trying to help, please stop."

Noah didn't comply. "Just like I didn't know that Rick would die."

All the air in Dylan's chest rushed out on a crushing *whoosh*. "Jesus, stop. Just fucking stop."

"I'm sorry, Dylan." Noah settled back, his arm resting on the ledge behind Dylan's shoulders. "You need to hear the truth right now. Coddling you will gain you nothing."

Dylan let out a scoff. "When have you ever coddled me?"

"When Rick was dying."

Dylan closed his eyes, but the spinning only got worse. He wasn't sure if he should blame Noah's words or the four beers he'd consumed.

"But don't worry," Noah went on, patting Dylan on the back. "You more than made up for that horrible day in the weeks that followed."

Dylan dropped his elbows to the table and pressed his palms against his eyes. Yeah, they'd taken turns falling apart. Dylan had been a basket case those last few days of Rick's life, forced to watch the only person on the planet he cared about slip away, in pain, with Dylan helpless to do a goddamn thing. Noah had kept Dylan together enough to keep him focused on Rick. But after Rick passed, Noah had crumbled. Seven days' worth of Noah crying and drinking had followed, culminating in a night where he'd made a move on Dylan. Wasn't hard to figure out the seduction attempt had been all about pain control. The alcohol certainly hadn't been doing the trick, for either one of them.

Dylan had almost felt bad for turning Noah down.

"You were my first attempt at seducing a straight," Noah said with a wistful smile.

Despite everything, Dylan's lips quirked. "Am I the one who got away?"

Noah threw back his head and laughed. "Oh, trust me, there've been others. But you were the first. A romantic figure I have no intention of changing."

"Glad I'm good for something."

"It's okay to be mad at Rick."

The words came out of the blue. But, deep down, Dylan knew the thought had been circling in his brain like a swarm of sharks growing closer and closer.

"Jesus, Noah. It's not like the man wanted to die."

"Yes," Noah said. "But we both know his choices played a role in contracting the virus."

"He didn't *have* any choices, man."

"Then why are you mad?"

The words came out like a fifty-mile-an-hour slide of bare skin across concrete. "I'm pissed at him because he left me *alone*."

Noah steadily met Dylan's gaze while Dylan's pulse pounded so hard the motion shook his chest. One of the teams on the widescreen scored a touchdown, and a rousing sound of cheers, and a few groans, filled the air. None of the noises, not a single one, seemed louder than Dylan's stomping heart.

When the din died away, Noah went on. "So quit taking your anger out on Alec. An anger you should have worked your way through ages ago."

Dylan let out a soft snort. "So says the guy who's been chasing unavailable men ever since."

Noah picked up his bottle of Perrier with a smug smile. "There's something deliciously forbidden about the impossible-to-obtain man. I've grown rather addicted to the chase."

Dylan shot his friend a look. Noah might appear pleased with himself, but Dylan knew better.

"Noah, you are a walking, talking, lying sack of shit."

Noah wrinkled his nose at the description. But Dylan noticed the way Noah's gaze slid from Dylan's eyes to somewhere over his shoulder.

"Your roughneck ways are usually intriguing." Noah wiped a nonexistent spill with his napkin. "Though currently I can't remember why."

Because you know I'm right.

"Besides"—Noah set his bottle down—"we're not talking about me, handsome. We're talking about you." Noah's brown gaze refused to back down. "And you've fallen, Dylan Blaine Booth, something I thought I'd never live to see, especially for another man, but there you go."

There you go echoed through Dylan's head until replaced by *you've fallen.*

The words paralyzed him, left him shit-scared and panicking.

Fallen.

Fuck. What a lame-ass description. He felt more like he'd plummeted helter-skelter from three thousand feet, life as he knew it splattering on the rocky ground below.

"Sorry to be the one to break it to you," Noah went on glibly, as if he hadn't just altered the course of Dylan's life forever. "I promise. If I ever fall again, you can rub the news in my face."

Dylan dragged his hands down his eyes. Jesus, he needed to find some better friends. Preferably ones more sympathetic.

"And how, exactly, does that promise help me now?" Dylan muttered through his fingers.

"Gives you something to look forward to, of course," he said cheerfully.

Implying, no doubt, just how much Dylan would need something to look forward to. Especially with his future looking so bleak and all.

Yep, he was definitely going to need new friends.

~~~***~~~

Two Wednesdays after the horrific end to the awards ceremony, soft country music greeted Alec as he entered the empty Front Street Clinic reception area. Sleep deprived, he clutched his latte. Fortunately the day had been long and grueling. Now he just needed to retrieve his laptop from his office before he could go home and collapse. He'd been pushing himself harder than usual, burying himself in his work and avoiding being alone with his thoughts. All of which centered on Dylan.

Chest aching, Alec wearily swept his hair behind an ear.

Computer. Home.

And then blissful escape in sleep.

Then he spied Martha, her back to him as she typed on her computer at the reception desk, and his heart sank. Hopefully the song on her radio would help him pass by without being detected. Exhausted, he couldn't deal with further interaction today.

Usually he split his week equally between the office and making the rounds in the mobile clinic, recruiting new patients and checking in with their regulars at the local soup kitchens. The clinic used food as incentive to keep their patient population coming back, because Maslow had been on to something when he listed out his hierarchy of needs.

According to the psychologist, the base of the triangle—the most fundamental of needs—included breathing, food, water, sleep, warmth, and sex. Dylan had learned to exist along the bottom rung, wringing all the pleasure possible from the very basics, like food and warmth and sex. He never really aspired to attain more, mostly because he didn't expect much out of life. A direct result of being given so little.

Alec gripped his coffee cup tight, hating how much that truth still hurt.

As far as his patients' priorities went, taking antiretroviral meds to treat HIV fell well below the need for food and a safe place to sleep. In addition, despite a van providing rides, the no-show rate for appointments at the office bordered on fifty percent.

This was why Alec had volunteered to spend long hours in their mobile clinic. Sitting around here with nothing to do, even for five minutes, left him with too much time on his hands. Too much time to contemplate the huge mess he'd made of his life and how much he missed Dylan.

Christ, he needed to get a grip.

Alec flicked his gaze between the hallway across the room and Martha's back. If quiet enough, he might be able to pull this off. He'd taken five steps when Martha spoke without looking around.

"Here's your appointment list for tomorrow." She swiveled in her seat and held out a clipboard. "Tyler's out in the RV, restocking supplies. You're supposed to stop by and see him before you leave."

Another person with too many questions. Unlike Martha, though, Tyler wouldn't hesitate to ask them.

Alec accepted the list and scanned the names. "What does Tyler want?"

Martha sent him her standard look, the one Alec imagined she made when coming across something in her refrigerator that looked iffy and smelled even worse.

"Haven't a clue," she said.

She paused, as if she wanted to say more. Alec took advantage of her hesitation and pivoted to leave.

"Wait."

Alec mentally groaned and turned to face the receptionist again.

Martha pushed her reading glasses up on her head, her salt and paper hair now sticking up at odd angles. "Haven't seen that boyfriend of yours around lately."

Numbed by the words, Alec waited for her to go on. He knew she was referring to Dylan. In the months since Tyler and Alec had broken up, not once had Martha made a comment. Everyone had known the moment Tyler had moved out, and most of the employees had either offered words of support and condolences or sent Alec sympathetic looks.

Not Martha.

Alec appreciated how the nurse/secretary/front-desk bulldog had been the single employee at the clinic who had kept her opinions and sympathies to herself—assuming, of course, sympathy was within her capabilities. She didn't believe in small talk or socializing. Nothing but work.

Until now.

"You tell him the next time he comes around he needs to park that motorcycle of his in the parking lot," she said. "Not on our walkway."

Despite the surge of sadness, Alec smiled at her grumpy way of wishing Alec luck with Dylan.

"Thanks, Martha," Alec said. "I appreciate it."

"Yeah?" She looked embarrassed at being caught being nice. "You might not be so grateful after you see the names on that list," she said, nodding at the clipboard. "The most disagreeable, noncompliant patients I could assemble." She propped a hand on her hip. "I suspect you need a little challenge right now."

"Thanks, Martha." Alec let out a small huff of humor. "I think."

Martha nodded brusquely at the side exit. "Tyler is waiting."

Gripping his latte, Alec set down the clipboard and headed outside into the fading afternoon light, crossing the sidewalk and stepping up into the RV that had been converted into a rolling clinic. The front of the vehicle contained two chairs for drawing blood to send for labs, the middle devoted to a tiny exam room complete with a patient table. The back consisted of a makeshift pharmacy where the medications were kept.

Testing was crucial, but if patients identified as HIV positive lacked access to medications, then the system failed in its most vital role. Alec would always be proud of what he and Tyler had built here.

A clinic that could have prolonged Rick's life.

Alec locked the sadness away and found Tyler in back squatting in front of an open cabinet, restocking their supply of brochures about safe sex. Alec had to smile. Even at the end of a long day, Tyler still looked impeccable, not a wrinkle to be found on his dress shirt, tie, or slacks.

"Hey." Alec leaned against the narrow doorway. "You wanted to see me?"

Tyler acknowledged Alec with a nod. "Logan and I broke up," he said before continuing with his task.

The coolly delivered words came as a shock. For a moment, Alec forgot to blink. He'd never even considered Tyler wanted to talk about himself.

"What happened?" Alec asked.

Tyler lined up the stacks of pamphlets with the same precision he applied to everything in his life. "His job," he said. "Turns out being an award-winning documentary film producer requires a lot of travel. And while I'm all for being monogamous, if your partner's gone most of the time, monogamy kind of sucks."

Alec absorbed the news as he finished his coffee and tossed the cup in the trash.

"I'm sorry," Alec said.

"Don't worry." Tyler paused to rest an arm on his thigh, and a hint of humor crept into his eyes. "I won't call your mother and tell her I'm a free man again."

Alec's lips twisted wryly. "Thank you."

Tyler's gray gaze held Alec's. Alec expected his ex to return to his task. Instead, after a brief pause, Tyler stood and faced him.

"We could try this again," Tyler said, leaning a hip against the counter. "Try *us* again."

The statement made an impressive landing, leaving Alec's mind reeling. Stunned, Alec stared out the RV window as a car roared by on the street beyond, the sound fading as the vehicle disappeared over the hill.

And what if Tyler claimed he wanted me back, Dylan? What would you say?

I'd say you don't belong with him.

"Think about it, Alec," Tyler went on. "We make sense."

In the days following their breakup, Alec would have given anything to hear those words.

In fact, if he hadn't met Dylan, Alec would be jumping at the offer right now. And he and Tyler might have made a real go at the relationship this time, even worked out their differences and been completely content. But contently happy could never replace soul-deep joy.

Dylan had taught him the difference.

Alec had never loved Tyler. Not the way he loved Dylan. Alec had been so focused on the idea of permanency, of getting married, that he'd clung to the idea of the relationship more than the man himself.

"I don't think..." Alec shifted his weight on his feet. "I don't think it's supposed to make sense."

A faint crinkle appeared on Tyler's brow.

"Dylan's not really gay," Alec said.

Tyler's crinkle grew deeper. "You mean he faked that too?"

"Yes," Alec said. "And no." He rubbed his forehead, realizing he sounded crazy. "I mean, he *was* sleeping with me, but—"

"Let me guess." One brow shifted marginally higher. "He's so deep into that walk-in-sized closet of his he couldn't find his way out with a flashlight, a GPS, and a search-and-rescue team."

"That's what I originally thought," Alec said. "But he truly has no hang-ups when it comes to labels. Gay, straight, bi, and every shade in between. He just doesn't care. It's almost funny." Alec watched the fading light filter through the trees outside, wishing he could laugh. "I'm the guy who's supposed to be protesting the limitation of labels. And yet, all along, I'm the one who tried to force Dylan to accept one."

"Most people need labels because they bring a measure of security."

"Exactly," Alec said.

Tyler crossed his arms. "Then what's the problem with Dylan?"

Stumped, Alec considered the question before letting out a self-chastising scoff.

"I guess it's another labeling issue. I want him to accept that we're in a relationship, and the idea freaks him out." Alec slowly blew out a breath. "He doesn't care if people know we eat dinner together every evening or that he spends most every night in my bed. But God forbid you call him my boyfriend."

"So he's afraid of being in a relationship."

Fear. The word did sum up the problem nicely. Dylan had learned to live with the loss of his mother and then his father. But Rick's death had been one loss too many.

"I just don't know where to go from here," Alec said.

"Well, I know how important being part of a couple is to you."

Pressure made Alec's throat ache as he looked at his ex. In the days that followed Tyler moving out, Alec had been too busy throwing a pity party to realize he was a major part of their problems. He'd mourned the loss of the couple label more than the loss of his partner.

God, I've been such a dick.

"I'm sorry, Tyler. I didn't mean to use you that way."

As always, Tyler's eyes remained cool and calm, but the muscle in his jaw clenched—the only sign of his discomfort. "It's okay," he said. "Took me a while to figure everything out. I wasn't exactly Mr. Perceptive."

"No, it's not okay. I ignored *us* in my focus on the clinic and ending Proposition 8. Essentially, I totally took you for granted. And you deserve better than that."

Tyler gave a single nod. "I do." He lifted a shoulder with his signature economy of movement. "Then again, doesn't everyone?"

They slipped into a companionable silence, and Alec leaned against the wall, grateful they'd managed to salvage their friendship. He was going to need all the friends he could get to survive the loneliness of the next few weeks. Months.

Years.

Christ. Alec fought the need to close his eyes against the painful thought.

Hip parked against the counter, Tyler crossed his ankles. "What are you going to do about Dylan?"

The sudden weight in Alec's chest made his heart's job difficult. That very question had been eating at him since Dylan took off. Alec was no closer to an answer now then he was back then.

"I don't know," Alec said.

He hated the way Tyler was looking at him. As if his ex knew Alec had waded into the deep-shit end of trouble and things were about to get worse.

"You love him," Tyler said.

"Yeah," Alec said. "I do."

Tyler's eyes remained steady, and two seconds ticked by before he spoke.

"I think you should go see Dylan," Tyler said. "Tell him how you feel."

"I already told him, and he left anyway. I don't think he wants to see me again."

"Who cares? Don't make the same mistake I did, Alec. Don't let him walk away without putting up a fight."

And although the words were delivered with a detached tone—Noah didn't call Tyler The Ice Man for nothing—clearly, when it came to Memphis Haines, Tyler had regrets.

"Do whatever it takes to fix things with Dylan, Alec." Tyler stepped closer, his colorless gray eyes as close to expressive as Alec had ever seen. "Before it's too late."

Chapter Sixteen

In the end, Alec decided he needed to call his mother before climbing on his motorcycle to hunt Dylan down. If he expected Dylan to stop closing himself off to the potential between them, then Alec needed to set his own affairs in order first. And that meant living a lie ended today.

He let out a scoff. Funny how the truth involved more than just where he stood in relation to the closet door.

"Hey, Mom," Alec said after she answered.

"Alec?" She sounded distracted, the sound of shuffling papers in the background. "Is something wrong?"

The answer sat on the tip of his tongue.

Everything.

He dropped onto his couch. "No," he said and then realized that was another lie. Where to begin? "Well, yes..."

"We never got to say goodbye to Dylan after the award ceremony."

A wry smile crept up his face. Sometimes his mother's obtuse nature in regards to social cues could be an advantage. Fortunately, his mother remained blissfully unaware that her question to Dylan had been a catalyst for disaster. A disaster of Alec's own making, of course.

Her words had simply lit the fuse to the bomb he'd built.

Phone pressed to his ear, he propped his elbows on his knees. "Technically, Dylan's not my boyfriend." He paused for a moment to let the confession sink in before forcing himself to go on. "I asked him to pretend."

"I don't understand." The background shuffle of papers ended, his mother most likely blinking furiously as she tried to process the news. "Why would you pretend you were serious about Dylan?"

"I'm not pretending. I *am* serious about Dylan." He'd never been more serious about anything in his life. Attempting to rub the furrows from his brow, he stared down at his bare feet, toes buried in the thick carpet. "He's just not my boyfriend."

The MD behind his name might stand for Massively Deluded, but one-way relationships were beyond even his delusional capabilities.

When she didn't respond, he went on. "I know you envisioned Tyler and me married. And I hate to disappoint you, but—"

"There's still a chance Tyler will choose to come back."

Alec closed his eyes. He could keep his mouth shut. Keeping the truth to himself would certainly make this conversation easier. But he'd been doing exactly that for years, trying to ease things between him and his mother, between him and the rest of the world. And he couldn't continue to hide those bits of himself, the most *important* bits, just to keep everyone happy.

"Tyler already asked me back, and I said no."

The silence from the other end of the phone pressed in on his chest.

When his mother finally spoke, he could sense her deep disappointment. "Why?"

"Because I'm in love with Dylan."

"But the two of you aren't even in a relationship."

A bitter scoff escaped, and Alec curled his toes deeper into the carpet. "I love you, Mom. And I appreciate all your efforts on my behalf. I really do. But..." He swallowed, forcing the words he should have said out loud years ago. "I can't live my life trying to please you."

"Alec." His mother's pause felt like forever. "You are better suited to marriage than most people I know. I worked hard to overturn DOMA and Proposition 8 because I wanted you happy."

"No, you wanted *you* happy."

Alec slammed his lids closed. He hadn't meant to be so blunt. Silence came from the other end of the phone, and he could picture his mother, that blank look on her face. A familiar guilt stabbed at Alec.

But he couldn't continue to let a sense of obligation rule his decisions.

"And I'm tired of feeling pressured to be your version of the perfect gay male," he said.

Christ, unloading those words felt good.

"I want to share my life with Dylan, yes," Alec said. "But I think you want me *married* because you feel a ring on my finger makes my being gay a little more acceptable."

"I..." A hush followed. "You..."

Alec let out a sigh, the uncomfortable pause answer enough. He'd struck gold with his words.

"I'm your mother, and I love you."

"I know."

"And I have absolutely nothing against homosexuals."

"I *know*."

Her tone defensive, she went on. "The gay community has come a long way, but that doesn't mean the prejudice has ended. Legitimizing your relationship—"

"What the world thinks about my personal relationship is not my problem."

And wasn't that the crux of the issue? Taking other people's ideals—his mother's, society's, even the gay community's—and letting them affect his decisions? He'd attended medical school because he wanted to practice medicine, but he'd been an overachiever to please his parents. He'd bypassed private practice and opened the clinic because he'd seen a need, but he knew the decision would make his family proud. And while he was thrilled the award money would expand the clinic's reach, the prestige had meant nothing to him...outside of satisfying his parents and hopefully reflecting well on the LGBTQ community.

He was living the life he wanted, but he'd let a sense of obligation to be the "perfect" gay color the details along the way. Even his decision to live with Tyler and his desire to make their relationship legal.

"I don't understand the sudden change of heart," his mother finally said. "You fought for months so you could get married."

"No." Frustrated, the words came out more forceful than he intended. "I was fighting for my right to *choose*." He reigned in the emotion, easing his tone. "There's a difference."

Alec scrubbed his face with his hand, letting the truth in his words sink in.

He knew his mother just wanted him happy. Unfortunately, she also believed society's opinions mattered to him. Or maybe they simply mattered to her. Either way, he couldn't afford to care anymore.

"But ultimately," Alec said, "I don't need a piece of paper with the government's stamp of approval to validate my feelings."

Labels.

Dylan was right. They didn't need labels. Or a title. He wanted to grow old with Dylan by his side, and saying "I do" in front of a judge wouldn't make Alec any more committed than he already was. Neither would Dylan defining himself as gay. Or bisexual. Or any other variant Dylan refused to choose. And if Dylan spent the rest of his life with Alec, all the while refusing to be called a "partner" or a "significant other," well, Alec would consider himself the luckiest guy on the planet.

When he stripped everything unnecessary away, all that remained was how he felt about Dylan. He was the other half of their matched set, the vital part Alec had sensed he was missing all along.

"Does Dylan love you?" she asked.

Alec's heart twisted painfully. "I think so, yes."

"Then what's the problem?"

"I'm saying, I'm hoping he'll take me back so I can spend the rest of my life with a man who'll never agree to marriage, Mom."

His mother's tone sounded doubtful. "And you could be happy with that, Alec?"

Every cell in his body screamed *yes*, forcing Alec to clutch his phone harder just to keep from losing his grip. He'd take a lifetime of uncertainty with Dylan over a sure-thing marriage to someone else. Christ, at this point, Alec couldn't even count on seeing Dylan again, much less fixing the problems between them.

His mother went on. "You'd be okay, ten years from now, with me still introducing him as your boyfriend?"

A small smile edged up his lips. "He might not even let you do that."

~~~***~~~

With Tyler's words in mind, Alec set about to do as suggested: achieve happiness. All in all, a fairly lofty goal for an unremarkable Wednesday evening.

Of course, the only way to truly achieve said condition was to win Dylan back.

With a knot of nerves in his stomach, Alec made his way up the street on his Harley. The knot grew tighter when he rounded the corner and spied the large red sign *Adams' Classic Motors*.

Conventional wisdom probably stated that, since Dylan was the one who'd left, he should be the one to come to Alec. Then again, Tyler had probably thought the same thing about Memphis. And that hadn't done Tyler any good.

So, screw conventional wisdom. Nothing about his and Dylan's relationship had been conventional. Why start now?

Alec rumbled up the driveway, parked the motorcycle, and stepped into the dim light of the garage. Despite the gaping garage door, the building was stuffy, the air humid. A hard rock song echoed in the space, but not so loud as to be obnoxious.

When Alec caught sight of Dylan squatting next to a decrepit motorcycle, inhaling and exhaling became a bit of a chore.

Sweat clung to Dylan's neck and dotted his T-shirt as he gripped a wrench, straining to loosen the bolt on the front tire. "Shit," Dylan muttered.

Alec's heart stalled in his chest, and he froze, convinced Dylan had seen him arrive.

Clearly oblivious, Dylan let out another string of curses as he leaned his weight down on the wrench. Given the amount of rust on the bike, Dylan's goal seemed hopeless.

Alec came to a stop a few feet from the motorcycle, waiting for Dylan to sense his presence. But, with his eyes tightly closed, his face scrunched in concentration, Dylan didn't notice. Instead, Dylan's biceps continued to bulge as he fought the bolt.

"She looks like a fickle one," Alec said.

The tool slipped from Dylan's hand and landed with a *clang*, skittering across the concrete. From his squatting position, Dylan met Alec's gaze, eyes wary as his hand rested on the motorcycle's exhaust pipe. Alec couldn't tell if the man was glad to see him, mad at the interruption, or just annoyed with the uncooperative bike in general.

"Yep," Dylan said, his voice careful. "She's trying my patience for sure."

"That's a Honda CB350." Alec knew he sounded as nervous as he felt. "One of the bestselling motorcycles worldwide in its time."

Dylan hiked a brow. "You got the full Wiki on every bike out there?"

Alec enjoyed the teasing a lot more when delivered with a smile. Right now he'd be happy with an easing of the tension around Dylan's eyes.

"No. Just thought about buying one during my research phase." Pausing, Alec decided to get down to business. "I spoke with my mother this morning."

Dylan blinked and then retrieved the wrench, starting in on the tire again.

Alec pushed on, hoping Dylan's attitude would improve with time. "I told her the truth. About Tyler. About you and me. About everything."

"That's great."

Not quite the reaction Alec had been hoping for. A little more enthusiasm would have been preferable.

Dylan reached for the toolbox lying just to his left, exchanging one wrench for another. "At least you don't have to keep pretending anymore."

Alec forced himself to at least *look* relaxed, leaning a hip against the Harley and crossing his arms. "Unfortunately, I have a new problem."

"Oh?"

Dylan continued to wrestle with the front tire, and his reluctance to meet Alec's gaze again only made the tension worse. Shit, the man didn't know how to give an inch. Alec considered walking out. Standing here with his heart pinned to his sleeve approached a form of torture.

But life without Dylan was worse.

"I can't sleep," Alec said. "My appetite is nonexistent. And I'm second-guessing every decision I've made over the last few weeks." A bitter scoff escaped. "Actually, I'm second-guessing just about every decision I've made since I turned sixteen and came out of the closet."

Dylan lifted a brow drily. "That's a hell of a lot of decisions."

Despite the tension, the corner of Alec's lip quirked. "Yes, it is."

"Could take you awhile to work your way through them all."

"I know, but none of them are as important as the one I already made about you."

After two heartbeats, Dylan rested his arm on his thigh and met Alec's gaze as if to say *go on*. And that small movement, the signal that Dylan was willing to listen, encouraged Alec to continue.

For the first time since Dylan had walked out of Alec's life, he allowed himself to hope.

"I know I've been hung up on labels. But, honestly, I don't care anymore. I just—" Alec shoved his hair back and sucked in a fortifying breath. "I just want to get back to the way things were. We don't need to call this a relationship. I don't need you to define yourself as my boyfriend. Or my partner. Or my significant other. Or whatever new term is applied to the role these days. I'm tired of settling, except..."

From his squatting position, Dylan stared up at him. "Except?"

"Except I just want to be with you. So I'll settle for whatever you're willing to give."

Dylan appeared to stop breathing, and Alec could just make out the emotional battle taking place behind the troubled green gaze.

"You—" With a frustrated look, Dylan frowned and returned his focus to the bike, staring at the tire. "You shouldn't *have* to settle."

The words sounded like the kiss of death to their relationship.

Oh God. Alec's heart pumped hard, and he fought to keep his expression under control.

"You kept asking how I felt about Rick," Dylan said. "And I kept saying I wasn't in love with him. But since the award ceremony, I've been doing a lot of thinking." He paused. "And remembering."

Alec forgot to take a breath in. "Remembering what?"

Dylan frowned again, eyes on the offending bolt.

"Rick and I...Well, it was more than just a simple friendship," Dylan said. "I never had any brothers, but I'm pretty sure we were more than that too." He gave a defeated shrug and tossed the wrench back into the box with a metallic *clink*. When he spoke again, his voice came out low. "Fuck, I don't know."

Alec waited for him to go on, and Dylan lifted his gaze to Alec.

"But on those nights when I huddled against Rick so we wouldn't freeze our asses off, the feelings were sometimes all mixed up. I think I might have felt...an   urge.   You   know"
—a sheepish look crossed Dylan's face, a novel expression for the man—"like a *sexual* urge. But I was never really sure what was a dream and what was real. It was all so confusing." Dylan sighed and looked away, sounding exhausted. "I'm still kind of confused."

He wearily wiped a hand down his face, leaving a small streak off grease on his temple. The smear left him looking vulnerable, and Alec's heart ached.

"But I was terrified of losing Rick as a friend," Dylan said. When he went on, his tone was bleak. "And I'd been so turned off by my experience with that asshole."

Alec had never seen him look so defeated and he fought the rising tide of anger, pain, and despair on Dylan's behalf. Not only had Dylan lost pieces of himself along the way, Alec suspected he'd buried some vital parts as well. Had he repressed his memories of his attraction to Rick? His real feelings for the friend he'd lost?

And, *Christ*, did any of this even matter anymore?

Dylan let out a scoff. "Then again, I was just so goddamned worried about surviving the next day. I could hardly think about anything else. We hadn't been in the apartment long before Rick met Noah. And I felt—"

Dylan hesitated, his mouth working, his expression focused and intense. He seemed to be struggling to articulate something. Something he didn't have the words to express. And, *dear God*, watching him wrestle with the process hurt.

Alec stepped closer. "Dylan, you don't have to do this."

"It's okay." He exhaled and rolled his head, as if to relieve taut muscles. "Shit. Only one way to describe it. There was Rick, and then there was the rest of the world. No one else ever came close." Dylan finally stood up, looking down at the Honda as he rubbed his finger across a tear in the seat.

His voice rough, Dylan said, "Until you came along."

Dylan met Alec's gaze. "Being with you was like being with Rick." A ghost of a smile came and went from the man's face. "Only there was great sex too."

The words expanded in Alec's chest, the potential killing him.

Dylan blinked. "And I..."

Dying to hear what came next, Alec couldn't move.

"And I want you back," Dylan finished.

Relief hit, leaving Alec's legs clumsy, but he managed to close the gap between them anyway. He moved fast enough that Dylan was still facing the Honda when Alec trapped Dylan's side against his chest. With a sigh, Alec pressed his forehead to Dylan's temple. Dylan closed his eyes and fisted his hand in the front of Alec's shirt.

"Whatever I have to do, man," Dylan said gruffly. "Whatever it takes."

With one great cosmic sigh of relief, Alec finally relaxed.

His out-of-control pulse slowed as he inhaled the scent of soap mixed with leather. A minute ticked by as neither moved.

"You don't have to do anything," Alec said. "Just don't walk out on me again."

In answer, Dylan turned his face and slotted their mouths together, his lower lip settling between Alec's. The touch was nothing more than a simple press of skin on skin, a shared, damp breath of exhalation.

And exaltation.

But the status didn't last. Needing more contact, more of *Dylan*, Alec tipped the man's head, his teeth and lips and tongue leaving a wet path along Dylan's throat. Dylan arched his neck in encouragement. The stubble was rough, the skin smooth. Alec reached the corner of Dylan's mouth and nipped—

"Fuck. Alec, wait."

Dylan turned his body until they were face-to-face and gripped Alec's hips, walking him backward until his shoulders hit the doorjamb. Dylan threaded his fingers in Alec's hair, holding his head still as the kiss changed. The intensity brought Alec ridiculously close to the edge.

Dylan pressed in firmly, opening Alec's mouth wide and then taking his time with each retreat, as though he were starving but didn't want to consume Alec too quickly. Forceful, yet unhurried. Soon Alec's jaw ached from the power behind the kisses, but he didn't mind. Desperate was good. Hungry was excellent.

Enjoying the moment... even better.

While Alec struggled to decide between a necessary breath to maintain brain function and continuing to kiss Dylan, Dylan made the decision for him.

Dylan's mouth landed on the pulse at Alec's neck, his voice hoarse. "Jesus, I've missed you."

Alec knew what he meant, could hear the truth in his voice. He might not be able to say it yet—in fact, the words might be a long time in coming—but Alec knew Dylan loved him. The idea scared the crap out of the man, but, as far as Alec was concerned, Dylan would just have to learn to adjust. Alec would teach him how.

"So show me," Alec said.

Dylan stuck his palms in Alec's back pockets and pulled, their cocks lining up beneath the denim. "Gladly."

Dylan arched his hips, and Alec moaned, Dylan swallowing the sound with his mouth. The rocking of their hips picked up speed, and what started out as partial hard-ons turned into raging fulls. The friction sent sparks of pleasure up his spine, and the thrusts became more demanding. Desperate, Alec nipped at Dylan's lower lip again.

Dylan hissed in approval and reached for the front of Alec's pants.

A honking horn sounded as a wolf whistle pierced the air, and Dylan's fingers froze. He glanced down at their tightly molded bodies, at his hand on Alec's zipper, and then at the door to his right, in full view of anyone driving by.

Dylan shot Alec a cocky look.

"I guess you can put me down in the bisexual camp," Dylan said with an amused tone. "Or at least somewhere on the sliding scale of bisexuality, whatever the hell that means." He punctuated the statement with a hard kiss and then pulled back. All humor gone, his expression grew serious. "And, uh, if you want to introduce me as your boyfriend, I guess I'm okay with that too."

"Are we retiring the 'backup' part?"

"I sure as hell hope so."

Alec gave the moment the consideration Dylan's concession deserved. "Actually, there's really only one thing I need you to call yourself."

Dylan tipped his head curiously. "What's that?"

"Mine."

A slow smile spread across Dylan's face. "That I can definitely do."

Epilogue

One Year Later

"Do you miss being in charge?" Alec asked.

Dylan sipped his beer on the deck of the restaurant, enjoying the sunset over the Pacific and the chatter of bikers after a good day's ride. The Sixth Annual Vintage Memorial Poker Run had already been deemed a success; the weather was perfect, participation at an all-time high. A salt-tinged breeze ruffled Alec's hair, his elbow pressed against Dylan's as they leaned against the wooden railing.

"I thought I was in charge last night," Dylan said.

Alec continued to scan the crowd, eyes crinkled in humor. "After all this time, your mind still resides firmly in the gutter, Dylan Booth."

"Hey, you might have rescued me from a garage, moved me into your home, and house-trained me, but life on the gutter side of things is fun." He fisted the front of Alec's shirt and leaned in to nip his shoulder before soothing the spot with his tongue. "As someone who visits me there daily, I'm not sure I understand the complaint."

Alec turned a smokin' blue gaze on Dylan. "I'm not complaining."

A thrum of awareness rippled just beneath Dylan's skin, and he reluctantly straightened up. This wasn't the time or place.

"I didn't think so." Dylan smoothed out the wrinkles he'd left on Alec's shirt. "And the answer to your original question is no. I don't miss being in charge of the poker run. Four years was enough. I'd rather enjoy myself than organize the sucker."

"Noah hasn't stopped bitching all day." Alec's mouth quirked. "I think you hurt his feelings when you hired an event planner."

Dylan cast a glance at Noah, now seated on the deck surrounded by participants sporting hardcore motorcycle gear. Unlike the chaps his tablemates wore, Noah's leather pants were sleek. *Chic* was the word Noah used, whatever the hell that meant. During lunch, Noah had shared the price he'd paid for his faux crocodile T-shirt, and Dylan had almost bitten his tongue in half, ruining Dylan's perfectly prepared hamburger with the taint of blood.

"Trust me," Dylan said. "Noah just likes to complain. He'd much rather spend his time working the crowd. Besides"—he waved his bottle in the direction of the satisfied bikers—"the participants are pleased with this year's arrangements. Especially the entertainment."

"It's definitely better than last year's."

Dylan groaned. "Don't remind me."

Noah never let Dylan forget that Destiny's Bitch had received a standing ovation after her rendition of "I Will Survive." Unfortunately, the reminder was more annoying than the incident itself. Every month or so since, Dylan's cell phone rang, blaring the tune. He hadn't figured out how Noah managed to keep swiping his phone on the sly and changing the ringtone. Or why the call always came at the most embarrassing moment possible, with the volume at full blast.

Last week, the old man behind Dylan in the NAPA Auto Parts store had nearly suffered a friggin' heart attack.

Dylan caught Noah's eye, and the man shot him a wink and a smile. Dylan volleyed back with a you're-not-funny look.

He knew Noah would wait until Dylan let down his guard again before the repeat offensive. But, *man*, how long could a guy remain on high alert? He'd assumed Noah would eventually grow bored with the prank. So far, no such luck. One more time and Dylan was changing the keyless entry to the front door and not giving Noah the combination.

Ever.

"Dylan!"

Dylan turned his head and saw Savannah Urban approaching.

The petite blond he'd hired to organize this year's event was a second year psychology student at Stanford, recommended to him by Jack Davis, an uncle of sorts. Besides the pretty features, sweet manner, and high-powered relative, the girl came with an added bonus: a twin named Sierra.

Two for the price of one, she'd said. And although Dylan had complained, trying to pay them both, Sierra had refused. What the two lacked in experience they'd more than made up for with enthusiasm, but sometimes their bubbly energy was almost too much.

Long ponytail pulled back through her visor, clip board in hand, Savannah—or was it Sierra?—approached Dylan. "I just wanted to go over tomorrow's schedule again."

"Savannah..." He hesitated, waiting for her to correct him, just in case he had the wrong twin. "I trust you. You and your sister have done a bang-up job. Today was spectacular. Everybody is saying this is the best year ever."

The fresh-faced blond blushed to her hairline. Seriously, had he ever been that young?

Dylan sent her a reassuring smile as he went on. "You don't need to keep checking in with me."

That's why he'd hired the two to begin with, to spare him from dealing with the details. With anyone else he might have felt annoyed, but she was just so friggin' earnest and adorable. And *wholesome*. Raising them would have been fun, and he finally understood why some people made the insane choice to have children.

Of course, with Dylan's genes, he'd probably wind up with a boy that was pure hell on wheels. He'd be better off raising Alec's kid.

Jesus, where had those thoughts come from?

But he knew. This wasn't the first time they'd popped into his head. The idea seemed to be following him around lately, nipping at his heels.

Savannah bit her lower lip. "Well," she said hesitantly, "Noah said I needed to—"

"Whoa." Dylan held up a hand. "Stop right there. I'm not one who attempts to offer advice or share wisdom or stupid shit like that. But, whatever you do, do *not* listen to Noah." He laid a reassuring hand on her shoulder. "I trust you way more than I trust him."

Savannah beamed, and Dylan didn't have the heart to tell her he trusted the deadlocked political system more than he trusted Noah Tanner.

"Are we good now?" Dylan asked.

Savannah's smile lit up her face. "We're good."

Dylan watched her weave her way back through the crowded tables and come to stop beside her sister. In matching visors, the twins huddled together for a moment, comparing clipboards.

"They're cute kids," Alec said. Dylan hiked a brow, and Alec shrugged as he continued. "Okay. *College* kids then."

"Yeah."

Funny how Alec had picked up on the same thought as Dylan. He returned his gaze to the two girls and pursed his lips, contemplating the thought dogging him for a while.

"You ever thought about having any?" Dylan asked.

"Any what?"

"Kids."

When Alec didn't respond, Dylan turned his head and met his partner's gaze.

Hip parked against the railing, Alec stared at him, his face reflecting the same shock present in those wide, blue eyes. Dylan never could decide which was more amusing, a tongue-tied Alec or the nervous, blabbering version. Looks like the topic of children had left Alec mute.

Fucking *adorably* mute.

A familiar warmth spread through Dylan's chest. He should be used to the feeling by now, but every time it felt like a novelty.

"Yeah," Alec said. "But..."

Those two short words seemed to have exhausted Alec's supply.

"Why haven't you ever mentioned the idea before?" Dylan said.

Alec blinked and crossed his arms, almost looking offended. "Maybe because of the way you initially freaked out about us. How was I supposed to bring up the subject when you weren't even capable of saying the words *I love you*."

Dylan scowled, but his heart wasn't in it. "I got over that in a few months."

"Try six."

"Okay." Dylan shrugged. "So I'm a slow learner."

"Are you serious?" Alec slowly cocked his head. "About the kids, I mean?"

Before Dylan could decide how to respond, a voice interrupted their private conversation.

"Hey, guys."

Tyler approached them with Logan at his side— the boomerang boyfriend, as so dubbed by Noah— and his gray eyes landed on the still stunned expression on his ex's face.

Tyler shifted his gaze between Alec and Dylan, his voice calm. Only the subject gave away his emotion. "Looks like Noah shared the news about next year's plans already."

Alec winced. "Sorry. I guess we shouldn't have agreed to give the annual bachelor bid two tries before giving up. I figured we'd make enough money the first time and you'd be safe."

Tyler's expression didn't budge, but Alec plowed on.

"You might as well agree to see Memphis about next year's attempt. Noah's going to hound you until you do." Alec's attention settled back on Dylan. After all that, Dylan could still hear the thread of amazement in Alec's tone. "But that's not what we were talking about."

"Then what were you two talking about?" Tyler said.

In a fit of evil, Dylan waited until Tyler took a sip of his beer before answering. "Having kids."

Tyler choked on his drink, coughing, and his eyes wide. Dylan bit back the grin of satisfaction. Nice to see the Ice Man occasionally lose his cool.

Unfortunately he recovered quickly, putting an end to Dylan's fun.

Tyler spoke slowly. "Are you kidding me?"

Alec watched Dylan with intent, clearly waiting on him to answer the question. Dylan ran the notion around in his head again, feeling it out. Testing the image in his brain. Before he met Alec, the thought used to conjure all kinds of horrors. But, lately, all Dylan pictured was a little girl or boy with Alec's blue eyes and his big heart. And maybe even his tendency to babble.

Dylan couldn't think of anything better.

"Nope," Dylan finally said. "Not kidding at all."

Alec shook his head, dazed, but clearly pleased. "I swear, Dylan." Alec pressed his forehead to Dylan's temple. "I could spend the rest of my life studying you and never figure you out."

Dylan grinned, wrapping his arm around Alec's shoulder and pulling him closer. "Sounds good to me."

Alec and Tyler began to talk about work, the housing fund, and next year's bachelor bid. But Dylan tuned them out, content to just hold Alec and enjoy the sun sinking into the Pacific.

"What would you call her?"

"Huh?" Dylan looked around and realized Tyler and Logan had gone.

Alec squeezed his waist, as if to get his attention. "If we had a girl, what would you name her?"

Surprised by the question, Dylan said, "I don't know."

"Well," Alec said, "at least a boy's name would be easy."

Curious, Dylan looked down at Alec where he was tucked against his side. The expression on Alec's face was more serious than Dylan had expected.

"What would you call him?" Dylan asked.

"Rick."

Dylan blinked, trying to clear the sudden pressure behind his lids. Jesus, his boyfriend really knew how to pack a punch. For a moment Dylan couldn't speak, gratitude and peace and something he couldn't identify, maybe joy, crowding the back of his throat.

And then Dylan's grin broke through. "That sounds perfect."

About the Author

By day, River works as a (mostly) mild mannered physician in a remote Alaskan town and has accumulated the wacky stories that come with the job. At night, her inner badass comes out to play. River likes to read and write edgy books that contain varying levels of humor and plenty of hot, steamy sex between two hunky men.

Word-of-mouth is important for any author to succeed. If you enjoyed the book, please consider leaving a review where you purchased it, or on Goodreads, even if it's only a line or two; it would make all the difference and would be very much appreciated.

Coming up next from River Jaymes

The Boyfriend Mandate

Read Tyler and Memphis's story in book two of The Boyfriend Chronicles.

If you would like to be notified when River's next book is released, please send an email to riverjaymes@gmail.com and we will add you to our list.

River Jaymes is also the author of:

Brad's Bachelor Party

In college, geeky med student Cole Winston fell for his best friend, Brad Kelly. The bold, brash charmer was everything Cole wasn't: confident, popular, and straight. Unfortunately Cole's secret blew up in his face, and he walked away.

Years later, when Brad needs help, he calls Cole. Now a respected trauma surgeon, Cole has learned not to risk his heart and is ready to be Brad's friend again. Things go well until Brad asks Cole to be his best man.

With both his parents dead, Brad never would have survived college or his brother's rounds of drug rehab without Cole. The five-year gap in their friendship was painful.

Now Brad's got his best friend back, a kick-ass job, and is engaged to the CEO's daughter. Life is great... until a hot encounter at his bachelor party leaves both men reeling. The sexual tension between the two is off the charts. Brad has commitments he needs to keep, but how can he go through with the wedding when he can't stop thinking about Cole?

And how can Cole stand beside his friend and watch him get married, especially now that he realizes he still loves Brad?

www.riverjaymes.com